Sarah Echavarre Smith _____
who wants to make the wor_____
story at a time. Her love of romance began when she was
eight and she discovered her auntie's stash of romance
novels. She's been hooked ever since. When she's not
writing, you can find her hiking, eating chocolate and
perfecting her lumpia recipe. Follow her on Instagram
and TikTok @authorsarahs

Much Ado
About
Hating You

Sarah Echavarre Smith

First Published in Great Britain 2025 by
Afterglow Books by Mills & Boon, an imprint of HarperCollins*Publishers* Ltd
1 London Bridge Street, London, SE1 9GF

www.harpercollins.co.uk

HarperCollins*Publishers*
Macken House, 39/40 Mayor Street Upper,
Dublin 1, D01 C9W8, Ireland

Much Ado About Hating You © 2025 Sarah Smith

ISBN: 978-0-263-39751-2

0525

For the bookworms and hot nerds

One

Aidan

I wasn't planning on kicking off the morning by writing an explicit sex scene, but here we are.

I skim over the last few paragraphs I've written.

Rome gently gripped Jia by the chin, hypnotized by the deep brown hue of her saucerlike eyes. The heavenly feel of her hot skin pressed against his body was enough to make him come right here, right now. But no way was that going to happen. He tensed his legs, focusing on the burn in his quads as he held his position above Jia. And then he gritted his teeth so hard, a sharp pain jolted through the back of his skull. That heat and pressure building inside of him started to fade. Good. He needed this pain, this distraction so he could last longer. He wanted to last as long as he could for her.

"Are you sure this is a good idea? Us together…like this?" Jia asked.

Her hot breath ghosted over Rome's lips as she traced a finger along his bottom lip. He closed his eyes and licked his lips right as she pulled her hand away, savoring the faint, sweet taste of her. And then he thrust inside of her, slow at first. The steady, measured movement was enough for her head to fall back as she let out a breathy moan.

"No, Jia. This is a terrible fucking idea." Rome tangled his fingers through her hair, her pants and moans of ecstasy spurring him on. His thrusts turned faster, harder, more desperate. Judging by the way Jia dug her finger-nails into his back and screamed his name over and over, she fucking loved it.

Once more Rome gripped Jia's chin to get her to look at him. Her eyes were cloudy with arousal. "Our fami-lies are sworn enemies. Your father's got a bounty on my head. But I don't fucking care. I love you, Jia. I'd gladly lose my head for one night with you."

Loosening my tie and clearing my throat, I'm grateful that Jason is gone on a coffee run instead of here in our shared of-fice. Damn. That was pretty hot. Not bad for a super nerd who looks the exact opposite of what you'd picture when you hear the words "erotic fanfic writer."

I catch my reflection in the framed glossy artwork hanging on the wall opposite me. I take in my thick-rimmed glasses and how rumpled this button-up dress shirt is—and how it makes me look like a grandpa. I tug a hand through my hair, wincing at the fact that I look like I'm cosplaying as a sixty-six-year-old man. And that's when I quietly observe how long my hair's gotten, how the curls are practically falling into my eyes. A new wardrobe *and* a haircut are in order. Christ.

I huff out a breath as I hit Save and continue typing on my laptop. All of that will have to wait until after the work week. Yeah, I should be grading essays right now, but I need a break. Don't get me wrong, I love my job as a professor in the English department here at East Nashville University and honestly love reading, critiquing my students' writing, and teaching them about classic literature.

But you know what I don't love? When the department chair sends out an email about a last-minute mandatory fac-ulty meeting that screws up my schedule for the day. I always set aside a sixty-minute block in the morning before my first class to grade papers and exams. But today I've got a pointless meeting to head to instead that's cutting into the majority of my grading time. So I figured doing a fifteen-minute creative-writing sprint would be a better use of my time.

A five-minute reminder for the meeting pops up. I do one more quick skim of what I just wrote, save it, then post it to my homepage on Scribble Share. Part of me still can't believe that I secretly do this. I'm an English professor who earns a living teaching British literature…who also writes erotic fanfic of my favorite Shakespeare plays under the username ShakespeareInLust on an online forum.

Yeah, that's probably a hell of a contradiction. But I can't help it. I've always loved reading and writing romance and erotica. And if the academia types that I'm constantly around weren't so judgmental about that genre, I'd happily talk about it. But it didn't take me long to figure out that sexy romance is looked down upon in my field. Pretty messed up when you think about it actually. My fellow professionals have no issue championing violent and depressing literature, but the second they read something with a sex scene or a happily-ever-after, they're ready to rip it apart. God, it's all so pretentious as hell sometimes.

I catch a few positive comments on my latest post, which is a mafia retelling of *Romeo and Juliet*—with the characters aged up to their twenties and a happily-ever-after, of course.

OMG hot! LOVE!!

Is anyone else totally in love with the Romeo and Juliet vibes?? Freaking adore this series!

If they let us read this kind of stuff in school, I wouldn't have skipped out on my English lit class so much LOL

There's a small burst of pride in my chest. I don't get a lot of compliments in my job, so reading these comments feels pretty damn good.

I grab my laptop, a notepad, and pen, and head down to the conference room. When I turn the corner, I spot Jason holding a giant mug of coffee.

"Wow." I gesture to his gigantic mug as we walk down the hall to the elevator.

He huffs out a breath. "I need it, man. I'm not in the mood for whatever doom and gloom this meeting is about to bring."

"How do you know it's gonna be all doom and gloom?"

The elevator dings. When the stainless-steel doors glide open, I hold back a groan at how crowded it is and how no one gets off. I sigh and follow Jason as we squeeze in. I accidentally bump my shoulder against someone whose face I can't see because I had to angle in diagonally to fit in and she's facing opposite me. All I can see is a ponytail of ridiculously shiny brown-black hair.

"Sorry," I say softly.

The faceless woman makes a scoffing noise.

"Come on, Aidan. You know this meeting's gonna be bad," Jason says. "Dr. Wauncho was vague as fuck in his email. I mean, what the hell else are we supposed to think when he says that he wants to address 'department efficiency' with some auditor dude that the university hired named Micah."

I try to shrug away the stress knot that's suddenly formed in my shoulder, but we're packed in here like sardines. I probably should have read that email more carefully because I only vaguely remember the mention of an auditor.

Jason leans in closer to me. "You know what that's code for, don't you? Layoffs."

Half of the elevator turns to look at him as he sips from his mug.

"Don't say that. You don't know that," I say.

"I hope I'm wrong. I really do. But I have a feeling we're about to walk into the lion's den so Micah the Auditor can annihilate our asses. And our jobs."

Jason's ability to turn even the smallest things into worst-case scenarios is legendary. He's always been like this in the five years that we've worked together. But I can't deny that he makes a valid point. Still though, I don't want to panic before we've even had the meeting.

"Let's not jump to conclusions, okay?"

My reassurance does little to quell Jason's obvious nervousness about the meeting judging by the deep frown etched in his face.

"What the hell kind of a name is Micah anyway?" I joke. "Ten bucks says he was some super religious homeschooled kid. I bet he ate paste too."

That cheap joke earns a chuckle from Jason. The elevator eases to a stop, and we walk to the conference room. All the chairs are taken by the time we make it in, so we stand against the wall in the cramped room. I don't miss the stern look Dr. Wauncho flashes as he shuts the door and clears his throat.

"Everyone, thank you for making this meeting. I apologize for the short notice, but this is a pressing matter," he says while standing at the head of the conference table. He tugs at the sleeve of his houndstooth blazer before folding his hands in front of him. "As you all know, the university budget is on the chopping block this year. Every department is being examined by auditors hired by the school. Which means there's a potential that we may have to make some cuts."

Grumbling echoes through the room.

"Wait, what about tenured faculty? Will we be part of the cuts too?" one of the tenured professors asks.

Dr. Wauncho winces. "Possibly. No one is immune when it comes to university financial issues."

I hear the professor mumble softly. I'm pretty sure he just cursed.

"Told you so, man," Jason mutters to me as he scrubs a hand over his cheek.

I let out a sharp exhale. This is definitely not good.

"Not to worry." Dr. Wauncho flashes a tight smile. "I truly believe that every member of the English department faculty is worth their weight in gold. I see this as an opportunity to showcase just how crucial we are to the university. And I'm certain that the auditor, Ms. Mila, will see that as soon as she gets started with her evaluation process."

"Who the hell is Ms. Mila? I thought the auditor was a guy named Micah?" Jason asks me.

"No clue." I strain to listen as he explains that the auditor will interview each of the faculty about their duties and course load and observe us in class. I grit my teeth in frustration. We're all essentially auditioning to keep our jobs. Just great.

Dr. Wauncho gestures to someone sitting at the far end of the table who I can't see from where I'm standing. "Now, if you'll all join me in giving Ms. Micah Mila a warm East Nashville University welcome."

The room is silent as a tall woman stands up. For a split second my eyes go wide as I take her in. Holy shit. She's beautiful. Big brown eyes, tan skin, full mouth. Is this what financial auditors look like? I figured they'd be nerdy dudes who look like me, not women who could moonlight as beauty queens. I banish the thought a second later. I sound like a creep, fixating on her looks.

When she turns her head, dread settles in the pit of my stomach. Instantly I recognize that ponytail…she's the one I bumped into in the elevator. We were shoulder to shoulder as I made fun of her name right to her face.

Her pinched expression doesn't budge as she does a quick

scan of the room. And then she locks eyes with me and her face shifts to a full-on glare.

This is Micah. And my career is currently in her hands. Fuck.

Two

Micah

For a second, all I can do is stand there and glare at the jerk from the elevator.

I take a slow, silent breath and try to keep my composure in this room full of people who undoubtedly hate me. I've done this almost every day for the three years that I've had this job. I'm used to the harsh stares and chilly response. It sucks, but it's part of being a financial auditor. It would be nice to work at a place where people didn't loathe me, but every job has its downsides. What I'm not used to is being made fun of straight to my face for such a petty reason.

Technically, it wasn't straight to my face given I was standing with my back to this guy. Still though. I was basically pressed up against him as he shit-talked my name. What an asshole. Yeah, I've gotten comments my whole life about how unusual it is for a girl to have a "boy" name. It's so damn annoying. But no one's straight-up made fun of my name since elementary school. I didn't expect to deal with this schoolyard crap as a thirty-two-year-old.

This *is* technically a school though—a university. So it's fitting in that way, I guess.

It takes an extra second for me to refocus and let the sting of this guy's insult roll off my back. Probably because he's got that hot-nerd look going for him—my personal weakness. I got a glimpse of his face in the reflection of the mirrored side panel of the elevator, but now I get to take in him face-to-face as he stands just a handful of feet away from me.

Wow. He's exceptionally good-looking. I take in his Buddy Holly glasses; his shaggy chestnut curls; how that dress shirt barely fits the broad, lean spread of his shoulders; how the sleeves are rolled halfway up those muscular, veiny forearms of his...

He looks like a handsome pro athlete who's cosplaying as a professor.

Shame heats my cheeks as I try to ignore that faint ache in my chest. It never feels good when someone hurts your feelings, but it cuts deeper when that someone is a person you find ridiculously attractive.

I have a lot of experience with that.

I clear my throat and refocus on the moment. Enough of this self-pity session. Forget this hot-nerd jerk. I've got a job to do.

"Good morning, everyone. Thank you, Dr. Wauncho, for that warm welcome."

He's the only person who acknowledges what I've said. He offers a polite nod while everyone else aims a hard stare at me. And honestly, I don't blame them. In a month and a half, some of the people standing in this room may not have a job because of me.

I ignore the churn in my stomach that thought causes. This isn't about feelings. This is about doing my job. And if everyone here is doing their own jobs well, they won't have anything to worry about.

"I'm sure all of you would prefer it if I keep pleasantries to a minimum and cut straight to the point, so here it is—for the next six weeks, I'll be conducting one-on-one meetings with all of you and observing you in your day-to-day roles as I determine just how effective you are in this department. At the end of my time here, I'll prepare a report with my recommendations and submit it to the head of the university."

"A report?" the hot nerd's blond friend asks. "What exactly will be in this report?"

"Many things. How many hours you put in per day at the university, how many classes you teach, how many students are enrolled in your classes, your retention rate, how many students drop your classes, what improvements you could make to your lesson plans in order to increase retention."

Blond Guy scoffs. Hot-Nerd Jerk frowns and pulls his lips into his mouth, like he wants to say something but is holding back. What's his name? His friend said it in the elevator, but I can't remember now.

Everyone else in the room grumbles or whispers to one another. Sweat beads dot along my spine. Already I can feel the anxiety sweat soaking through my blouse.

This is your job, Micah. Who cares if they don't like you? This isn't a popularity contest.

I notice Hot-Nerd Jerk pursing his lips as his blond friend mutters something I can't hear to him. Hot-Nerd Jerk shakes his head and rolls his eyes.

"Look, I understand that none of you are thrilled about my being here," I say, pleased at how steady and firm my tone is despite the nerves firing inside of me. "But here's the truth— your university is hemorrhaging money, and I've been asked to help solve this problem."

Hot-Nerd Jerk grumbles loudly to his friend once more. Then he glances over at me before looking back at his friend and smirking. Like he's shit-talking me right in front of my face. Again. Irritation burns hot inside of me.

"Is there something you'd like to say to me?"

It takes a second before he realizes I'm speaking to him. His brow hits his hairline as he looks back over at me. "Are you talking to me?"

"Yes. You seem to have a lot to say to your friend. If you have a question, ask me. If you'd prefer to gossip, you can leave this meeting instead of being rude enough to whisper while I'm trying to address you and your colleagues."

His friend winces and says, "Sorry, Aidan" in a low voice.

For a second, all Aidan does is look at me, his blue eyes hard. And then he chuckles. He fucking *chuckles*. Like this is all a joke to him.

"Okay, sure, I've got a question—what did you study in college?"

I pause. I wasn't expecting that.

"I have an MBA," I say.

I don't miss the tight set of his jaw as he bites down, clearly displeased with my answer. "Did you also study English or literature?"

"I didn't." I took writing classes and have always loved reading and writing for fun, but I don't mention that. Because I know that wouldn't make a difference to a pretentious jerk like him. He'd only care about my opinion if I had an impressive degree in the subject to back it up.

Kind of like my ex.

An ugly feeling pools in the pit of my stomach. That's the second time this guy has reminded me of him. Definitely a bad sign.

I push away the thought. My douchebag ex doesn't deserve to take up any more space in my brain.

"So what makes you think that you're qualified to make recommendations about something you know nothing about?" Aidan asks.

I start to speak, but he cuts me off.

"We're supposed to trust that you and your MBA know better about literature coursework than actual professors with degrees in this subject?"

His tone borders on taunting as he says *MBA*. My skin pricks as the irritation inside of me bubbles over. It's not till the base of my skull starts to ache that I realize just how hard I'm biting down.

"Maybe it's not the worst thing in the world to get an outsider's perspective on things, given the status of your budget and less than desirable student enrollment numbers," I say.

He works his jaw like he's trying to decide between screaming or grunting. "Is putting people out of work a passion pursuit for you? Or do you get a bonus for each faculty member you help get fired?"

Gasps follow Hot-Nerd Jerk's smart-ass question. I almost choke at his audacity, but I manage to keep my mouth closed. That burn of irritation is now a full-on bonfire in my belly. This guy. Fine if he's not happy about me being here, but he has no right to be an unprofessional asshole.

"Professor Scott, that tone isn't necessary," Dr. Wauncho says.

"I disagree," Hot-Nerd Jerk aka Professor Scott says. "We could all be out of a job in just over a month because of Ms. Mila. I think we have a right to express how we feel about that."

Dr. Wauncho starts to speak, but I stop him.

"I'm happy to address Professor Scott." I pin him with my gaze. "I do this because it's my job. Kind of like how you're here because it's your job."

"I'm not like you," he bites. The sting of his tone takes me by surprise. I don't even know this guy and he's already doing a number on my self-esteem. "I do this job because I'm passionate about literature and I think it's important to teach my students the classics. Not that I'd expect *you* to understand anything about appreciating the value of something like literature since, you know, you can't assign a dollar amount to it."

My skin flashes hot. The anger brewing inside of me has seeped through my pores with that pretentious-as-fuck dig at me. "I assure you, Professor Scott, by the end of my audit, I'll have figured out the exact value of you and this department."

I spot the fury the moment it flashes in his icy blue eyes. I can see it clear as day even though I'm standing a dozen feet from him.

The room is dead silent as we glare at each other. Usually I'd be fighting the urge to crawl out of my skin in a moment like this, trading insults with a stranger in a room full of onlookers. But I'm too pissed to feel anything other than rage right now. And determination.

I sit back down, the meeting ends, and I march out of the room.

This guy hates me. Good. That's going to make my job a lot easier.

Three

Micah

My phone buzzes on the kitchen table where I'm working on my laptop. When I see it's my dad calling for the second time this evening, I let out a heavy sigh. I can't keep ignoring him.

I take a second to clear my throat. I haven't spoken since my meeting this morning at East Nashville University. I don't want him to think anything is wrong if I sound hoarse or squeaky.

"Hey, Dad. What's up?"

"Oh, nothing much. Just wanted to check on you and see how you're doing."

"I'm fine."

He chuckles. "You say that every time I call you."

"Well, you've called me almost every day this week. My life is pretty boring, so I don't really have much else to say."

"Right…"

There's a pinch in my chest at the slight defeat in his tone. I need to watch my tone. I sound so irritated when he's just trying to check on me.

"Sorry, Dad," I say, making sure my voice is lighter this time. "Work's just been busy. I want to make sure I do a good job on this audit."

"You're going to do a great job, honey. You've always had an amazing work ethic."

The confidence in my dad's tone stings. His belief in me almost hurts at this point. After everything I screwed up—and after everything he and Mom gave me to help dig me out of the hole I got myself into—I'd rather he be skeptical than un-waveringly supportive. I don't deserve it.

A quiet moment follows, and I'm almost certain he's holding back from saying another encouraging comment. He knows I can't stand it.

"Did you make sure to eat dinner?" he asks.

"Of course I did."

"What did you have? And please don't tell me it was some-thing you microwaved. You're young and need to nourish yourself with proper home-cooked food."

I chuckle, feeling the slightest bit lighter this time. Most thirty-two-year-olds would be annoyed with their parents fuss-ing over their eating habits, but it always makes me laugh. It reminds me of when I was a kid and he'd ask me what I had for lunch at school and I'd say something ridiculous, like di-nosaur meat. He'd counter with his own made-up meal, like unicorn steak or mud pies, and we'd go back and forth, nam-ing silly foods until we laughed so hard we could barely speak.

"Unicorn steak, of course," I say, smiling.

"What a coincidence. So did I."

We both laugh.

"I made a yummy veggie chili actually. And cornbread. That was from a box, though, because you know how much I hate baking. Still. I think that's a pretty good meal for someone of my cooking-skill level."

Dad lets out a low whistle. "Well, look at you, Iron Chef."

We share another laugh. Then he pauses and clears his throat. "Honey, you're always welcome to come over for dinner. You know how your mom and I always cook way too much. It was my turn to cook tonight, and you should see the pile of *pansit* that's left on the stove. We always love having you."

That familiar sting hits once more. I glance around the cozy space of this luxury loft in the Gulch—this luxury loft that isn't mine. It belongs to my super successful twin sister,

Jordan, who is out of the country for the next six months and needed a house sitter, so I'm taking care of her place for her. And because she's an angel, she's not even charging me rent.

"I'm good, Dad. You don't need to offer to feed me every night."

"I know that," he says quickly. "It's just that we're your parents, we love you to bits, and we'll take any excuse to see you, kiddo."

I smile despite the shame that heats me from the inside out. My whole family has done more than enough for me this past year. My parents helped me pay off the credit-card debt I piled up after my breakup, and my sister gave me a place to live. They're the reason I'm doing well right now.

I'm beyond grateful for them. Without them, I'd be living in a roach-infested apartment with an empty bank account. But it's also why I'm so adamant about not going over to see my parents all the time. I want to show them that I don't need to rely on them for everything. I want to show them that I won't always need their help and that I'm capable of making it on my own, even after making the biggest mistake of my life.

I close my eyes, and a flash of that awful day appears. How I lost my place, my savings, and my fiancé in a single day. All because I let myself get too comfortable…because I was stupid. I should have seen it coming.

When my eyes start to burn, I quickly blink. "I appreciate it, Dad. Really. But I've got a good routine going here."

"Sure, honey. I get it."

"How about I stop by Sunday? I'll be in the mood for some *pansit* and leftovers by then for sure."

"Honey, that would be wonderful." I can hear the smile in his voice. God, my dad is so kind and loving, I could cry.

I manage to hold it together while we exchange *I love you*s and tell each other good night. But as I finish up my work, my brain goes to the one place I know it shouldn't.

Ashton.

As I shower and get ready for bed, I can't help but think about what he's doing. No doubt he's with Bianca. Probably cuddled on the couch reading together. Or in bed...

I press my eyes shut so hard, they start to burn. Why the hell do I do this to myself? I don't even want to be with Ashton anymore, that cheating, manipulative prick. But if I'm being honest, I miss the stability of our life together, of feeling happy.

Actually, *thinking* I was happy is more accurate. Because if I had known everything he was doing behind my back, I would have left him long before that afternoon from hell when I found out everything and my entire world came crashing down...

I shuffle to the kitchen and down a glass of water, somehow swallowing past the lump in my throat. No more wallowing. I've done enough of that to last a lifetime. My breakup with Ashton was a wake-up call. No more giving my heart to some guy who seems amazing only to get screwed over seven ways to Sunday. Over my dead body will I ever get into another romantic relationship anytime soon.

By the time I crawl into the massive king-size bed with a pillow-top mattress, I know I'm too wound up to sleep. I need a distraction. I grab my phone and pull up my favorite way to take my mind off my pathetic life.

I tap the Scribble Share app and navigate to the profile of my favorite writer on the platform: *ShakespeareInLust.*

I smile when I read the username, like I do every time I see it. Ridiculously cute and clever. This author rewrites Shakespeare's famous plays as steamy erotica stories with happily-ever-afters. I may be anti-romance in my personal life, but I'm a total fangirl for their stories. They're currently rewriting *Romeo and Juliet* as mafia erotica, and I'm tearing through the chapters—they're so steamy and so freaking good.

When I see they've posted a new chapter to their story, I

crack a smile. The tension in my neck and shoulders melts as I sink into my plush pillows and comforter.

I'm one sentence in before my eyes go wide.

"Jia, baby, do you understand just how badly I've been craving you?"

Rome dipped his head back down between Jia's legs, dusting a kiss on her left inner thigh, then her right. He savored the delicate twitch of her leg muscles, how her body responded so greedily to the slightest touch from him. A shuddery breath fell from her lips as she started to speak, but Rome gently scraped his teeth against that supersensitive patch of skin. This time Jia's breath turned ragged. By the time his tongue made it to her clit, her entire body was trembling.

Jia moaned, her eyes rolling to the back of her head. "But what…what about…"

Rome ran his tongue slowly up, then down, rendering Jia speechless. When he began making delicate swirls around her sensitive bud, she yelped. She tugged her fingers through his midnight-black hair before pulling his face away.

"Rome," she panted.

His entire body ached at the loss of contact. Already he was desperate for more of her sweet taste, and he had only been without it for two seconds.

Jia gazed down at Rome, her burnt-sienna eyes hazy with arousal. "My dad…he's going to murder you, Rome…"

Rome quirked an eyebrow at the same time as a taunting smirk tugged at his lips. He lowered his head back down between her legs. He slipped a finger inside her, moaning at how warm and wet she was.

"Here's the thing, Jia. I don't fucking care."

He worked his tongue against her until she was screaming with ecstasy, until her brain forgot about everything
and everyone that wasn't Rome. As she exploded around
his tongue and fingers, she realized that she didn't care
either. All she wanted, all she needed was Rome Montez.

My breath is shallow when I finish reading. Wow. That
was hot as hell.

My entire body is flushed by the time I turn my phone on
silent and reach to turn off the lamp. I contemplate breaking
out the vibrator from the nearby nightstand, but I don't. It's
past eleven now. I need to go to sleep.

I burrow into my comforter and catch myself thinking
about the writer behind ShakespeareInLust. I'm guessing she's
a woman. So many amazing erotica writers are women.

As I drift off to sleep, I catch my delirious brain wishing
I could bring Rome or any of her male characters to life. I'd
happily trade in any of the real-life douchebags I've dated for
Rome or any of ShakespeareInLust's romance heroes. I let out
a sleepy chuckle. If only.

Four

Aidan

When I walk into my classroom to teach my Shakespeare Yesterday and Today class, I see Micah sitting at one of the empty desks. I choke on the coffee I just sipped. She stares at me with a horrified look on her face as I cough and thump my fist against my chest. Glad none of my students are here yet to witness this mess of a scene.

She starts to stand up and move toward me, but I hold up a hand.

"What are you doing here?" I choke out.

She leans back, like she's offended that I asked her such a question.

"I'm observing your class for my audit. We talked about this in yesterday's faculty meeting, remember?" She purses her lips as she stands there and watches me cough and clear my throat.

I walk over to the desk and set my things down before taking a long gulp of coffee.

"Do you think that's a good idea?" she asks, frowning at the mug in my hand.

I ignore her very obvious dig at me and resist the natural urge to roll my eyes. "Shouldn't you have told me that you'd be interrupting my class this morning?"

She looks shocked at what I've said. Then she blinks and she's back to glaring at me. "I didn't realize I needed your permission to do my job, Professor Scott."

"I'm not telling you how to do your job," I say, matching

her hard tone. "I just would have liked a heads-up that you'd be observing me today."

"That's not how I operate. I've already made it clear what my goals here are, and when I spoke to Dr. Wauncho, he said that I'm free to observe all the faculty as I please these next six weeks. I find that's the best way to get an accurate read on day-to-day operations. It's no good if I tell you I'm observing so you can prepare some inauthentic performance."

"'Inauthentic performance'?" I repeat, trying my hardest to hold in the incredulous laugh I'm aching to let out. "Are you seriously saying that I'd fake my work performance in front of you? In front of my students?"

"It's possible." She doesn't even blink.

I huff out a breath. Barely eight in the morning and already my day is ruined because Micah the Auditor decided to show up to my class unannounced. Actually, these next six weeks are ruined knowing that she's going to be hovering above me, poring over my every flaw and using that as cause to potentially recommend that the dean of the university fire me.

I think back to what she said at yesterday's meeting.

By the end of my audit, I'll have figured out the exact value of you and this department.

It was professional speak for *I'm going to fucking end you.* My skin pricks as the frustration builds inside of me. It's clear she's hell-bent on destroying me.

But more than that, it's the way her words reminded of my biggest insecurity…my biggest pain…

The moment she said that, I was instantly transported back to that summer after freshman year of college, to that standoff I had with my dad in his living room. I can still see the disappointment etched deep in his face as we talked.

"*You can't be serious, Aidan. You're quitting hockey? To become a teacher?*"

"*I'm serious, Dad.*"

"Think about what you're giving up. I know you won't be a super-star if you ever make it to the NHL, but you'll still be a solid player. Even if you get bounced back to the minors every year or so, you'll still get to play pro."

"I spent my whole life destroying my body for a sport I don't care about anymore. I'm done."

"You think that because you got A's in all your English classes, you're a genius? You suddenly think your value is in your brain instead of your body now? Pathetic."

Pain radiates in my chest as I think about that memory and the fact that I've barely spoken to my dad since that day.

I shove it all away, refocusing on the moment. This isn't about my dad. This is about my job and trying to reason with this auditor.

I check the time, noting that students will start filtering in in a few minutes.

"Look, would it help if we cleared the air a bit?"

She frowns. "What are you talking about?"

"I'm sorry about what I said in the elevator yesterday. About your name."

She looks surprised at what I've said. "It's fine," she mutters.

"It's not. I was rude and unprofessional. I'm sorry."

"I said it's fine."

I sigh and shake my head. Clearly none of this is fine.

We stand there for a silent few seconds. I notice she's look-ing at me expectantly.

"What?" I finally ask.

"Is that the only thing you want to apologize for?"

I frown, confused. "Yeah…"

She stares at me. I'm not sure why. Is she waiting for me to apologize for getting into it with her at the staff meeting yes-terday? She's the one who came in guns a-blazing, rubbing ev-eryone the wrong way with her curt, unsympathetic attitude. How else was I supposed to react?

Micah lets out a bitter chuckle. "Okay. Never mind."

She starts to turn away.

"Wait, what do you mean?"

"It's nothing," she says without even looking at me.

I step toward her. "No, really. Did I do or say something else that upset you? Because if I did…"

When she spins around, I'm taken aback at the flash of pain in her eyes. "I said never mind, Professor Scott. I'm going to observe you during today's class. We'll have a brief meeting afterward so I can give you my feedback."

I take in the embarrassed look in her eyes as she turns back to her desk and sits down.

"You don't have to keep calling me Professor Scott. You can call me Aidan."

She ignores me as she scribbles something in her notepad. A second later students start filtering into the classroom. Guilt gnaws at the pit of my gut. Clearly I hurt her feelings. I think back to the argument we had yesterday during the faculty meeting, but I'm struggling to remember everything. Things definitely got heated, and I can't remember exactly what I said to her. We were both pissed and snapped at each other.

A minute later the room is full with students. I clench my jaw before forcing out a breath. I can't think about this now— I've got a class to teach.

"Morning, everyone." I take my usual spot in the class, which is to lean-sit against the front of the desk. "Let's dive right in, shall we?"

I swipe my paperback copy of *Romeo and Juliet* and hold it up. "What did we all think?"

When the room of twenty students stays quiet, I start to get nervous. Getting the silent treatment this early in the morning from a group of nineteen- and twenty-year-olds isn't a surprise. I'm used to it, honestly. It normally takes a bit for them to warm up and start speaking. But knowing that Micah is sitting here, observing my every move, documenting everything that happens so she can use it to evaluate me—and that it could determine whether or not I keep my job—has me sweating.

Out of the corner of my eye, I spot her scribbling something on a notepad. Probably about how it's crickets in my class so far. Fantastic.

I do my best to push aside the doubt trying so hard to seep in. I make sure my tone is light when I speak again. "Tough crowd this early in the morning. No one's excited to chat about this classic? I'm excited. I even brought my favorite *Romeo and Juliet* pun cup."

I hold up my thermos, which sports a sticker of cartoon knife with a smiling face on it. "'O happy dagger'? No laughs? Really?"

A few chuckles follow.

"Most of you already read this in high school, right?" I ask. They all nod.

"What did you think of it then?"

When everyone is quiet yet again, I let out a loud groan that earns me a loud laugh.

"Come on, guys. Throw me a bone here. Honestly, what did you think of this play when you read it as a fourteen-year-old?"

A student in the front raises her hand, and I call on her.

"Honestly? I didn't really understand it at that age. I thought it was boring."

"Fair," I say.

The student behind her raises his hand. "I agree. I didn't really get it either. I thought it was kind of dumb that these two kids thought they were in love and were willing to kill themselves after knowing each other for not very long."

Mumbles of agreement follow.

"Also fair," I say.

A student in the back hesitates before raising her hand. "I, uh, always thought it was so awful how so many people called this play a romance. It's, like, one of the least romantic things I've ever read."

"I definitely see your point. Let me ask you all this—has your opinion changed about this play after reading it years later?"

I get a mix of reactions. Mostly shrugs with a few yeses and noes.

"We've got a good mix of reactions. Always exciting." I pause. "Okay, so I think we all can agree that *Romeo and Juliet* isn't a great relationship handbook, right?"

Almost everyone laughs. Except Micah, of course, who's glaring at her notepad as she scribbles furiously.

"Do you remember what it was like falling in love for the first time?"

Affirming noises follow.

"You didn't do anything as tragic as these two did. Thankfully." I hold up the book. "But I bet some of you thought that you were head over heels in love after not knowing that person very long, right?"

It's quiet before a good chunk of the class nod their heads in agreement.

"Tell me about it."

"I can definitely relate to that feeling," a student in the front says with a shy laugh. "I was totally in love with my high school boyfriend. We're not together anymore, but fourteen-year-old me thought we'd be together forever. It's pretty silly to think about now."

"It's not," I say. "That's the very definition of young love. It's your first time feeling that way. It's your first time feeling that heart-pounding excitement, that attraction, that intoxicating surge of emotions. That first time holding hands, that first kiss." I make a mock-explosion sound while gesturing with my hands, which earns me a good laugh. "You thought about them all the time. You couldn't get them out of your mind if you tried, right?"

They all nod. A couple more students share how they felt the first time they fell in love.

"How did it feel when people like teachers or parents questioned your relationship or your feelings for your partner?" I ask. "When they said stuff like, *It's never going to last—you're too young.* Or that what you were feeling was just hormones and not real love."

Multiple students remark how hurt and mad they were.

"You can kind of understand where they're coming from now though, can't you? Looking back at yourself as a teenager, you can see why some of your relationships didn't work out, right?"

Almost everyone says they agree.

"It's still kind of a dick move though, to tell someone that their feelings aren't valid just because they're young, don't you think?"

Everyone either nods or says "Yeah."

I hold up the book once more. "I know this play is chock-full of flaws and it's old as hell and it's hard to relate to in modern times, for sure. All of those criticisms are valid. But I honestly think the emotions of the characters stand the test of time. Because we all know what it's like to be young and in love and feel like it's going to last forever. And we all know how bad it hurts when that love ends—when you get your heart broken for the first time."

The entire class nods in agreement. Even Micah is looking at me. She's not nodding, but she's not actively glaring at me. I'll count that as a win.

"Yeah, this play is a tough sell because the characters are young, and they haven't known each other for very long before they're willing to die for their love for one another. A bit dramatic and unrealistic, for sure. But there's an emotional significance there that I think is pretty relatable when it comes to falling into and out of love. Maybe we don't have to take this play literally for it to be meaningful. Maybe its value is in the raw emotions that it makes us feel when we think about our own experiences of being young and in love. That's why this class is called Shakespeare Yesterday and Today. Yeah, he's old-fashioned. Not to mention dead. But I think his writing still holds a lot of value even today. To me, that's what makes literature special, when it can conjure up genuine feelings within you while you read it, no matter how old the text is."

The students nod in agreement with what I've said.

"Enough of my yammering. Let's break into groups so you all can discuss that more on your own."

I break the class into small groups and tell them to chat about their thoughts on the play. Before class ends, I assign them the next play to read. When everyone leaves, I walk over to Micah, who's still scribbling.

She looks up at me. "Would you like to go over my notes here or in your office?"

I'm thrown off by how no-nonsense her tone is. I shouldn't be. Her entire demeanor is the definition of *no-nonsense*. But I guess the hopeful part of me wanted her to be affected by what I said in class today.

"Here is fine." I sit down at the desk next to her.

"Did you realize that you didn't take attendance?"

I pause, surprised at her out-of-the-blue question. "What?"

"You didn't take attendance at the beginning of class," she repeats.

"I don't take attendance this far into the semester anymore."

"Why not?"

She doesn't even blink. It's like she's got all of her questions loaded up and ready to go. She's like a damn machine.

"Because at this point I know who's showing up to my class."

She pulls a sheet of paper out of her notebook and shows it to me. "It says on your class roster that there were four more students who were enrolled in this class, but I only counted twenty today."

I skim the paper. "Those four students stopped showing up after the first week. It's pretty common for some students to start a class, decide it's not for them or they can't handle the course load, then drop."

More furiously scribbling. Jesus, is she writing an essay?

After a long moment, Micah looks back at me. "You're clearly well-liked among your students. And you do a good job of breathing new life into such antiquated literature. But I can't ignore the fact that you're not good at retaining your students, Professor Scott."

My mouth is open as I process everything she's said. Damn, if that wasn't some epic back-handed complimenting.

I shake my head. "Wait, so you're using the fact that a few students have dropped my class as a reason to criticize me as an educator."

"If that's how you want to phrase it, go right ahead," she says as she straightens her stack of papers. "And it's not just this class. I looked through your rosters over the past couple of years. You've had a handful of students drop almost all of the courses you teach."

"Most professors lose a handful of students each semester, no matter the class." I can't believe how blunt and short-sighted Micah is being. "I-I don't understand…"

This time when she looks at me, she pins me with a hard, unyielding stare. "Tuition is the main source of revenue for a university, Professor Scott. The more students you enroll, the more tuition the university earns, the more money it makes. If a student drops a class, they don't have to pay for it. That's less money that the university makes."

Frustration gnaws at me. "I know that. I'm not an idiot."

"There's no need to get hostile, Professor Scott."

Frustration turns to anger. "You come into my classroom

and insult the material I'm teaching and make it seem like I'm some moron who's costing the university money because I don't think to take attendance every day, and *I'm* the hostile one?"

I stand up from the desk and start to gather my things.

Behind me, I hear Micah let out a heavy sigh. "I'm not trying to upset you, Professor Scott. I'm just trying to help."

I spin around to face her. "I said call me Aidan."

Her saucer like eyes widen the slightest bit at the bite in my tone. "I'd prefer to keep this as professional and cordial as possible, Professor Scott."

"Of course you would," I mutter as I finish grabbing all my stuff off the desk.

"Excuse me, but what is that supposed to mean?"

"It means that all your fixation on professionalism is BS. It doesn't take away from the fact that you don't care about anything other than nitpicking at any random thing you can find for your little audit."

She scoffs. "How dare you say that. I'm just doing my job."

I look her dead in the eye. "That's crap and you know it."

When her mouth falls open and all she can do is stand there and stare at me, I feel the tiniest burst of satisfaction.

After a few seconds, she resumes her signature hard stare. "With all due respect, Professor Scott, I'm trying my hardest to do a good job, whether you believe me or not."

It's not till she finishes speaking that I realize just how close we're standing to each other. The tip of my shoe is touching the tip of her high heel. Our faces are just a handful of inches apart. I inhale to steady myself, but that's a huge fucking mistake because I breathe in a lungful of whatever perfume she's wearing. It smells like candy and flowers, and goddamn, it's intoxicating.

A second later my brain catches up. That familiar surge of frustration bubbles in my chest, and I look her in the eye.

"With all due respect, Ms. Mila, you're right—I don't believe you. You're the worst thing that's happened to this university."

Her brow hits her hairline as I stomp out of the room, fuming.

Five

Micah

I stand in this empty classroom, rattled and stunned by Aidan's insult. And pissed. Really fucking pissed.

I throw my pen on top of my notepad and tug a hand through my hair.

You're the worst thing that's happened to this university.

This isn't the first time someone has lobbed a critical comment my way during an audit. I normally can take comments like that in stride. It's the nature of this job. People are never happy when there's an auditor in their workplace, observing and evaluating them. I expect them to be mad and irritated at me.

But to be disrespectful? That's crossing a line.

And that's exactly what Aidan did when he said I was the worst thing that's happened to this college.

I make myself take a slow, deep breath. I can't let him rattle me like this. I'm here to do my work, not make friends.

I almost laugh when I think back to before class started, when he said he wanted to clear the air. When he apologized for making fun of my name in the elevator, I started to get my hopes up. I actually thought that was a friendly gesture from him. And I thought that he was going to apologize for how hostile he was to me during yesterday morning's meeting too.

But no. I was wrong.

And when I hinted at it, he looked at me like he was totally clueless. Like he had no idea what I was talking about.

And that's when it dawned on me. He didn't apologize because he doesn't think what he did was wrong. He didn't see anything wrong with mocking my degree and my qualifications in front of a room full of people.

Anger and frustration steamroll my insides.

I can accept that he doesn't like that I'm here. I can even accept that he doesn't like me.

But what I refuse to accept is the way he's treating me. Like I'm nothing, like he knows better, like I don't matter.

My heart pounds in my chest. God, he's a jerk.

I scoop up my things and walk out of the room, down the hall toward the next classroom I'm due to observe.

I can't keep thinking about him. I force myself to take another long, silent breath in an attempt to calm myself. I need to refocus so I can go into my next class observation with a clear head…

"…she's a menace, Dr. Wauncho. Her presence is a blight on this department. And she's only been here a day."

I stop dead in my tracks at the sound of Professor Scott complaining about me to his boss.

I glance ahead and see an open office door a half dozen feet ahead of me.

"Professor Scott, I understand your concern. But there's not a lot I can do about this," he says. "Ms. Mila's presence here is mandatory. She was hired by the university. It's out of my control."

"Oh, come on, Ronald."

I jolt back at the jump in volume in Aidan's voice.

"There must be something you can do. She's bringing everyone down. Morale is at an all-time low. Not a single one of us in the English department is happy she's here. You heard how dismissive she was in yesterday's meeting. It's obvious she doesn't value what we do here. She doesn't care about literature or the arts."

"I understand you're upset," Dr. Wauncho says in a placating tone. "But my hands are tied. Ms. Mila is here to stay for the next six weeks."

"I can't believe this," Aidan mutters. "There's got to be some way to get rid of her."

I frown at his blunt phrasing.

Get rid of her.

Like I'm a pest.

Rage pulses through me.

"Can we file a complaint with her boss? Maybe if we complain about her enough we can get her fired."

My jaw drops. Is he fucking serious?

Anger and adrenaline surge through me. I stomp up to the open office door, step into the doorway, and see Dr. Wauncho sitting at his desk. Professor Scott is standing in front of him, his back to me.

"You're brainstorming ways to get me fired?" I blurt.

Aidan whips his head around to face me. His blue eyes are wide with shock, but a half second later he's glaring at me.

He crosses his arms over his broad chest. "Yeah. I am. Feels pretty awful when someone tries to mess with your job, doesn't it?"

I step toward him. "I'm not messing with your job. I'm here to observe you in your position and bring my findings to your university. I'm not actively trying to get you fired. Don't you dare say that."

He rolls his eyes. "Don't insult me, Micah. You and I both know that's a bunch of corporate BS you recite so that you feel better about what is it you do for a living. Because admitting that the whole point of your job is to make other people lose theirs is just too on the nose, isn't it?"

My jaw falls open. The fucking audacity of this guy.

He tilts his head at me. It's a slight move, but it screams *condescending*.

"Did I hit a nerve?" he asks.

The anger and frustration inside of me morphs into raw determination. I start to smile. The satisfied look on his face fades. He frowns like he's confused.

I shake my head. "Nope. In fact…"

I grab my phone and pull up the number of my boss, Carl, at the firm I work for.

I move to hand my phone to him. "You can call my firm right now and tell them whatever complaint you have about me."

Aidan frowns at the phone in my hand. "What?"

"I'd love for you to talk to my boss. His name's Carl, by the way."

"You would?"

I nod at him. "I want to stand here and listen while you tell him whatever excuse you've made up about me to get me fired. Because I'm certain it's absolute crap. And I'm certain my boss will laugh in your face."

Aidan's frown turns into a full-on glare.

"And I'm going to laugh in your face too, Professor Scott. Because clearly you have nothing on me. There's not a single thing I've done in the day and a half that I've been here at your university that would warrant me getting fired. I've been professional and honest with you. And the hard truth of the situation is simply that you don't like it. You don't like me."

Intensity flashes in those soft blue eyes. His gaze falls to the phone in my hand, but I know he's not going to take it and report me to my boss. Because I know he's got nothing on me.

He's just a cranky, entitled jerk who's mad that someone is challenging him for once.

I drop my hand at my side and take a step forward, closing the space between us. "It's completely fine that you don't like me, Professor Scott. I don't like you either. But that has no bearing on how I do my job. So why don't you devote less time inventing ways to get me fired and spend more time focusing on your own job so you actually have a chance of re-taining it at the end of this audit?"

When I see his eyebrow lift, I'm surprised. He almost looks intrigued. Actually, more like impressed at what I've said—the way I've stood up to him.

Out of the corner of my eye, I see Dr. Wauncho stand up and round his desk toward us.

"All right, you two, why don't we take a second to cool off."

Aidan blinks, and that hard expression returns.

"No need," I say, turning to leave.

When I step out of the office, I stop, surprised to see a dozen heads peering out of every doorway in this hallway, looking in my direction.

They must have overheard us...or we must have been louder than I thought...

I clear my throat and walk down the hall. I ignore the stares and make my way to my next classroom, my heart racing from the adrenaline rush of confronting Aidan.

I'm glad I stood up for myself, but I hate feeling like I just made a scene. How embarrassing.

When I walk into the classroom, I'm relieved to see it's empty. I have some time to collect myself before the profes-sor and students walk in. I set my things on a nearby desk and take a moment to close my eyes and breathe. It takes a few sec-onds for my heart to stop pounding. I can feel the adrenaline leave my body as the seconds pass, but then I start to feel antsy.

I let out a heavy sigh at the thought of powering through the rest of the day. But then I think about going home tonight and unwinding with a glass of wine and bingeing my favorite stories from ShakespeareInLust on Scribble Share. The perfect reward for a crummy day at work, and I instantly feel better.

Six

Aidan

Jason glances at me after sipping from his beer bottle. "You okay?"

I nod.

He frowns at me. "Seriously though. Are you?"

I sigh. "I'm fine, Jason."

He shakes his head like he doesn't believe me. Which is understandable because I'm lying.

I take a drink from my water glass while pretending to watch the game on the TV above us at the sports bar we're at. But I have a hell of a time paying attention. My focus is shot. It has been ever since Micah and I got into it this morning within earshot of the entire English department.

"Micah was pretty harsh with you, man," Jason says. "The way she called your bluff." He lets out a low whistle and shakes his head. His shaggy blond hair sways with the movement.

I frown at him. "I don't need a play-by-play. I was there when it happened."

He pats my shoulder. "Sorry, man. You tried your best to get one over on her. You've got my respect for that. But she won this time."

"We don't need to keep talking about this."

I still can't believe Micah had the nerve to call me out like that. I mean, I guess she was within her right to do that. I had nothing on her to get her fired. Still though. It sucked being ridiculed, especially by someone who hates me. And who I know, without a doubt, wants to get me fired, no matter what she claims.

But the weirdest part about what happened? Part of me was kind of…excited by it.

When I think about my argument with Micah from this morning, I have to fight back a cringe. Yeah, it was unprofessional of me to complain loudly about her and to suggest that we get her fired, but I was at my wits' end. Micah clearly has it out for me. It's obvious from how apathetic she was when she observed my class that she doesn't actually care about how well I do my job or how much the students enjoy my class. All she cares about is numbers. Enrollment, attendance, retention, tuition. And if that's all she uses to evaluate me as a teacher—if she's going to ignore my actual teaching methods and the rapport I have with my students—then there's no point in ever trying to get her to see my point. She'll always be against me.

I think back to how she called my bluff and offered her phone up to me to call her boss. I was so thrown off, I couldn't think of anything to say. So I just stood there and took in the visual of this woman—this gorgeous, feisty woman, going toe-to-toe with me and handing me my ass…

An unfamiliar restlessness courses through me when I think about that moment. It's the same restlessness that hit me when she and I went toe-to-toe in my classroom after the students left…when we were standing so close to each other that I could feel the tension sparking in the air between us…

A strange, excited feeling whooshes through me. What the hell?

I can feel my face heat with shame even as I think about it now. Jesus, what does that say about the kind of person I am? What kind of guy gets excited when an attractive woman who can't stand him tells him off?

Just then, Kendall, our friend and fellow English professor, walks into the bar and spots us. We wave her over. She swipes her dark brown hair out of her face and sits down on the stool next to me.

She aims a pitying expression at me. "How are you holding up?"

I let out a frustrated laugh. "God, did everyone in the English department hear Micah rip me a new asshole? Did you tell all the other departments about it too?"

The server stops by, and Kendall orders a beer and three shots of tequila.

She pats my arm. "We're going to toast to you with tequila. You were brave enough to take on the big bad auditor, and for that we salute you."

I chuckle and tell her thanks.

"You were just brave enough to say what we all were thinking," Jason says to me.

Kendall nods in agreement. "I've been racking my brain to think of a legitimate way to get rid of Micah so we can save our jobs."

"Well, if you think of it, let me know. I know how to get ahold of her boss," I joke.

Jason and Kendall offer sad chuckles. The server drops off a beer for Kendall and the tequila shots.

She raises her shot glass and looks at me. "To Aidan, for taking on the evil auditor."

"To you, man," Jason says as he raises his shot glass.

I raise mine too. "Thanks, guys."

Together we knock back the shots and set our empty glasses on the tabletop.

"So how was Micah when she observed your class this afternoon?" I ask Kendall.

She groans, her expression twisted like she's in pain. "Awful. She grilled me about my attendance rates and how many students have dropped my class so far this semester."

I nod once. "Sounds about right." I pat her shoulder. "Sorry."

"She's terrifying. She didn't smile once in my class," Kendall says. "And I was teaching comedy writing in my composition class today. All the students were laughing. But her? Not even once. I even tried to bond with her. We're both Filipino, so I made a joke about karaoke. She didn't even smile."

Her shoulders sink.

"I'm sorry," I say.

"Yeah, sorry, Kendall." Jason winces.

She takes a long pull of her beer.

As Jason and Kendall talk about their plans for spring break in a couple of months, I grab my phone and pull up the Scribble Share app. I check on my latest story, which I posted this afternoon, after my fight with Micah.

I was so tense and worked up, and writing was the only way I could expend that energy. I had a free hour between classes, so I holed up in my office and wrote a scene where Rome defends Jia against an attacker. And as weird as it sounds, I felt a lot better after writing it.

I smile when I see how many likes it's gotten so far. It's early evening, so it's only been up a few hours.

I do a quick skim of the comments.

Pure hotness! WOW WOW WOW!

Yes, Rome! Fight for your woman!

I don't care what anyone says, it's always super hot when a man is willing to throw down and protect you without hesitation

Hottest thing on the planet is when a man goes in full-on feral protector mode and defends his lady

My mood instantly lifts. The readers on this platform are the best. Always supportive and kind.

I put my phone away so I don't come off as that jerk who is glued to his phone when he should be paying attention to his friends. A hand claps on my shoulder. I look up and see my little brother, Liam, grinning down at me.

I should probably stop calling him little. At six foot three, he's an inch taller and has at least twenty-five pounds of muscle on me.

"Hey." I smile up at him. "What are you doing here?"

"Getting some drinks with the guys after practice." He nods to the far side of the bar, where a few of his hockey teammates are.

"I didn't know guzzling alcohol was part of your pro-athlete regimen."

Liam laughs and pats his stomach. "It is for as long as I can get away with it."

I roll my eyes. "You and your twenty-eight-year-old metabolism can fuck right off," I joke.

He bursts out laughing. "Aww, come on, big brother. You're not *that* much older than me."

He frowns at the top of my head. "Actually, I take that back. I think I see some gray hairs. Damn, I didn't know you could have gray hair at thirty-two."

I chuckle. "You asshole."

My brother runs a hand through his wavy dark blond hair. "Good thing I got the blond genes in the family. Gray blends way better with blond," he teases.

I shove him, and he laughs. Jason laughs too. I notice Kendall frowning at Liam.

Liam notices too because he grins at her. "You miss me, darlin'? I mean, I can't blame you. It *has* been a few months since we've seen each other."

She wrinkles her nose. "Shut up, Liam."

My brother clutches his chest with his hand and stumbles back a step. "You know just what to say to get me going, firecracker."

When she flips him off, I roll my eyes.

Despite the fact that Kendall can't stand Liam, he still constantly teases her. These two have been like this ever since we were all enrolled in at the same college together. I was in graduate school and became friends with Kendall, who was in undergrad at the time. When she and Liam first met, they got along fine.

Then we all went to a house party together thrown by one of his hockey teammates after a big win during the season. Everyone got pretty wasted, and the next morning Kendall was giving Liam the cold shoulder. When I asked her what was up, she said it was nothing. That was years ago, and I haven't pried since.

I just figured my brother's obnoxious personality finally got to her. I don't blame her. He's always joking and doesn't take a damn thing seriously. I could see how he would get on someone's nerves. He gets on mine constantly.

Kendall's frown deepens when Liam sits down on the stool next to me.

"Won't your teammates notice you're gone?" I ask.

"Nah, they're all pretty drunk," he says.

Kendall makes an annoyed sound. "I have to pee."

When she gets up to leave and walks off, I notice Liam's gaze following her.

I elbow him. "You should really stop giving her such a hard time. She clearly hates it."

He flashes a lopsided grin. "Nah. I like it when she's mean to me. It gets me hot."

"You're a pig," I mutter.

"So what's new with you guys?" Liam asks.

"We're being audited at the university," Jason says. "We'll probably get fired."

Liam's brow hits his hairline. He turns to me. "Seriously?"

"It's too soon to tell what's going to happen, but it's not great news. It feels like we're all auditioning to keep our jobs."

I explain to Liam about Micah and how she's been hired by the university to observe our department to see where the school can make cuts to save money.

He looks dazed as he shakes his head. "Sorry, dude. That really sucks."

"Yeah. It does." I down more beer.

"So this auditor…" Liam says while stretching out his shoulder. "Is she hot?"

I roll my eyes. My brother is an idiot. But given the fact that next to hockey, his second-favorite activity is hooking up with any woman who gives him an enthusiastic yes, I shouldn't be surprised by his question.

I look at him. "What does that have to do with anything?"

He shrugs. "Just curious."

"She is really pretty," Jason says. "She's also terrifying. A total hard ass. She gives off this vibe that if you cross her, she'll tear you to shreds."

Liam grins. "That's kinda sexy."

Frowning, I shake my head at him. "You are a caveman."

My brother shrugs. "I can't help it. I love it when a gorgeous woman isn't afraid to fight with me. It means she's passionate. And that keeps things fun and exciting, if you know what I mean." He winks at me, and I punch his shoulder.

But as I let my mind wander to earlier today and think about how attracted I was to Micah during our fight, I silently admit that maybe my little brother has a point.

Seven

Micah

"That professor sounds like a grade-A dickhead. Want me to kill him?"

I choke on the sip of tea I just took as I laugh at what my sister just said.

"Crap, sorry," Jordan says on the other line of the phone. "I didn't mean for you to choke to death."

I cough a few more times, then take another sip of tea.

"It's okay," I say, my throat raw. "It was worth it."

I've just arrived home to Jordan's condo. We're having our weekly video chat, and I've just finished venting to her about how Aidan was trying to get me fired.

"Seriously though, I'll buy a plane ticket right now and kick his ass for being such a jerk to you," Jordan says.

I soften at the conviction in her tone. Having a twin sister who's ready to drop everything to defend me is something I'm grateful for. Jordan's been this way our entire lives. She's always been protective of the people she loves, especially me.

"Will you pull the same move you did when we were in kindergarten and that boy pushed me off the swing?" I tease.

Even now I can picture Jordan running up to that kid and kicking him in the balls.

"You know me. Always aim for the jewels. Always," she says.

I laugh. "As enticing as that is, I'll have to decline. Thanks though."

"Oh, come on," she whines. "I've been going extra hard in my boxing-fitness classes. I want to put my skills to practical use. Kicking your work bully's ass would be a perfect way to do that."

"You're the best, you know that?"

"So are you."

"How's London?" I ask.

"Amazing, I assume. Can't really say though because I've been holed up in my office working ever since I got here."

"You're such a workaholic."

"I love my job. There's a difference," she says pointedly.

My sister is a corporate lawyer who recently moved to London to work on a huge international case for her firm.

"Please tell me you're at least getting home at a reasonable hour and not working through the night at your office," I say.

"I've only done that twice. Okay, three times." She pauses. "Fine, four."

"Yeah, you're totally not a workaholic," I joke.

"Shut up," she says through a chuckle.

"Seriously though, Jordan. Be sure to take a break every once in a while, okay? Make some time for yourself. It's not good for you to work all the time."

She sighs. "Okay, okay. I will."

"Promise me you'll do something fun this weekend. Something touristy. Like ride on the London Eye. Or take a selfie in front of Buckingham Palace."

My sister groans.

"Promise me."

She sighs. "I'll go check out Big Ben Saturday morning, but that's the best I can do."

I smile. "Perfect. Send me a selfie for proof."

"You're such a stickler."

"I'm an auditor. I can't help it."

We both laugh.

"I really needed this vent session, Jordan. Thanks for this."

"Always. No matter what."

I tuck my feet under my legs as I lounge on her plush sofa and glance out the floor-to-ceiling window of her top-floor condo. City lights from the buildings nearby twinkle against the indigo night sky. This place is ridiculously nice, and my sister is a saint for letting me stay here rent-free.

"Thank you again for letting me stay at your place," I say softly. "I swear, I'll pay you back once I build my savings back up—"

"No way, Micah."

I let out a heavy breath. "Come on, Jordan. I feel like I'm taking advantage of you."

She laughs like I've just said the most ridiculous thing ever.

"Don't even try it. Micah, I own my condo. I don't make mortgage payments on it anymore, so that would be pretty messed up of me to make my own sister give me money for staying there. Besides, you're doing me a favor by looking after the place while I'm gone. With you there I'm not stressed about a pipe bursting or something catching on fire."

I feel the slightest bit comforted. "Thanks, Jordan. Really."

After ending things with Ashton, I had almost no savings and moved into a place I could barely afford and racked up so much credit-card debt just to pay my bills. As soon as my sister and parents found out about my financial situation, they swooped in to help me. Jordan insisted I move into her place for free while she was away in England. And my parents gave me money to pay off my debt. I'm so lucky to have them.

Jordan is quiet for a second. "So… Fuckface hasn't tried to bother you again, right?"

I smile at my sister's nickname for my ex. "No. He hasn't."

"Good." She's quiet again. "You know, Micah, all you have to do is say the word and I'm happy to go all psycho lawyer on him. He deserves it for what he did to you."

A cocktail of pain and shame whirls through me like a tornado.

"Jordan, I told you. I don't want to deal with him anymore. I want to just leave him in the past, where he belongs."

A heavy sigh echoes from her end of the line. "Micah, he was an asshole to you. He broke your heart and he screwed you over. He deserves to have his ass nailed to the wall."

I close my eyes, my chest squeezing when I think about my relationship with Ashton. We dated for two years. After a year together, I moved into his house and started paying him rent. From the moment I met him, I was in awe of him. He was a successful author who had won awards for his books. I was so excited that someone so accomplished and brilliant was interested in me. And when I told him about my dreams to be a writer someday, he was sweet and supportive. He encouraged me to write in my spare time and even offered to read and critique my work.

My stomach churns when I think back to the first time I let him read my writing. I had written a short story. I've always loved reading romance, so I thought it was only natural that I write one.

I can still remember how he cackled when he read it. Like it was a joke.

I remember exactly what he said. I'll remember it forever.

Sweetie, this is cute, but come on. This is smut. Utter trash. So lowbrow. You can do better than this.

The worst part was how instead of standing up for myself, I felt embarrassed and ashamed. Because in that moment, I thought he was right. I thought that since he was a brilliant author, he knew better than me.

I forced out a laugh to hide how I really felt and said he was right. And then I stopped writing altogether. Just like that, I abandoned what I loved. I haven't written anything since.

Pain stabs through my chest when I think about the day I came home early from work and saw his phone on the coffee table.

I didn't mean to snoop, but as I sat down on the couch, he got a text. It was a photo of his assistant, Bianca, topless.

For a second, I froze, my eyes wide as I stared at the photo. And before I could tell myself not to, I grabbed his phone and read the text she sent along with the image.

Aching for you.

I shot up to my feet a second later and ran to the bathroom to vomit. I couldn't believe it. Ashton was cheating on me.

"Micah, you paid Fuckface's mortgage for a full year." My sister's voice jolts me back to the present. "You helped pay for his renovations with your savings too."

God, I was so, so stupid to do all that, to give him all my money. We weren't even married.

"And the whole time he was cheating on you. That asshole owes you thousands of dollars."

I close my eyes and shake my head. "I know. Believe me, I know…but legally, I don't have any claim to that money. You know I don't. My name wasn't on the mortgage. He doesn't owe me anything."

Jordan exhales sharply, then goes quiet again.

"I'm sorry," she finally says. "I didn't mean to rehash all this—I just… I love you, Micah. You're my twin sister, and my instinct is to fight for you. Always."

A sad smile tugs at my lips. "I love you for that."

"And I know you don't like it when I pry, but have you dated anyone since ending things with him?"

I shake my head.

Jordan stares at me. "Come on, Micah. It's been almost a year."

"I know. It's just…the thought of dating again freaks me out. What if I fall for someone and they screw me over again?"

"Then don't date. Just hook up."

I laugh at how she says it, like it's a no-brainer.

"I don't know if I'm built for hookups. Sex always feels so personal to me. I'm not interested in having sex casually."

"Then just do mouth stuff and hand stuff."

I burst out laughing. "I can't believe you just said that."

She shrugs and smiles. "I'm a lawyer. I'm always to-the-point about everything."

When I finally stop laughing, I think about what she said.

"Okay, I'll admit it would be fun to be with someone who I could mess around with. A guy who would be okay with something casual but not full-on sex. But that's so specific. No one would be on board with that."

"Micah, come on. You're gorgeous, smart, funny, and a blast to be around. Guys would line up around the block to be your almost-fuck buddy."

I laugh again, then glance at the clock on the wall. "Shoot, it's almost eleven your time. Sorry for keeping you up so late."

"Don't be. You know I'm a night owl."

"I hate this time difference between us."

She sighs. "Same. But I'm only here till the summer. Then I'm back and we can meet in person for our weekly vent sessions like we normally do."

I smile. "Can't wait."

"If you change your mind about wanting me to come home and kick Professor Douche Canoe's ass, let me know."

I chuckle. It feels good to laugh after reliving all those ugly feelings from my breakup.

"I promise I will."

"I'm proud of you for standing up for yourself," Jordan says. "And hey, don't be afraid to get petty if he keeps being a jerk to you."

"We don't have to take it that far, Jordan."

She scoffs. "We absolutely do. He tried to get you fired, Micah. And you did nothing wrong. You were just doing your job. If he's going to play dirty, then you're allowed to play dirty too."

I'm quiet as I mull over my sister's words. I've never had a problem standing up for myself in uncomfortable work situations. I never crossed the line though, no matter how rude or mean a client or coworker has been to me.

"I don't know if I have it in me to play dirty, Jordan."

"That's why you have a scrappy twin sister. Think of all the stuff I was exposed to in law school. I'm full of ideas."

When I think back to everything my sister told me she dealt with as a law student at Vanderbilt, I still can't believe it. I thought all you had to do to succeed at a top law school was study hard and perform well in class. I was wrong.

Jordan told me that some of her classmates were downright psycho with the way they tried to sabotage each other. *Cutthroat* doesn't even begin to describe it. They hid textbooks at the library, stole study guides, and posted the wrong dates for the finals schedule on online student forums. One student even tried to poison his rival during a test because he wanted to ensure he got the top grade in the class. His rival was allergic to nuts, so the guy splashed peanut oil into his coffee when he wasn't looking. During the test, he had a severe allergic reaction. Paramedics were called, and thankfully the student survived. The psycho student was caught and arrested and kicked out of law school.

"I want to avoid jail time, so I'm going to stick to the professional route," I say.

"Such a rule follower," she teases. "So what's your plan, then?"

"I'm going to ask to meet with him one-on-one tomorrow morning so we can clear the air. And then we can move on like professionals."

"Good luck with that."

We tell each other goodbye, and I hang up and cook myself

a quick dinner. I sit down at the table and pull up the Scribble Share app on my phone so I can binge-read ShakespeareIn-Lust's fanfic while I eat.

When I see a brand-new post, I smile, eager to dive in.

Lava blasted through Rome's veins as he took in the sight in front of him.

Casio stood just a dozen feet away, his hand gripped around Jia's wrist, pressing her up against a wall.

Jia's face was twisted in pain. "Don't touch me."

Casio flashed a smirk as he leered down at Jia. "I can touch you all I want. Your father said so."

Jia tried to pull away, but his grip on her wrist was too tight. She winced in pain. "He would never say that."

Casio lowered his face to Jia's. "Your father said to bring you back to him by any means necessary." With his free hand, he grabbed her chin roughly and jerked her face up to look at him. "And in my opinion, this is necessary. You're a feisty one."

Something inside Rome snapped. Never in his life had he cleared a dozen feet of space so quickly. It didn't even take a second for him to make it to Casio. Powered by adrenaline and rage, Rome grabbed Casio by the neck, pulling him off of Jia.

Casio stumbled back, quickly righting himself. Rome moved in front of Jia, creating a barrier between the woman he loved and the man he wanted to rip apart with his bare hands.

Rage pumped hot in his veins as he glowered at the man who dared to put his hands on Jia. His Jia.

"Don't fucking touch her," Rome growled.

"Too late. Already did."

The muscles in Rome's hands ached to strangle him. "You're going to fucking die for hurting her."

A bitter laugh fell from Casio's evil smirk. "Someone's jealous," he taunted. A second later, he pulled a knife from his pocket.

Behind Rome, Jia gasped. He wanted more than anything to turn around and comfort her, to tell her this would all be okay. But he couldn't look away from Casio. He needed to keep his eyes on him to protect himself—to protect Jia.

Casio brandished the knife. "I'm taking her with me."

"The fuck you are."

Another evil laugh fell from Casio's lips. "I'm gonna enjoy gutting you like a fucking fish."

Rome stepped forward, closing the space between them.

Casio blinked at him, clearly surprised. He lunged forward, the knife in hand, but Rome was quick to react. With the outside of his forearm, he blocked Casio by hitting the inside of his bicep while punching him in the stomach with his free hand.

Casio hunched over in pain but straightened back up a second later. He lunged forward and slashed at Rome, cutting his shoulder.

Jia yelled, but Rome was unfazed. It was like he didn't even feel it. Because he didn't. All he felt was the urge to protect Jia. It was the single driving force in his body. His brain, his muscles, his bones, his blood—everything in his body worked together for a single goal.

Protect Jia.

Rome moved liked a machine. He ducked and dodged Casio's blade, then landed a punch to his side, then another to his jaw.

Casio wobbled on unsteady feet. Even with his knife, he was powerless against Rome's rage and fury.

Casio lunged forward, but Rome ducked to the side.

Losing his balance, Casio fell to the ground, dropping the knife. A split second later, Rome jumped on top of him. He pummeled him over and over again until his face was a bloody pulp, until his knuckles were raw, until Casio was just a mound of unmoving flesh on the concrete.

His heart pounding in his chest, Rome stood up, panting hard in an attempt to catch his breath.

"Rome…"

Jia whispering his name snapped him out of his rage-fueled trance.

He looked at her, taking in the worried look on her beautiful face, her chestnut hair in her face, the tears tumbling down her cheeks.

She stepped up to him, hugging her arms around him tight. When he groaned, she let go of him.

Her deep brown eyes were wide with concern. "I'm so sorry. I didn't mean to hurt you."

Emotion bloomed in his chest as he gazed down at Jia. She was safe. She was in his arms again. Nothing else mattered.

He pulled her back into his chest and kissed the top of her head.

"Don't worry about me, Jia. I'm just fine."

It's not till I finish reading that I realize I've been holding my breath. I exhale.

"Wow…" I smile to myself. I've never been a fan of violence on TV shows and movies, but there's just something about a protective romance hero who's willing to fight for his love interest that drives me wild in the best way. It's like catnip.

When I see all the glowing comments at the end of the post, I'm not surprised. That was superhot to read.

It must feel amazing to have so many people adore your writing. I wonder how ShakespeareInLust feels when they see this reaction. If I were brave enough to post my writing on this app and people actually liked it, I'd be over the moon. It would be a nice change from being treated like enemy number one at my job.

But no way do I have the guts to do that after Ashton's criticism.

I tap the comment box and start typing. I'm terrible about remembering to leave comments after reading, even though I know I should. I'm sure the authors appreciate the positive feedback from their readers. But sometimes I just get so caught up in the story that I forget. And honestly, I get nervous that the authors will read my comments and think that they're silly. I bet ShakespeareInLust doesn't even read all the comments they get anyway, given their popularity. They probably won't even see mine.

I'm overthinking this. I finally type a comment.

Okay, @ShakespeareInLust. It's official. You've unleashed a new kink for me. I had no idea that "Don't fucking touch her" and "You're going to die for hurting her" could get me so hot! AMAZING!

I chuckle as I read back my comment. And my username: Hot4Hermia. I came up with that when I first joined the app. If ShakespeareInLust ends up seeing my comment, I wonder if they'll like the reference to *A Midsummer Night's Dream*.

I set my phone aside to clean my dishes at the sink. When I go back to the table, an alert pops on my phone screen.

When I read it, I gasp.

ShakepeareInLust just replied to my comment.

Eight

Aidan

I'm smiling like an idiot at my phone screen. I can't help it.
The comment I just read is awesome.

Okay, @ShakespeareInLust. It's official. You've unleashed a
new kink for me. I had no idea that "Don't fucking touch her"
and "You're going to die for hurting her" could get me so
hot! AMAZING!

I don't always reply to comments on Scribble Share, but
tonight I have some free time before I head to the gym with
Jason for a late-evening workout.

But more than that, reading this person's comment made
me chuckle. And it feels really good to laugh after the crappy
day at work I had.

Aww really? I'm thrilled to hear that. Gotta love a hero who
isn't afraid to throw down for his lady! Also, I adore your name.
Hermia is one of my favorite characters from A Midsummer
Night's Dream :)

I can't help but smile. *HotForHermia* is really clever and cute.

I stand up from my couch and head to my kitchen to grab
a quick snack. I'm demolishing a granola bar when I see that
Hermia replied to my comment.

Hot4Hermia: OMFG YES! The "touch her and die" trope is one of my favorites! I am *trash* for it! And really? You're team Hermia? A lot of the people who've read A Midsummer Night's Dream tend to sympathize with Helena more than Hermia

ShakespeareInLust: One hundred percent team Hermia. I mean, nothing against Helena. They both get put through the ringer. I feel for the two of them. I just always thought Hermia was the prettier name. I know that's probably really weird and random.

Hot4Hermia: Not at all! I think so too! Haha look at us geeking out about Shakespeare LOL

ShakespeareInLust: Shakespeare FTW!

I hit Reply and immediately wish I hadn't. I sound like a loser. And then I notice we're taking over the entire comment section with our conversation. That must be really annoying for everyone who's not part of this conversation.

I navigate to the Message option of Scribble Share and type out a message to Hot4Hermia.

ShakespeareInLust: Hey! I figured it would be better to continue geeking out about Shakespeare via DM, we were kind of taking over the comment section with our conversation haha

Hot4Hermia: Oops haha. Good call :)

Hot4Hermia: Speaking of geeking out, I just have to say, I adore your stories. You're an incredible writer. I didn't think anyone could turn Shakespearean tragedies into compelling fanfic with happily-ever-afters, but you are so good at it. I'm seriously addicted to your writing. Whenever I have a bad or stressful day at work, reading your stories makes me feel better instantly. So thank you for that :)

For a second, I just stare at my phone screen, blown away at this person's compliment. Work was a shit show today, and I've been in a low mood the rest of the day because of it. Reading this person's message was the boost I didn't know I needed.

Before I can type a response, she sends another message.

Hot4Hermia: I hope that wasn't totally weird that I said all that! I probably sound like a psycho fangirl. I promise I'm not! LOL

I laugh as I type a message in return.

ShakespeareInLust: First of all, don't even worry, I don't think you're a psycho. And second, thank you. That was honestly one of the kindest things anyone has said to me. It made my day :)

Hot4Hermia: Really?

ShakespeareInLust: Really :)

It's not till my face starts to ache that I realize how wide I'm smiling. Whoever this person is has totally turned around my night. I came home all stressed and pissed from that argument with Micah this morning, and now my mood has changed completely.

ShakespeareInLust: I had a terrible day at work and you turned it around. Thank you for doing that.

Hot4Hermia: You're welcome :)

Hot4Hermia: And sorry to hear about the crummy day at work. That always sucks :(

ShakespeareInLust: Ehhh it's okay, it happens. Writing on Scribble Share has been a helpful way to decompress honestly.

Hot4Hermia: If it makes you feel any better, work sucked for me too today

ShakespeareInLust: Shoot, really? I'm sorry

ShakespeareInLust: Are you dealing with an annoying boss? Did they dump a bunch of work on you?

Hot4Hermia: Nothing like that thankfully, just the coworker from hell

ShakespeareInLust: Wow, really? Me too

ShakespeareInLust: Annoying coworkers are THE WORST

Hot4Hermia: No way, you too?!

ShakespeareInLust: Yuuuupppp

Hot4Hermia: UGH

ShakespeareInLust: UGH is correct

Hot4Hermia: This person is just… I don't know if I've ever met anyone so obnoxious. Just fights me every step of the way when I'm just trying to do my job

ShakespeareInLust: I'm sorry you're going through that. I can relate, it's a frustrating and maddening feeling.

Hot4Hermia: It is!

Hot4Hermia: But it feels nice to vent a bit about it, so thanks for that :)

ShakespeareInLust: Of course! I'm always here to vent and complain about coworkers from hell :)

My phone buzzes with a text. It's Jason telling me he's on his way to the gym. Shoot. I'm gonna be late to meet him.

ShakespeareInLust: Sorry, but I'm late meeting my friend, so I should go. Just didn't want you to think I'm ghosting you!

Hot4Hermia: No worries. Have fun with your friend! And I hope tomorrow is a better day for you!

ShakespeareInLust: Thanks! I hope the same for you!

Hot4Hermia: And I also hope that we get another hot story from you soon! I'm dying for it! No pressure though :)

ShakespeareInLust: Promise I'll post again soon! Have a good night!

Hot4Hermia: You too!

I grab my wallet from the kitchen counter, head out the door to my garage, and hop into my car. The whole car ride to the gym, I'm smiling.

Nine

Micah

As I walk through the East Nashville University campus, I catch myself smiling.

I still can't believe I had such a fun conversation with ShakespeareInLust last night. I expected them to be annoyed at my fangirling, but they were so sweet and gracious about it. And even when I started complaining about my workday, they were such a good sport. They even vented about work too.

It was such a fun conversation—everything flowed so naturally. It felt like talking to an old friend, and it put me in the best mood.

I take a second to breathe in the crisp January air. Despite how chilly it is, the sky is a beautiful shade of cornflower blue and there's not a cloud in sight.

I'm due to observe another one of Aidan's classes today. My smile drops. Just the thought of being in the same room with that guy has all the muscles in my neck and shoulders tensing.

I take a deep breath as I walk into the building that houses the English department. It's a beautiful winter day, I'm in a good mood, and I'm not going to let him ruin it.

I make my way to the elevator and hit the button for the floor where Aidan's office is. When I walk up to his open door, I take a breath to steady myself before I knock.

"Come in." His low, gravelly voice hits my ears. I close my eyes. God, I hate that I like the sound of his voice so much.

When I step inside, he's frowning at something on his laptop screen. He looks up at me and his frown etches deeper into his handsome face.

He's pissed to see me.

That makes two of us, buddy.

I walk up to his desk. "About our argument yesterday. I'm not going to let it affect our time together here at the university."

He blinks at me. Then he scoffs. "Okay."

He looks back down at his computer. That familiar mix of frustration and anger simmers inside of me. If that wasn't the most passive-aggressive dismissal I've ever seen.

I unbutton my coat. "That's all you have to say? 'Okay'?"

"Yeah, Micah," he says through a heavy, annoyed exhale. "That's all I have to say." He doesn't even look at me when he speaks. It's like he doesn't even think I'm worthy of eye contact.

I clench my jaw. This jackass. I can't stand him either, but I would never speak to him like this.

I place my palms on his desk and lean down so I'm hovering over him.

"Do you think you could pay me the slightest bit of courtesy, Professor Scott, and look at me when you speak to me?"

He closes his eyes and clenches his jaw. He takes a breath. And then two seconds later, he finally opens his eyes.

He starts to look up from his laptop, but his gaze snags on my torso. His eyes go wide.

For a second, all I can do is stand there in shock.

Is he…is he gawking at my chest?

A million invisible needles prick all over my body. I want to crawl out of my skin.

I should probably be used to this. Guys have been staring at my chest since puberty hit. Ever since I was a teenager, I've had a larger-than-average chest…and men have always seemed to want to stare at it.

Every muscle in my body twitches with the urge to cross my arms over my chest, to shrink and hide myself.

But I don't. I stay standing over his desk. I shouldn't have to cover myself because he can't seem to handle himself around a woman's body.

"You're a pig," I mutter, my voice low and hard.

Aidan blinks and shakes his head, like he's coming out of a trance.

He finally looks me in the eye. "N-No, I wasn't… I mean…"

His face is fire-engine red. Good. I hope he overheats from embarrassment.

He blinks again, his blue eyes wide with panic. "Your blouse is unbuttoned," he blurts.

Dread rockets through me. I look down and instantly wish the ground would open up and swallow me whole.

Because the entire top part of my blouse is wide open, exposing my black lace bra.

I gasp when I see how the tops of my boobs are practically spilling out of the cups. You can almost see my nipples…

Oh god no…

I stumble back and turn my body away as I quickly button it back up. And then I button up my wool coat, even though I'm inside, just to cover myself even more.

Even though I'm sweating out of sheer embarrassment.

"I-I-I didn't mean to…" he stammers.

Anger slices through the fog of humiliation. I spin around. He's standing up now, but he's still behind his desk.

I glare at him. "You didn't mean to? Are you serious?"

His cheeks are still bright red as he opens his mouth, then closes it, then opens it, then closes it again.

Finally, he huffs out a breath. "Of course I'm serious," he says. "I just…couldn't really help it…"

My mouth falls open. The fucking audacity of this guy to gawk at my breasts and then feed me the lamest excuse possible.

"You couldn't help it?" I almost laugh. "You've got to be kidding."

He tugs a hand through those chestnut curls. "I mean… you were leaning over my desk…" He flings his arm toward his desk. "And they were… I mean *you* were…kind of in my face…"

My mouth falls open as I stare at him. "You're accusing me of purposely shoving my boobs in your face?"

That panicked expression reappears. He shakes his head furiously. "No! I know you weren't trying to shove…yourself in my face. I just meant that it was jarring to see…"

My head falls back as I groan. "I can't believe the way you're acting right now."

"What's that supposed to mean?"

I scoff at how indignant his tone is. "You're acting like you saw a car accident and couldn't help but stare."

He shrugs. "Well, I mean, yeah, that's kind of how it felt."

I let out a laugh of pure disbelief. "Oh my god. You can't be serious."

Aidan flashes that lethal frown once more. "I think you're overreacting."

I step toward him. "And I think you're disgusting. Because based on what you're saying, you can't seem to control yourself. Apparently your eyes have a mind of their own and just have to gawk anytime they see a pair of breasts."

His gaze on me sharpens. He clenches his jaw. "I'm offended that you'd imply such a thing."

"It's true."

"You know, this entire problem could have been avoided had you just buttoned up your blouse properly."

My jaw falls to the floor. He's blaming *me* for this?

"So you're saying it's my fault that you can't help but gawk at me like a creep?"

He exhales sharply. "Look, if Jason had walked in here with his shirt half-open, I would have gawked too."

I stare at him. "Somehow I doubt that." I turn to leave. I still have to observe his class later today. Just the thought of being around him after this whole awful incident makes me want to scream.

I can't avoid it though. I have a job to do.

When I get to his office door, I stop and turn back around to him. "I don't ever want to mention this again. Okay?"

He folds his muscled forearms across his chest and aims a hard stare at me. "Fine."

"And don't ever look at my chest again."

Aidan quirks an eyebrow. "That won't be a problem. As long as you can remember to put your clothes on properly."

My jaw plummets to the floor. I can't believe he just said that.

He sits back down at his desk, ignoring me as he hammers away on his laptop.

I stomp out of his office, fuming. Seriously, fuck this guy.

Ten

Aidan

"Wow. You're really off your game today, big brother."

Liam weaves around me on the ice, taking the puck with him. I spin around and try to chase after him, but he's too fast.

He flicks his stick and sinks the puck into the net. He fist-pumps the air.

I stop and hunch over, bracing my free hand on my leg as I catch my breath. "It's pretty lame how you, a pro hockey player, celebrate scoring against me, not a pro hockey player."

He laughs. As I straighten back up, he skates past me.

Every week, Liam and I meet up at a rink to play one-on-one and run some other drills. It helps keep me in shape, and he does it as part of his training.

"Come on. One more. You can get it past me this time," he says.

I wipe the sweat from my brow and groan but square up with him anyway. He drops the puck onto the ice, and I snatch it and skate off. He's on my ass as I sprint to the net.

I know my little brother is taking it easy on me, but I still want to make this shot.

He starts to close in on me, and I slap the puck with my stick. When it lands at the back of the net, Liam yells.

"Nice! See? I knew you could do it."

I head to the edge of the rink, grab my water bottle, and chug.

I take a second to catch my breath. "You let me have that one."

Liam offers a crooked smile and shakes his head. "Nah, man. I was tired. You earned it."

"Yeah, right."

"If this were ten years ago and you were still playing college hockey, you would have smoked my ass, no problem."

"Maybe."

Just Liam mentioning college hockey makes me think of our dad. How he would lecture me after every game I played and what I did wrong. If he were here, he'd probably chew me out about what I could have done better, how much faster I should have skated, how I could have handled the puck better.

A weird relief pulls at my chest. It makes me even more grateful that I gave this up and focused on teaching. I'm a lot happier playing hockey just for fun.

A tinge of sadness hits me. If only that were good enough for my dad...

He was a hockey dad to the extreme, and I hated it. For most of my life, he felt more like a coach than a father. I remember him saying *Good game* more often than *I love you* as a kid. He only ever wanted to talk to me about hockey. He didn't care if I was interested in other hobbies. Whenever I tried to talk about anything else, he would half pay attention or tell me that I should focus more on playing better. All that mattered to him was for me to be a hockey star.

I glance at Liam and wait for him to mention our dad, but he doesn't.

Liam's still on good terms with him and sees him regularly, which is fine. I don't want my brother to cut things off with him just because I have. But I don't want to listen to him tell me for the millionth time that I should be the bigger person and try to fix things with our dad. He just doesn't get it. Our dad's always been happy with Liam since he made hockey his whole life. He doesn't know what it's like to be the one that our dad will forever be disappointed in.

Thankfully, other than that, the issues I have with our dad haven't affected our relationship as brothers. We bicker and get on each other's nerves, like all brothers do, but we care about each other and genuinely get along.

We head to one of the benches outside of the rink and unlace our skates.

Liam looks over at me. "Seriously though. You've been quieter than normal today. Everything okay?"

I huff out a breath and think about that disaster meeting with Micah in my office yesterday morning. How it all started when I looked up and saw her boobs just inches from my face…

How I stared at her for way, way too long…

Shame flashes through me.

She was right when she called me a creep. That was unquestionably wrong of me to stare at her chest.

But honestly? I wasn't lying when I said that I couldn't help it. It was like my brain had gone offline. Micah has the most incredible pair of breasts I've ever seen.

Even now I can picture them perfectly, spilling out of that sexy-as-hell black lace bra…

I press my eyes shut and shake my head.

For fuck's sake, Aidan. Can you stop picturing her boobs?

A sinking feeling hits me. I think about how angry and upset Micah was when she caught me looking at her. As much as I don't like her, it's still messed up what I did. Yeah, it was an accident, and I truly didn't mean to stare at her chest like that, but that doesn't make it okay.

I was still a jerk with how I reacted. I should have just apologized and let her lash out at me instead of getting so defensive.

"Work stuff has just been kind of stressful," I finally say.

Liam offers a sympathetic look. "Sorry, man."

I shrug. "It is what it is."

We start to throw our gear into our bags.

"Is it that hot auditor again?"

When I see my brother smirking at me, I roll my eyes.

"Oh damn, it is." He laughs. "What'd she do this time?"

I hesitate for a second. "It wasn't her. It was me," I mutter.

"What do you mean?"

I hesitate again, debating whether I should even tell him this. He's going give me endless shit for it. But honestly? I deserve it. I deserve to get shit on for how I handled things yesterday.

I run a hand through my sweaty hair. "So, uh, she came to my office yesterday, and when I looked up at her, I noticed her shirt was unbuttoned."

Liam's eyes go wide. "Seriously?"

I nod.

"You saw her boobs?"

"She was wearing a bra, but…yeah, I could see, um, a lot."

He blinks. A second later, he starts to smile. "She's got a nice rack, huh?"

I shove him. "Could you for once not act like a hard-up frat boy?"

He holds up a hand. "Okay, I'm sorry."

I let out a breath. "I couldn't help but stare at her. She got upset, and we argued. It was pretty fucking awkward and uncomfortable."

Liam's quiet as we finish packing up. We stand up and head to the entrance of the rink.

"So what are you gonna do?" he asks.

"Nothing. She said she didn't want to talk about it again."

"Then why are you so bothered by this?"

I stop walking and look at him. "Seriously? You don't understand why I'm a little thrown off after what went down between Micah and me?"

"You said yourself she wants you two to forget it. But here you are, still talking about it."

I'm quiet for a second. My dumbass little brother has a point.

"Maybe that means something," Liam says.

"Like what?"

He grins. "Maybe you're into her."

I frown at my brother. "I mean, yeah, she's attractive. But she doesn't even like me. Just like I don't like her."

Still grinning, my brother shakes his head like he doesn't believe me. "Like has nothing to do with attraction, Aidan. Do you how many times I've had hate sex? It's fucking hot."

I laugh, astounded by my brother's brashness. "You can't be serious."

"I'm dead serious. You don't have to like someone to have a good time in bed with them. Sometimes that fire and tension from hating each other is all you need."

I roll my eyes.

He pats my shoulder. "Think about it."

"You're out of your mind," I say as we walk out of the rink and into the parking lot.

But, annoyingly, my brother's words stick in my head.

I never thought I'd be into that sort of thing. With every woman I've dated, we liked each other right off the bat. Before meeting Micah, I never thought I could even be attracted to someone I despised.

Sometimes that fire and tension from hating each other is all you need.

I catch myself wondering if that's true.

Eleven

Micah

"So Professor Douche Canoe just sat there and stared at your chest?"

I sigh. "Yeah. He did."

Jordan makes a disgusted scoffing noise. "That prick."

I take a sip of my tea, then set it on the coffee table. I grab a blanket from the end of the couch and drape it over me while I give my sister a play-by-play of my blowup with Aidan yesterday.

"You have to retaliate, Micah. No more Ms. Professional Auditor. That creep objectified you to your face. He needs to pay."

I groan. "Jordan, I don't know…"

"He can't get away with this, Micah."

"He apologized."

"He gave you a half-assed apology, and then he blamed you for what he did. That's beyond messed up."

I'm quiet for a second. "Well, when you put it that way."

"Exactly. Screw that guy."

"Jordan, what exactly do you want me to do? Key his car? Egg his office? We still have to work together. If I try to go after him, I'll get fired."

She lets out an evil chuckle. "No, no, no. Nothing like that. You have to think strategically. Don't do anything that can be traced back to you."

I shake my head, impressed and a little scared by my sister's calculating thought process.

I look at the clock on the wall. "It's getting late where you are. I'll let you go."

"No, I want to plot revenge with you," she whines.

I chuckle. "Venting to you was exactly what I needed. I don't want to do anything more than that."

She makes a huffy noise. "Fine."

We say goodbye and hang up. A minute later she texts me.

Jordan: I know you said no revenge, but just in case you change your mind, here are some ideas:
    -laxatives in his coffee
    -anonymous glitter bomb delivered to his office
    -Carolina reaper sauce in his lunch

Me: Wow…you came up with those reeeaaaallll quick

Jordan: Old law school habits die hard

Jordan: Promise me if Professor Douche Canoe does one more disrespectful thing to you, you won't stand for it. You'll get back at him.

Me: I promise

I finish my tea, knowing full well that I don't have the guts to get revenge on Aidan.

But as I reread my sister's text, I can't help but think about how satisfying it would feel to get back at him.

I let out a sigh and shake my head. No way can I do that.

I walk into the English department, my body tense as I pass Aidan's office. We haven't spoken for the past few days, not since I caught him staring at my chest.

I know I have more class observations and meetings with him coming up, but I don't want to think about that right now. Right now, I just want to focus on getting ready for today's meetings and enjoy not having to deal with Aidan.

I reach the end of the hall and turn the corner, almost bumping into Dr. Wauncho.

"Sorry about that," I say.

"Not a problem. These hallway corners are quite sharp." He chuckles. "Say, you don't have any meetings or class observations right now, do you?"

"No, I'm free for the next half hour or so. Did you want to meet with me about something?"

He shakes his head. "I was thinking you could join us for some coffee and bagels. It's an English department tradition. Every Wednesday morning."

"Oh…" No way. Aidan will be there, and I can't handle even looking at him right now.

But it's not just the idea of running into Aidan that makes me not want to go. It's also that no one would want me to show up at their gathering, other than him.

"I really shouldn't."

"Oh, come now." He flashes a jolly smile. "We'd love for you to join. I'm the one who brought the bagels today, so I can promise they're good. Thank goodness you missed it last week when Jason brought them. He picked them up from a gas station. Can you imagine? Gas-station bagels?" His face twists in disgust.

I force a polite smile. "Dr. Wauncho, I appreciate the invitation, but let's not beat around the bush. No one in your department even wants me here. I'm certain they'd be upset if I just showed up during what, I'm assuming, is supposed to be a fun time for the department faculty."

His smile fades, and he nods. "I understand. How about you just stop by and grab one, then you can leave?"

I let out a sigh and try to maintain my polite smile. He's not going to give up.

"Okay. Thank you."

I follow him to the conference room. The second I walk through the doorway, conversation stops. Everyone is glaring at me. I instantly get that needle-in-the-skin feeling that always hits when I'm uncomfortable.

Yup. Just as I suspected. I'm still enemy number one. Everyone still hates me.

Disappointment flashes through me. It would be nice to have a job where I'm not so hated. I think back to how when I first started working as an auditor, I wasn't fazed by this sort of thing. I guess it's finally catching up to me.

I glance to the side and catch eyes with Aidan.

He blinks and shakes his head before his gaze falls to the floor.

"I brought too many bagels, so I invited Micah to grab one on her way to her workspace," Dr. Wauncho explains to everyone.

I flash a weak smile at him in thanks.

He grabs an empty paper cup and offers to pour me a coffee. I thank him. He starts to grab the decaf pot, but I stop him.

"Regular coffee please," I say. "I need at least a pot of coffee a day, or I get a headache," I joke.

Everyone around me is silent. That needle-in-the-skin feeling intensifies. I didn't really think I'd be able to make them laugh, did I?

He chuckles and hands me the coffee. "I'm the same way too. I should know better."

I tell him thanks. Conversation resumes in hushed tones as I walk to the table with the bagel spread.

There's a gagging noise. I whip my head up and see Jason coughing and wiping his mouth. He chugs from the water bottle in his other hand.

"You okay?" Aidan asks him.

Jason shakes his head and looks at Dr. Wauncho. "What the... Why is the cream cheese so spicy?"

He frowns at him, confused. A second later, his brow lifts. "Oh, you must have tried the ghost-pepper cream cheese. It's got a nice little kick, don't you think?"

Jason groans, his face red from coughing and chugs more water. He offers the half of his bagel that he hasn't eaten to Aidan, but Aidan shakes his head.

"You know I can't stand spicy stuff."

Jason drops the bagel half into the trash and walks out of the room, still coughing.

Dr. Wauncho chuckles and glances at me. "Some folks just can't handle a little heat."

I offer a polite smile and grab a napkin and do a quick scan of the food. I'm not even hungry—I just want to get out of here as quickly as I can, so I swipe the bagel closest to me.

I start to turn, but Dr. Wauncho stops me.

"Blueberry! Excellent choice! You must try it with the honey-nut cream cheese! It's divine."

I hold back a groan and nod politely, then step over to the container of honey-nut cream cheese, grab a knife, and smear some onto my bagel.

As I look up, I catch Aidan staring at my chest. Again.

Fury burns through me like a wildfire. Is he fucking serious?

A beat later, his gaze lifts to my face. His eyes widen when he sees me glaring at him.

And just like before, his stubbled cheeks turn fire-engine red. He opens his mouth, then closes it quickly. And then he walks off.

Can he really not keep his eyes off my chest? I'm wearing a sweater today. None of my skin is even exposed for him to look at.

I murmur a quick "Thank you" to Dr. Wauncho as I walk

out of the conference room and back down the hall to my workspace. The second I'm inside, I shut the door and drop my bagel into the trash can. I feel bad since he was so nice to treat me, but I can't even bear to look at it. My appetite is long gone after being ogled by Aidan yet again.

With my arms at my sides, I ball my hands into loose fists. The nerve of that jerk to gawk at my chest. He was so obvious about it too. He didn't even try to be discreet.

I tug a hand through my hair, annoyed and frustrated and pissed off all at once. All the muscles in my neck and shoulders are tight.

How can I make it any clearer to him to keep his eyes above my neck when he looks at me?

The conversation I had with Jordan the other night pops into my head.

Promise me if Professor Douche Canoe does one more disrespectful thing to you, you won't stand for it. You'll get back at him.

I stand there and let my sister's words marinate.

Revenge.

Yeah, it's petty and unprofessional. But I don't care. Aidan made it clear just how unprofessional he is when he shamelessly stared at my chest. Twice.

I take a breath and stretch out my neck. I glance down and see the discarded bagel in the trash can.

A second later, the most brilliant idea pops into my head.

Twelve

Aidan

It doesn't matter how many times I make myself look at the screen at the front of the conference room. I can't focus.

Yeah, I see words and pictures, but trying to comprehend what I'm looking at just isn't happening.

I focus on Dr. Wauncho standing at the front, gesturing through his presentation during this staff lunch meeting. But again, nothing registers.

My brain is too distracted.

I think back to this morning when I saw Micah again… when I stared at her chest. Again.

I press my eyes shut, the burn of shame roasting me from the inside out. I tug at the collar of my shirt. I'm tempted to rip it off, I'm so uncomfortable.

I can't believe I did that.

I let out a slow, heavy sigh. Thankfully, none of my co-workers sitting around me seem to notice how distracted and uncomfortable I am.

I didn't mean to stare at Micah's chest again. I know that's such a cop-out, but it's the truth.

When she walked into the conference room this morning, I had every intention of ignoring her. And I did at first.

But while she was leaning over and grabbing a bagel, I dropped my napkin and bent over to pick it up, and as I looked up, I was at eye level with her chest again.

And then, because I'm the most fucking awkward human on the planet, I froze. And that's when she saw me looking at her.

I blink and see the death glare she aimed at me.

I didn't even apologize or explain myself in the moment because we were surrounded by the entire English department, and I didn't want to draw even more attention to that fucking awkward moment.

Even if I had, I doubt she would have believed me. And I don't blame her. The last two times we've seen each other, she's caught me looking at her boobs. I have zero doubt she hates me with every cell in her body.

I let out a quiet sigh when I think about how this is going to make things worse between us. How awkward and uncomfortable will things be when she observes another one of my classes or needs to meet one-on-one with me?

I sigh and force myself to focus on what Dr. Wauncho is saying.

"…and with that, I'll wrap things up. Any questions?"

A pang of guilt hits me when I realize I missed all of his presentation. He was so excited to tell us about the conference he attended, and I spent the entire time thinking about Micah.

A handful of people ask Dr. Wauncho some questions. I ask if he can send me a copy of his presentation so I can read it over again later. He says of course.

The department secretary pops into the doorway and tells everyone that our lunch delivery has arrived.

Dr. Wauncho claps his hands. "Fantastic! Why don't we hand out everyone's orders, and then I can finish up answering questions."

Two food-delivery people walk in with bags of food in both hands. I stand up and help collect the bags and start handing them out to people. When he grabs his wallet to tip the delivery people, I stop him and grab cash from my pocket.

Dr. Wauncho starts to tell me that it's not necessary, that it's his treat for us attending the presentation, but I insist and hand the cash to the delivery people.

He pats my shoulder. "That's quite generous of you," he says.

I say it's my pleasure. It's the least I can do for not paying attention during his presentation.

I grab the turkey club I ordered and take my seat at the table while things continue.

I grab one half of the sandwich, nodding along with Jason as he asks another question.

"So with that new grading software, will the tech support be twenty-four-seven? Because that would be really helpful," he says. "In the past whenever I had a problem with our current grading software and Tech Support isn't available, Aidan's been my go-to guy. He's gonna be thrilled I won't be bothering him as much."

He looks at me and chuckles. I flash a thumbs-up. "Always here for you, buddy."

Everyone chuckles. I take a bite of my sandwich and chew. A second later, my tongue starts to burn.

I stop chewing. A second after that, it feels like my mouth is on fire. I swallow, and the fire spreads down my throat and slowly down my chest.

I start to cough. After a few seconds, I can't stop. The more I cough, the more raw my mouth and throat feel. I try to stop, but I can't. It's like my body is trying to hack through the sudden burn.

My eyes burn with hot tears, blurring my vision.

I press my eyes shut for a second, but that just makes it burn worse. I open my eyes, blinking furiously.

Jason turns to look at me. "Are you okay?"

I nod, even though it still sounds like I'm hacking up a lung. I grab my water bottle and chug some water, but that doesn't even dull the burning.

"Are you choking?" Jason asks.

I shake my head. "Spice…" I hiss between coughs. "Too spicy…"

He frowns at me, then looks at my sandwich. "Why'd you order a spicy sandwich?"

"I didn't," I rasp, then cough some more.

By now the entire room has gone quiet. Everyone is gawking at me with concerned expressions as I hack and cough.

I grip the base of my neck, as if that's going to soothe my coughing. It doesn't.

Still hacking, I glance down at my sandwich half. I ordered a plain turkey club. It shouldn't be spicy at all.

When I peel away the bread from the sandwich, my eyes go wide. It's covered in hot sauce.

"I think you got the wrong order," Jason says.

I glare at him. "You think?" I sputter before pushing my chair from the table and hunching over as I continue hacking. My chest aches, I'm coughing so hard. I manage a deep breath between coughs, but then I swallow some saliva, and that only makes me cough harder.

Everyone around me gets up and starts to freak out.

"Get him some water!"

"He already drank water. It didn't even help."

"Water doesn't alleviate spice. It spreads it to other parts of your mouth, making it worse."

"What alleviates spice, then?"

"Dairy! Any kind of dairy!"

"Does anyone have milk or yogurt or—"

I look up just in time to see Dr. Wauncho barreling toward me.

"Here, drink this!" He cracks open a small container of skim milk and shoves it into my hand.

I grab it and chug it. I close my eyes as the cool liquid coats my throat. I hum as I swallow. Fuck, that's soothing.

I drain the container and set it on the table. Then I rest my elbows on my knees and take a second to catch my breath. Snot is dripping from my nose. My entire face is covered in sweat. Even the lenses of my glasses are wet. I glance down, horrified when I see a sweat spot in the center of my chest and under both armpits.

When I look up, the entire conference room is standing around me, staring.

A wave of embarrassment crashes through me.

When I clear my throat, I wince, it's so raw.

"Sorry, everyone. I, uh, I'm kind of a wuss when it comes to spicy food," I manage to say, my voice soft and watery.

Jason pats my shoulder. "For a second there I thought we were gonna have to call paramedics." He lets out a nervous chuckle.

I try to smile, but my throat and chest ache so much that even that small movement kills.

I glance up at Dr. Wauncho. A worried frown is etched in his skin as he looks down at me.

"Thanks for the milk," I rasp.

"Of course. Goodness, you gave us quite a scare." He looks at the destroyed half of my sandwich still sitting in its to-go container. "You didn't order your sandwich spicy?"

"Nope." Someone hands me a napkin, and I whisper a thanks as I dab at my face and mouth.

Dr. Wauncho removes his glasses and bites the earpiece as he studies my sandwich, deep in thought. "What an unfortunate mix-up," he says.

"You're telling me," I mutter. My mouth is still on fire.

"I should call the bistro and complain," he says.

I shake my head. "No, don't do that. It was just a mix-up. I don't want anyone to get into…"

The soothing feeling from the dairy fades, and I start to cough again. I cover my mouth with my hand as I struggle to swallow back the fiery burn creeping up my chest and throat.

Is this what it's like to eat spicy food? How the hell do people enjoy this?

I stand up and jog out of the conference room toward the bathrooms down the hall so I can cough and hack without an audience. Everyone jumps away from me, clearing a path from me to the doorway instantly. I'd be impressed at the spontaneous synchronicity if my mouth, throat, and chest weren't currently on fire.

Micah rounds the corner, and I nearly run her over as I hit the men's bathroom.

She lets out a shriek as she jumps out of the way, bumping into the wall.

I hunch over the nearest sink and rinse my mouth with cold water. I gargle and spit icy water over and over. After a solid minute, the fiery burn starts to dial back.

I rip a paper towel from the nearby dispenser and wipe my nose and mouth, then take off my glasses. For a few seconds, I just stand there and catch my breath between coughs. I'm breathing like I just did hockey suicide drills.

I take off my glasses and splash cold water onto my face before rinsing out my mouth yet again. I almost gag at the sour taste of hot sauce lingering in my mouth. I hack for a few seconds, then glance up at my reflection in the mirror. Jesus. My face is red, my eyes are watery, and my cheeks are hollowed out. I look like hell.

And then I hear something. I have to strain for a few seconds to make out what I'm hearing. And when I do, I'm fucking livid.

Because that's the sound of Micah laughing at me behind the door.

Thirteen

Micah

Aidan Scott is coughing his brains out, and I'm giddy.

I know that makes me a jerk. I don't care.

He's the one who ogled my chest, refused to apologize for it, blamed it on the way I was dressed, then did it again when I told him not to.

Maybe sneaking hot sauce into his sandwich wasn't the most mature thing in the world. It was honestly probably pretty cruel.

But he deserved it. If he's going to treat me like a piece of meat, I'm not going to just stand there and take it.

I'm going to get back at him.

I cover my mouth as I stand outside the door of the men's bathroom.

I'll admit laughing about it is pretty messed up. But he's done some pretty messed-up stuff to me too. So I guess we'll call this even.

Just then the door flies open, revealing Aidan's flushed face glaring at me.

I step back, jolted.

I stare up at him, mesmerized. His square jaw is bulging as he bites down. His nostrils are flaring. His chest is heaving with each breath he takes. His eyes are two inky pools of black ringed in ice blue, and there's a sheen of sweat glistening along his forehead.

He looks…really hot when he's pissed and sweaty.

My brain slingshots to a place it shouldn't go. It imagines

Aidan on top of me, that same intense, furious look on his face, breathing hard.

Except he's not mad. He's turned on. By me.

I press my eyes shut and shake my head, willing the visual away.

What the hell was that?

"You think this is funny?" he barks, his tone hard and sharp.

I jolt back to the present. Oh, right. Right now we're about to fight because he's angry that I'm laughing at him while he coughed up his lungs.

I clear my throat and straighten up to my full height. "Maybe."

Fury flashes in his eyes as he glowers at me. "You're a real piece of work, Micah."

I glare at him. "I could say the same about you."

He grips the door frame, leaning closer to me. "And what the hell do you mean by that?"

I cross my arms. "Do you think I missed the way you looked at me this morning? Specifically at my chest?"

He exhales, his gaze on my sharpening. "That was an accident. I dropped my napkin and you happened to be in my line of sight, and—"

"Oh my god, you really are pathetic. The first time you look at my chest, you say it was my fault, that you couldn't help it. And the second time it happens, it's a mistake. I guess nothing is ever your fault, is it?" I toss up my hands in frustration. "You're just a helpless man being bombarded with all these distracting visuals."

He purses his lips, clearly pissed at how I'm mocking him. He tugs a hand through those thick chestnut waves. He leans his face closer to mine. "It's the truth, whether you want to believe it or not."

Anger pummels my insides. This guy. Either he thinks I'm

a complete idiot or he's brash and arrogant enough to lie to me while looking me dead in the eye. It's probably both, honestly.

Aidan narrows his gaze at me. "Some advice for you, Micah—grow the hell up. It's rude to laugh at people when they're sick. It makes you look like a callous psycho. So whatever you need to do to get that part of yourself under control, do it. It's pathetic."

My jaw falls to the floor. The fucking nerve of this guy to speak to me like that.

The corner of his mouth drags up in a smug smirk. He looks so pleased with himself for rendering me speechless.

But I take a breath. I bite back the urge to call him every awful name I can think of. Instead, I take a page out of his book.

I look him in the eye as I smirk at him and say, "I have some advice for you too—you should double-check your food before you eat it. You have no idea the lengths people will go to get back at you for the way you've mistreated them."

I savor the two seconds that Aidan's eyes widen with recognition. And then I turn around and walk away before he can say another word to me.

"Holy shit! You did it, Micah! You actually did it." Jordan beams at me from my phone screen. "You went hardcore revenge on Professor Douche Canoe." She rests her palm on her chest and aims a joking wistful expression at me. "I've never been this proud of you."

I shake my head and laugh. "I still can't believe I put hot sauce in his sandwich. It was so…evil. And sneaky."

She shakes her head. "Sneaky? Yes. Evil? Not even close."

I start to say otherwise, but she stops me.

"Evil is doing something wicked and cruel for no reason. Like purposely starving someone to death. Or conning someone out of their life savings. You would never do anything even close to that, not in a million years. What you did was get him back for being a creep to you. That's not evil. That's justice."

I take in the pointed look on her face. We're not identical twins, but we still look a lot alike. Same big brown eyes, same button nose, same full mouth, same black-brown hair. Jordan has bangs though and cut her hair to her shoulders, while mine is long and all one length.

I sigh. "Maybe you're right. Still though. As satisfying as it felt to get back at Aidan, part of me can't overlook how messed up it was to do it."

Jordan waves a hand, completely unbothered by what I've said. "You only feel that way because you're a good person, Micah. You're reasonable and fair and don't spend your time thinking of ways to screw people over. So the one time you do something to get back at someone for mistreating you, you feel unsettled about it. It's understandable. It's also proof that you're not evil," my sister says matter-of-factly.

I nod, despite the trepidation whirling inside of me. Do I regret putting hot sauce in Aidan's lunch? No—he deserved it. But I still think it's an objectively messed-up thing to do. This entire dynamic between us is screwed up.

"Thanks for the pep talk, but I'm ready to move on from it now and just focus on my job," I say.

Jordan nods once. "How it's going? Other than Professor Douche Canoe, of course?"

I tell her about the presentation I have in a couple of days in front of the English department.

"I'm giving the faculty and staff an early progress report of my findings," I say. "Hopefully they'll take it seriously and adjust things so that when it comes time for my final report, I won't have to recommend cutting as much from the department."

My sister holds up a mug in cheers to me. "You'll kick ass like you always do."

I try to smile despite how nervous I feel. I've done presentations like this a million times before in my job, but I always get nervous beforehand. It never feels good to stand in front of a group of people who you know hate you as you try to persuade them to take you seriously.

But it's my job. This is what I'm good at. I'm good at observing and analyzing. The one time I tried to veer from that I failed miserably. So now I know better. I need to stick to what I know and leave the big dreams to those who can handle it.

Jordan and I chat for a few more minutes before we end our call, and I spend the rest of the night putting the finishing touches on my presentation.

Fourteen

Aidan

"No way." Liam blinks at me with wide unbelieving eyes as we climb out of his luxury SUV and step into his garage. "Are you sure it was Micah? Like, you're positive she's the one who put hot sauce in your sandwich?"

"Of course I'm positive," I say.

I follow Liam into his town house. When I walk inside, I immediately trip over his gear bag and almost stumble over a toolbox.

I quickly right myself and glance around the kitchen floor, which is littered in random crap. In addition to his hockey gear bag and toolbox, there's a giant container of protein powder, an empty cardboard box, a package of bottled water, and a wet towel lying on the floor.

"How the hell do you live like this?"

He shrugs. "I'm used to it."

I roll my eyes at him. "You're living like a frat boy. Jesus." I frown at the unopened air fryer I got him for Christmas, which is sitting on his kitchen island. "You haven't opened that yet?"

He stares at the box, like it's the first time he's seen it. "Huh. I forgot that was there." He laughs. I punch his shoulder, and he laughs harder.

"What? I travel a lot for work. And when I'm in town, I'm playing or at practice or training. I haven't had the time to unpack and get settled in."

I roll my eyes. "Liam, you moved into this place months

ago. It would take one day to unpack if you just blocked out the time and did it."

He grins at me. "Maybe you could do it for me."

I scoff. "No way. Look, why don't you just stay in tonight and unpack. I'll tell Mom. She'll understand."

Liam shakes his head. "And miss a free home-cooked meal? No way."

We're supposed to have dinner with our mom tonight. Liam is usually busy during hockey season, but every once in a while, he gets a free night and our mom insists that we make a family night out of it and come over for dinner. I always offer to cook or pick up food from a restaurant, but she insists on cooking for Liam and me. The one thing she leaves for us to sort out are the drinks, and it's Liam's turn to bring wine tonight, so we stopped by his place to get it on the way.

He mentions something about how the team he plays for has staff that the players can hire as personal assistants.

I stare at him. "You need to hire a personal assistant to unpack your kitchen? Are you kidding me?"

He flashes that pretty-boy smile that gets him out of anything. "Why not hire someone to do the stuff I hate doing anyway? I get paid enough."

I think back to when we were kids and the two of us started mowing lawns for the neighbors to earn extra money. He was terrible at it, always cutting the grass too short and missing entire patches in people's yards. When our neighbors would look at the awful job that Liam did, he'd give them that same smile and say that he was sorry it wasn't better and that he was still learning. It worked every time. They'd laugh and say no big deal before paying him and leaving a tip. It always drove me nuts.

"Pretty awesome perk of my job, right?" He grins, then opens his refrigerator door and pulls out a beer bottle. He hands it to me and fills a glass of water for himself.

"No beer for you?" I ask.

He shakes his head. "Nope. Gotta hydrate for tomorrow's training session."

I start to give back the beer, but my brother shakes his head. "You sound like you could use a beer after the day you had."

I put the beer back into the fridge and instead grab an electrolyte drink. I crack it open and take a long pull, wincing at the sweet taste.

"I should probably just stick to water and this stuff." I take another sip.

Liam leans against the kitchen island, shaking his head. "I still can't believe Micah put hot sauce in your sandwich. That's some hardcore shit."

I sigh. "Yeah. It was."

On the drive to my brother's town house, I tell him everything that went down today.

I chug more electrolyte drink and notice him squinting at me. "What?"

"You sure it was an accident that you stared at her chest again?" Liam asks.

I shove his shoulder. "Of course it was an accident. It was just bad timing." I set the bottle on the counter. "Really, really bad timing."

Liam looks at me like he doesn't believe me. "If you say so."

He motions for me to move aside and grabs a bottle from the wine rack.

"You think this'll be enough?" he asks.

I nod. "Neither of us are drinking. That'll be plenty for Mom and Aunt Ricki if she shows up too."

I start to walk to the garage door, but I notice Liam lingering the kitchen.

He clears his throat as he looks at me. "So, uh, Dad called me today."

I feel the muscles in my neck and shoulders tighten. "What did he want?"

Liam hesitates for a second. "He asked about you. Wanted to know how you were doing."

I grit my teeth, annoyed. "Not sure why he'd be interested in how I'm doing. He made it clear to me after I quit playing hockey in college that he had no interest in my life anymore."

Liam frowns. "Come on, Aidan. That was a long time ago that you two fell out. Yeah, Dad was a jerk back then, but—"

"I don't care," I bark. "I'm not interested in speaking to him."

Liam purses his lips, even though I know he wants to say more. But I don't want to hear whatever our dad told him to say to me.

Ever since that day in college, he made his disappointment and disinterest in me crystal clear. He barely spoke to me. He stopped calling me. He and our mom have been divorced since Liam and I were little, so it's not like I had to see him much anyway. He focused all his energy and attention on Liam, who could actually fulfill his dreams of having a superstar athlete for a son. Whenever I attended one of Liam's games, I made sure to sit far away from him.

I take in the pained look on my brother's face. Guilt throttles me. I hate that the rift between our Dad and me affects him too.

"Hey. I'm sorry," I say, my voice quiet. "I shouldn't have lashed out on you like that."

He shakes his head. "It's okay. I shouldn't push you. I know things between you two have been strained for a long time. And I know it's his fault. I'm sorry for making it sound like I was putting it on you."

"It's okay." I sigh. "I'm sorry he puts you in the middle of us like that. It's not fair to you."

Liam opens his mouth like he's going to say something, but

instead he stays quiet. "We should get going, or we'll be late and Mom will chew our asses."

We both chuckle, and the tension in the air between us fades.

We walk back out to the garage and hop into my brother's car. Liam drives us to our mom's house in Franklin, a picturesque town just outside of Nashville.

I check my phone and pull up the Scribble Share app. When I see a message from Hot4Hermia, I read it immediately.

Comfort reading your stories again to unwind from work :) Hope you're having a good week! And hope you haven't had to deal with that obnoxious coworker!

I start to smile. It's nice to hear from her after the shit day I've had. I type a quick response.

Hey! Thanks so much for rereading :) And I wish I could say I was able to avoid them...but sadly, we had a run-in. It was pretty unpleasant.

I'm about to exit the app, but I see that she replies right away.

Hot4Hermia: Oh no! Crap, I'm sorry to hear that :(

ShakespeareInLust: I'm just glad to be done with work for the day.

Hot4Hermia: I hope you're doing something fun to take your mind off work stuff!

ShakespeareInLust: Dinner with family should do the trick :) How are you? How's work going for you?

Hot4Hermia: Doing well. I managed to get a tiny little win over that coworker that's been annoying the crap out of me, so I'm currently riding the high of that.

ShakespeareInLust: Really? Way to go! Glad one of us is winning the battle against the obnoxious coworkers

Hot4Hermia: *laughing emoji*

Liam eases to stop at a red light and glances over at me. "You could just apologize to Micah, you know."

I put my phone away and turn to him, annoyed that he brought up Micah. "Why? She's the one who doused my sandwich in hot sauce. She's the reason I embarrassed myself in front of everyone I work with. I shouldn't have to say sorry to her."

My face heats when I think about how loud I was while coughing and choking. The whole building heard me. So fucking mortifying.

Liam runs a hand through his gold-blond hair as he checks out his reflection in the mirror and chuckles. "What are you gonna do, then? Poison her back?"

"Of course not."

He pats my shoulder. "Yeah, I know, you're not the vengeful type."

My brother speeds ahead. He's right. I'm not the vengeful type. But I'm not a doormat either. I can't just let Micah get away with what she did.

Liam stops at a Starbucks drive-through.

"It's six thirty in the evening," I tell him when he pulls up to order.

"Mom's making turkey pot pie. You know a plate of that

knocks me out cold. I need the caffeine to keep from passing out at the dinner table."

I chuckle. And it hits me: the perfect way to get back at Micah.

Fifteen

Micah

I blink at my laptop screen, struggling to focus through a splitting headache.

I close my eyes and press my fingertips to my temples and gently massage, but it doesn't do much to ease the dull pain in my skull.

It's been three days of battling this on-and-off headache, and I have no idea what brought it on.

I press the back of my hand to my forehead, wondering if I'm running a temperature, but my skin doesn't feel hot.

Leaning back in the chair in my workspace, I let out a sigh.

I think back to my routine over the past few days. Nothing's changed. I wake up and start my day with a cup of coffee and water, then I hop onto the exercise bike in Jordan's workout room, eat breakfast, get dressed, and head to work. And that's usually when my headache kicks in. It doesn't matter how much coffee I drink or how many breaks I take, it doesn't go away until I come back home and have an evening cup of black tea. Then it's gone. And then it starts all over again in the morning.

I glance around the tiny, dingy space that I've been working in over the past two weeks, ever since I started working at East Nashville College. I let out a heavy sigh. Maybe that's the culprit. Maybe I'm so stressed from this job—from all the arguing with Aidan—that it's finally taking a toll on my body.

Not a whole lot I can do to fix that though. I'm stuck here, dealing with Aidan, for the next month.

My shoulders slump as I let out a heavy sigh. I just need to power through this…even though the timing couldn't be worse.

This afternoon I'm giving my presentation to the English department about my findings so far. My back tenses as I picture all the glares that await me.

I take another swig of coffee and force away my nerves. I just need to get through this presentation—then I can go home and decompress.

Head throbbing, I skim through the rest of my slides. But after a minute of staring at my laptop screen, my eyes start to cross. I press my eyes shut. This isn't helping. I've been over this enough times; I'm sure it's all good to go.

I set a timer on my phone for fifteen minutes so I can take a quick nap, then rest my head on my desk.

My phone blares, jolting me awake. My eyelids are so heavy that it takes a few seconds for me to fully open my eyes. I turn off the alarm and check the time on my phone screen, surprised at how quickly fifteen minutes passed. It felt like seconds.

I grab my things and head for the conference room. It's empty when I get there, which I'm grateful for. I wanted to be early so I could set up and take a few minutes for myself.

I hook up my laptop to the projector, then set out the packets I put together on the tables for everyone to read through and follow along during my presentation.

Once I finish, my head is throbbing. I take a drink of water before downing the rest of my coffee. Maybe I need to stop drinking so much coffee. Maybe my body is finally putting up a fight against all that caffeine I've been shoving into it all these years.

People start filtering into the room. I stand awkwardly at the front, trying to keep my expression neutral. I'm sure they don't want a fake smile from the auditor who could possibly put them out of a job.

I'm not even sure I have the energy to move my face muscles, honestly. This headache is zapping up the last of my stamina.

Minutes later, Dr. Wauncho comes in and walks up to me.

"I'm very much looking forward to your presentation," he says.

"Thank you. I'm eager to share my findings with everyone."

His eyebrows wrinkle slightly, his expression concerned. "Are you all right? You look a bit tired."

This headache is really doing me in. I glance off to the side and catch my reflection in the nearby window. My skin looks ruddy and some pretty sizable bags have set up camp under my eyes. I take in the million flyaways that have escaped from my ponytail.

Wow. I look wrecked.

I smooth a chunk of loose hair behind my ear. "I'm fine."

"I'd hate to think we're running you ragged." Dr. Wauncho chuckles, right as Aidan walks in. "I know this department can be a handful at times."

Aidan looks over at me. The corner of his mouth hooks up in an amused smile before he turns away and sits down at one of the tables.

Why does he so look so happy?

Maybe he's thrilled to see me look so run-down and haggard.

I straighten up, despite how I feel. Maybe I look like crap, but I'm not going to let that affect the way I do my job.

I force a smile. "Everything is great. I appreciate you checking in."

Once he takes his seat, I get started. "Thank you all for coming this afternoon. I know my presence has been quite an adjustment, but I'm hoping that after I share my progress report with you all today, you'll find it helpful."

I tap the keyboard of my laptop and pull up the first slide. "As you can see on this first chart, I compiled all the data re-

garding enrollment in the department, attendance, and retention rate at the start of last semester, and then…"

I trail off when Kendall raises her hand. "Yes?"

"The numbers on the screen don't match with the numbers
on the packet I have," she says.

I frown. "What?"

She walks up to me and shows me her paper. She's right.

"Oh…" My head throbs. "I'm sorry. I don't know how I
missed that."

Kendall stands there and looks at me, the expression on her
face expectant.

"Um, just disregard that page in the handout," I say after a
second. "I'll email an updated copy to you all later."

She sits back down and I continue, until Dr. Wauncho speaks
up.

"I apologize for interrupting you, Ms. Mila, but this looks
like an entirely different infographic," he says.

I walk over to where he's sitting at the front row. I have to
stare at his handout for what feels like a full minute before I
make sense of the text and numbers on the page.

He's right. That's the wrong graphic. How did I mess that
up too?

"Crap…" I press a fist to the side of my head in attempt to
relive the pressure building in my skull. I look up. "Do all of
you have the wrong graphic?"

Half of the room nods. A handful say they have the correct
one in their packet.

My brain feels like it's trapped in a fog. Why can't I seem
to think straight?

A sea of unhappy and confused frowns looks back at me.

It's bad enough that everyone in this room hates me. But
now I also look like an incompetent jackass in front of them.

My pulse rockets. Sweat breaks out the back of my neck.

With a packet in hand, I hurry back to the front and hunch down at my laptop, my heart racing and my anxiety amping up.

"I'm so sorry, everyone," I say quickly as I look between the printout and my laptop. "I've been feeling a bit under the weather and I thought I double-checked everything, but I guess I must have missed a few things…"

Murmurs echo throughout the room. I can't hear what they're saying, but I'd bet anything they're talking about what a disaster I am.

The door to the conference room opens. Jason walks in with a Starbucks cup in hand. He mumbles an apology for being late as he walks by me to go sit in the free chair next to Aidan.

"What did I miss?" Jason whispers.

"Just the beginnings of an utter shit show," Aidan says softly. The people around him chuckle.

A wave of shames bubbles up inside of me. I know I'm a mess right now, but does he really have to rub it in like that? Such a jerk.

"I had to sneak out and get my caffeine fix," I hear Jason say to Aidan. "Hopefully Food and Beverage Service will restock the caffeinated coffee soon."

My head pops up. "Restock the caffeinated coffee?" I say to Jason.

He aims a wide-eyed gaze at me. "Yeah. It's been rough going without proper coffee in the break room for the past few days."

I look at him as my brain struggles to put the pieces together. "Wait, the coffee in the break room is decaf?"

"Yeah…" The drawn-out way he says it implies that I should know this. "Didn't you see the email?"

"No, I didn't see the email," I snap. "I'm not a staff member, so I'm not on the email list. I never got it."

"Oh." Jason blinks. "I guess I figured someone would have told you."

"Professor Scott told me that he'd tell you," Dr. Wauncho says as he looks between us, clearly confused.

Aidan aims a pointed stare at me. The corner of his mouth quirks up before he pulls his lips into his mouth, clearly trying to stop himself from laughing. "I must have forgotten. Oops."

Muffled laughter echoes in the room. Dr. Wauncho aims a disapproving stare at Aidan, but it doesn't faze him. He just sits there, smug satisfaction written all over his face.

That's why I've felt off this week. That's why I've had a splitting headache every day I've been here—my caffeine-addicted body has been running on decaf this whole time.

Aidan planned for this to happen.

That bastard.

I take a breath before addressing the room. "I'm so sorry, but I'm going to have to reschedule."

Everyone gets up to leave, not one bit disappointed about ending this meeting early.

As Aidan walks by, I stop him.

"I'd like to speak to you." I try to keep my voice low since there are people all around us, but the bite in my tone is crystal clear. I mean fucking business.

And everyone seems to know that, judging by how quickly they scurry out of the room.

When Aidan turns to shut the door after the last person leaves, I catch the tail end of an eye roll.

I walk up to Aidan right as he spins around. He falls back into the door, his brow hitting his hairline.

Clearly he wasn't expecting me to corner him, but I don't care.

This guy has blasted through my last nerve. I'm fucking done.

Sixteen

Aidan

I jolt back at the sight of Micah backing me against the door, hitting my head against the hardwood. "What the…"

"You did that on purpose, didn't you?" Micah bites. "You didn't tell me about the decaf coffee in the break room because you knew I drink a pot of coffee a day, and you knew the caffeine withdrawal would screw me up."

My lips twitch, aching to laugh.

Yeah, I know I'm a dick for laughing in her face when she's struggling.

But feels really, really good to see Micah off her game after how she laughed while I coughed my guts out the other day.

I lean forward and look her straight in the eye. "Like I said before, it slipped my mind."

Micah's deep umber gaze turns fiery as she glowers at me. She wags her finger in my face. "You're a liar. And a jerk."

"So are you," I growl. "You think I was just going to let you get away with dousing my sandwich in hot sauce, then laughing about it while I coughed my brains out?"

Her tan skin flushes as she purses her lips. She drops her hand to her side. "At least I had a legitimate reason for doing that to you. You were looking at my chest again after I told you not to."

I lean my head back against the door, yank a hand through my hair, and let out a frustrated groan. "Micah, for the millionth time, I told you that was an accident. It was bad timing. Your chest just happened to be in my line of vision."

She throws her head back and lets out the most frustrated sounding laugh. "Oh my god, I can't believe you're still sticking with that lie."

I grit my teeth as irritation rockets through me. I can't take one more second of this woman calling me a liar when I'm telling the truth.

"I'm not going to stand here while you call me a liar," I mutter.

I move to step around her, but she plants her hand on my chest. "We're not done."

I still instantly, glancing down at her hand on my body.

Her warm, soft hand…

Even through the fabric of my shirt, I can feel how hot her skin is.

My pulse kicks up as she stands there touching me. Goose bumps flash up and down my skin.

I blink down at Micah. She's looking at her hand on my chest. I watch as the skin on her slender, delicate neck flushes pink. She swallows, and I keep watching her, mesmerized by the slow movement along her throat.

That anger from seconds ago has transformed completely. Now, instead of feeling pissed off, I feel intrigued. And hot. Really, really hot.

Well. This is…different.

Still staring at my chest, she sinks her teeth into her bottom lip. Something in my belly flickers.

Fuck, that's sexy.

A long moment passes before I notice the change in the air between us. It's still thick with tension…but a different kind of tension.

Before I can think more about it, she quickly pulls her hand away. Like she just got caught touching a hot stove.

Her chest heaves as she takes a breath. My gaze lands on her collarbone, how the skin above her chest is flushed now too.

She looks up at me. "I wouldn't call you a liar if you would just tell me the truth." Her voice is softer now, but the conviction is still there.

And that's when I know that she can feel this change in the air between us now too.

That flicker in my chest intensifies.

"You want to know the truth, Micah?" My voice is low and rough.

Her gaze falls to my mouth for a split second. She licks her lips before look up at my eyes again. Something flashes in her gorgeous deep brown gaze. It takes a second before I figure out what it is.

It's lust.

I think Micah wants me. Which is convenient because I want her too.

I let my gaze drag across her plush lips. My mouth waters.

My brain feels like it's short-circuiting with how quickly things have changed course between us in the span of just a couple of minutes.

I'm not normally like this. In the past, when I've argued with a partner, I've never felt anywhere close to being turned on.

But I've never argued like this before. I've never been backed against a wall by a beautiful woman who I'm insanely attracted to but who I also can't stand…

What the hell his happening?

"I want the truth," Micah says in a breathy voice.

It feels like firecrackers are going off in my chest. It ignites the last of my nerve enough to tell her what I've been holding back these past several days.

"Okay. Here it is—you have fantastic breasts, Micah. There, I said it. Your perfect breasts were inches from my face, spilling out of your bra, and I couldn't stop myself from staring that first time. And the second time it happened, it was just awful timing. I really didn't mean to look, but I did. Because you're the most beautiful woman I've ever seen in my life, and from the first moment I saw you, I can't get you out of my head. How's that for the truth?"

Her mouth falls open as she stares at me. In the quiet few moments that follow, my heart thrashes in my chest. It's beating so hard, I can feel it in my ears.

Holy shit... I can't believe I just said all that.

She blinks quickly. "Wait, you...you think I'm beautiful?"

I'm confused by how surprised she sounds. "Yeah."

She just stares at me. I almost laugh. Does she not know what she looks like?

"I think you're hot," she blurts.

I fall back into the door again, stunned. "You do?"

She nods. "Of course I do."

Now it's my turn to feel surprised. I start to laugh out of sheer disbelief.

"I wasn't expecting you to say that," I finally say.

That pink flush painting her cheeks and chest intensifies. "Well. It's the truth. You told me yours. It's only fair I tell you mine."

Her gaze falls to my mouth once again.

I can't help but smile. "You keep looking at my mouth."

Her eyes cut to mine. "So do you."

She bites her bottom lip once more, then runs her candy-pink tongue along the seam of her mouth.

My dick pulses. That mouth and that tongue have told me off, they've called me names...

And it only makes me want her more.

I try to swallow back a groan, but it comes out sounding like a growl. "Stop doing that."

"Stop doing what?" There's a teasing lilt to her voice. She's fucking with me. She's fucking with me, and I love it.

"Biting your lip. Licking your mouth. It makes me wild. It makes me want to kiss you, Micah."

The corner of her mouth quirks up, like she knows exactly what she's doing to me.

I lean my head closer to her. Our faces are barely two inches apart now.

"I'm warning you, Micah. If you bite your lip again, I'm going to kiss you."

Her mouth parts open. She exhales, her hot, wet breath sheeting across my skin. I tap my tongue against my top lip, and I swear I can taste her. The faintest hint of sugar and coffee.

My mouth waters just imagining what her perfect, plush mouth would taste like.

And then she looks me dead in the eye and bites her lip.

I crash my mouth against hers.

She teases her tongue against mine and moans into my mouth. My dick throbs.

That moan. That hot little moan.

The things I would do to hear Micah make that sound over and over and over…

Fuck.

She claws at my shirt, and I grip a hand around her waist, pulling her against me.

Micah is desperate and rough with her kiss, and fuck, I love it. It's just like her personality: feisty, bold, brazen.

With my other hand, I gently grip her chin and tilt her face up, deepening our kiss. Her lips and tongue are just as sweet as I suspected. I hum, savoring her taste.

With each passing second our tongues and mouths get filthier and filthier. Air whooshes out of my lungs. It feels like the floor is tilting beneath my feet.

Holy *fuck*, this kiss. This kiss is enough to wreck me.

This woman is going to wreck me.

Maybe that's why I was so attracted to her. Maybe my cave-man brain knew that this woman could fucking destroy me with a single kiss.

I breathe in a lungful of that intoxicating vanilla-orange scent she's wearing. When I'm this close to her, the scent mingles with her natural smell, and fuck, if it's not the most incredible scent in this entire world.

My head spins as I pull her tighter against me. I can't get enough of her. Her body, her mouth, her scent…

She whimpers into my mouth before breaking our kiss and pausing to catch her breath. Her hands are fisted into my shirt as she presses the softest, sweetest kiss to my mouth. Then another. And another.

Like she's showing me how soft and playful she can be.

She gazes up at me, and that's when I see it: a flash of something warm and raw in those gorgeous mahogany eyes.

Micah is feisty and fierce, but she's also soft and sweet. I see it right there inside of her.

She hates me, but she's looking at me like I'm the only one she wants.

I'm dizzy as I stand there, holding her, breathing in lungfuls of her vanilla-orange perfume, her sweet taste lingering on my lips and tongue.

Nothing about this, nothing about us makes sense right now. But I don't care.

She smells incredible and tastes incredible, and all I want is more of her.

"Fuck…" she murmurs.

I let out a low chuckle. "Yeah. Fuck."

I cup my hand over her cheek. "Is that all you want, Micah? Just a kiss?"

She shakes her head. "I want more."

Seventeen

Aidan

A second later, I sink to my knees and push her skirt up. Her breath catches as she gazes down at me, a drunken haze in her eyes.

"Is this what you want? My mouth on your pussy?"

Her mouth falls open, like she's surprised at what I've said. She nods.

I shake my head. "I want to hear you say it."

She lets out a shaky breath. "I want your mouth on my pussy."

I grin up at her, then lower my gaze. I groan when I see how wet her panties are.

"All this for me?"

"Yes," she whimpers.

I growl at the need in her voice. Then I bury my face between her thighs. "Fuck, baby. You're soaked."

She inhales sharply above me.

I flick my tongue along the crotch of her panties. Her inner thigh muscles twitch against my face.

I drag my tongue up and down her slit roughly. My dick is throbbing in my pants. Jesus. Just a few seconds of licking her outside of her panties has me hard as steel, ready to blow. I need to pace myself.

Above me, Micah's breaths grow desperate and ragged. After a minute of rough teasing, I lean back and look up at her. Those beautiful brown eyes are dazed and drunk. Her chest is bright red and heaving with each breath she takes.

For a second all I can do is stand there and look at her. She looks so undone and so fucking beautiful.

My breath comes out in a slow hiss. "Put your back against the wall," I growl.

Her eyebrows lift slightly at my command. But then there's a flash in her eyes. The corner of her mouth lifts. Well, then. I think she likes it when I'm a little bossy.

She backs up to the nearby wall, and I follow. I reach up and slowly pull her panties down her mile-long legs.

I glance down at the wetness of the fabric, my dick getting harder by the second at seeing just how turned on Micah is—how turned on she is by me.

I glance up and smirk at her. "So fucking wet."

She bites back a grin, her full cheeks flushed. She nods.

I run my thumb along the fabric. "For me."

Her mouth parts open. "Yeah."

My dick swells right along with my head. Micah hates me, but she loves my mouth on her pussy. She loves how good I make her feel.

I rest my palms on her thighs and slowly glide up. My gaze still locked with hers, I lean my face into her pussy. And then I lick.

Her eyes roll and her head falls back. "Oh my god…"

I run my tongue along her soaking-wet slick, groaning at how drenched she is, how sweet she tastes. She tugs a hand through my hair, and I grunt at the flash of pain.

Fuck, I love it when a woman pulls my hair when I go down on her. It means she likes what I'm doing. It means my tongue is making her feel really fucking good.

I run my tongue gently over Micah's swollen clit. She gasps; her inner thigh muscles tense. She pulls my hair even tighter.

I take that as my cue to keep going. I swirl my tongue softly over her clit, keeping a steady rhythm.

"Aidan…"

I smile against her pussy. My dick throbs at the satisfaction of hearing her finally say my name.

After a minute, she lifts her right leg and rests it on my shoulder, giving me more access. With my tongue still working her clit, I slide a finger into her pussy. She mutters a breathy curse, her leg buckling over me. But I straighten my back, holding her up with the help of the wall.

Her breathing quickens. It's not even a minute before she's panting. She tugs her fingers through my hair harder. I look up at her and see that flash of panic in her eyes.

She's close.

I lean back but keep my fingers inside of her pussy, pumping hard. I look her in the eye. "Say my name again," I command.

She runs her tongue along the seam of her lips.

"Aidan." She moans it. Pleasure rushes through my dick. Fuck, I like the sound of that.

"Do you want me to make you come, Micah?" I know the answer, but I want to hear her say it.

She nods. I shake my head and stop moving my fingers.

"Not until you say it," I growl.

Her chest rises with the breath she takes, and she blinks quickly, like she's frustrated. "Make me come, Aidan. Please."

My knees buckle. I can barely take this, watching this tough and put-together woman come undone for me.

"I need your tongue," she whines. "Will you please give it to me?"

My cock is on the verge of ripping through my pants. I'm gonna lose it, hearing Micah begging for my tongue, begging for me to make her come.

I move my face back between her thighs and flick my tongue over her clit while I pump my fingers inside of her once more.

Thirty seconds later she comes. Above me, I hear muffled screams and moans. Her legs wobble around me. I wrap my free hand around her thigh, holding her steady between me and the wall.

She unravels for what feels like a minute. I groan into her perfect pussy, pleased at how she has to cover her own mouth to keep from screaming too loud because that's how hard I'm making her come.

When her movements begin to ease, I back off. I press a kiss to the inside of her thigh before I look up at her.

Those burnt-umber eyes are wide as saucers as she peers down at me, like she can't believe that happened.

I stand up and stare at her. A pink-red flush paints her tan skin, her hair is a mess, she's soaked from her pussy all the way to her thighs, and she's never looked so beautiful.

My heart thrashes in my chest as she grips my chin in her hand, kissing me until I'm gasping for air.

And then she looks me dead in the eye and says, "I need to suck your cock."

Eighteen

Micah

I stare at Aidan, dizzy with arousal, my entire body vibrating.

Never in my life have I ever done anything like this.

I've never hooked up with a guy at work. I've never even dated someone I've worked with.

I'm stunned at what's just happened between us. We were arguing, things got heated, and Aidan admitted he was attracted to me. I was so surprised that I admitted I was attracted to him too.

And then it was like a switch flipped. All that fury and frustration morphed into raw passion. I've never felt that before.

And then we kissed, and holy *shit*, I can't remember ever having a kiss like that. So desperate, so rabid. Practically feral.

And then Aidan dropped to his knees and went down on me.

My pussy is still throbbing at how good he was with his mouth. And all the filthy things he said to me…

Teasing me about how wet I was, telling me to say his name, ordering me to stand against the wall…

My clit pulses.

I had no idea Aidan would be like this. So filthy and so bossy.

And I'm so turned on that I need to suck his cock.

And that's when I realize my headache is long gone. It disappeared the second he kissed me.

Nothing like a surprise hookup and a soul-shaking orgasm to make my body forget that it's in caffeine withdrawal.

Aidan looks at me. His throat works as he swallows. The corner of his mouth quirks up, amusement flashing in his eyes.

"You wanna suck my cock?" he rasps.

I nod.

"Then get on your knees, Micah."

I bite back a smile. I really, really like Bossy Aidan.

I drop to my knees and reach up to unzip his pants. He pushes them down a bit, and I catch sight of the impressive bulge at the front of his gray boxer briefs.

I bite my lip. When I yank down his boxer briefs and pull out his dick, my mouth waters.

"Wow," I murmur, gripping the base of his thick cock.

He groans. I look at up at him, relishing the bulge at the side of his jaw and the way his chest rises and falls with the breath that he takes. I'm just holding his dick and already he looks like he can barely hold it together.

A wave of satisfaction flashes through me. I smile up at him and pump him once in my hand. His eyebrows crash together as he grunts.

I grip him harder and pump again. His head falls back against the wall.

"Micah…" he rasps.

"You want my mouth on your cock?"

Head still back, he nods. A giddy feeling whooshes through me. Now it's my turn to be in control, to make him beg for my mouth.

"Say it."

He looks down at me, his eyes cloudy with arousal. "I need your mouth on my cock, Micah. Please."

Something flickers low in my belly at the pleading in Aidan's voice, at hearing just how much he wants me to make him feel good. I think back to just a few minutes ago when he did the same to me.

We don't even like each other, and here we are, on our knees, begging for each other.

This is so messed up…but I like it. I like it a lot.

My clit aches with need. I'm still so wet.

I swirl my tongue around the head of his cock. Above me, he mutters a curse. For a minute, I keep at it, licking and swirling the head until his breaths have turned desperate and broken.

"Fuck, Micah…that mouth…you're incredible."

I smile as I pull back. I glance up and watch him as he tugs a hand through his chestnut waves. So worked up. So turned on.

I take him into my mouth, gliding my tongue along the underside of his rock-hard dick. He makes a choking sound and swears.

"Holy shit," he mutters. I smile around his dick.

I glide up and down his cock while I pump the base of him with my hand.

"Baby…"

My stomach flips at hearing him call me that. I'm surprised at how much I like it. There's so much affection, so much sweetness in his tone.

"Baby, you're dangerous with that mouth."

My eyelids flutter. Wow. Aidan is all about praise when he's turned on. God, that's sweet. And such a turn-on.

With my free hand, I push his shirt up so I can get a view of his body.

HOT DAMN.

Aidan is *ripped*. I clock an actual six-pack. His chest is chiseled too. *God.*

He flashed a smug smile. "Enjoying the view?"

I hum and relax my mouth, taking him deeper. A low grunt rips from his throat. His thighs tense. I work him faster in my mouth and hand. After a few seconds, he threads his fingers through my hair, pulling gently. I moan at the burn against my scalp.

"I'm gonna come," he groans.

I moan. A dozen seconds later, he unloads into my mouth with a muffled growl. I relax my throat and take it all.

When he finishes, I release him and fall back onto my heels. I touch my fingers to my lips as I glance up at him. His hands are in his hair and his chest is heaving. He looks down at me and blinks.

For a moment, we stay like that, quietly staring at each other as we catch our breath.

When I stand up, I get a better look his expression. That drunk-aroused look is gone, and he's looking at me like he's freaked out.

Like he made a mistake.

Like he made a mistake by hooking up with me.

My stomach falls to my feet.

"I should get back to my office," he mutters.

I blink at him, stunned. Is that really all he has to say after what we did?

I open my mouth to say something, but he takes a step back. His gaze falls to the floor and his shoulders hunch as he straightens his clothing. He clearly doesn't want to talk to me. He just wants to get dressed and get away. From me.

I quickly pull my panties back up and straighten my skirt, embarrassed.

I clear my throat. "Yeah. I should leave too."

He looks at me and opens his mouth like he's going to say something, but he stops himself. He starts for the door, but then turns around.

"You should wait a minute after I leave before heading out." He frowns. "I don't want people to think we were messing around in here."

Aidan's words are like a punch to the gut. But I command my face muscles to stay neutral. I nod. "Okay."

He slips out. I wait for a minute, and then I leave too. I head back to my workspace, in a daze, feeling so foolish and so stupid as I struggle to focus on my work the rest of the day.

As hurt as I am at Aidan's reaction, I can't bring myself to regret what we did. It was really, really hot. And exactly what I needed.

But that doesn't matter. Because clearly it meant nothing to him.

His words from minutes ago echo in my mind.

I don't want people to think we were messing around in here.

That gut-punch feeling is back.

Message received, loud and clear. Aidan wants to forget what we did. He wants to move on and pretend like nothing happened.

Fine. I'll go back to acting like the heartless auditor he thinks I am. He's not going to like it, but I don't care. It's what he said he wanted.

Nineteen

Aidan

I stare at my laptop screen in my office, my focus shot.

It's been that way ever since Micah and I hooked up in the conference room two days ago.

I still can't believe we did that. I can't believe *I* did that.

I yank my tie loose from around my neck and force out a breath.

I've never done anything even close to that in my entire life.

Before the other day, if someone had told me that I'd have a hookup in the conference room of my workplace, I would have laughed in their face.

Not a chance in hell.

But it happened. With Micah, a woman who can't stand the sight of me.

My brain pulls up the image of Micah gazing down at me, her thighs twitching, her chest heaving, her skin hot, her pussy wet...

My pulse kicks up. I tap my tongue on my upper lip, remembering how sweet her pussy tasted...

My dick begins to stir. A hard swallow moves down my throat.

I blink, and all I see is Micah's pouty, plush mouth. I see her biting her bottom lip. I see her licking her lips...

I remember her on her knees, taking me into her mouth, teasing me, working that heavenly tongue up and down my shaft until I couldn't take it any longer and spilled down her throat...

My cock hardens.

My hand twitches to pull myself out of my pants and take care of myself. But I don't because I'm at work and I shouldn't be jerking off in my office like some fucking heathen.

I huff out a breath. We also shouldn't have gone down on each other in the conference room.

No shit. But you did. And it was the hottest moment of your life.

I make myself take a long, slow breath. Not like jerking off would make those filthy thoughts disappear. The day we hooked up, as soon as I got home from work, I jerked off. And then I did it again that night in the shower. And again yesterday morning when I woke up before work. And again last night.

And then I logged into my Scribble Share account and wrote a hot sex scene inspired by our hookup. None of it has helped. I can't stop thinking about Micah. I still want her, I still crave her…

I yank my hand through my hair, annoyed at myself.

I constantly give my brother a hard time about how sex-obsessed he is, but it turns out I'm no better. Because apparently all it takes for me to lose my control is seeing Micah bite her lip while she's lashing out at me.

I lean back in my chair and shake my head at myself. That's a hell of a kink.

I think back to how when we were finished in the conference room, I just stood there, staring at her. I couldn't help it. She had just given me the hottest blow job of my life. I had lost the ability to speak and think clearly. But when I did, I panicked. I didn't want someone to walk into the conference room and see us. We would have gotten fired.

It was more than that though…my mind was blown at just how insane the sexual chemistry between Micah and me was. I've never felt that way with anyone before. Ever. I've never had a hookup in a public place. I've never had sex with anyone I wasn't in a relationship with.

But there I was, standing there with my cock out after having the hottest sex of my life with a woman who hates my guts, and it threw me off.

So I blurted out that I should head back to my office. I cringe when I think about how blunt and uncaring I sounded, like I didn't give a shit about Micah or how she felt.

My chest aches. I did care though. Yeah, we fight and we can't stand each other, but I cared about how she was doing in that moment. I wanted to ask how she was feeling and if she was okay with what we'd just done. But I was so overwhelmed and freaked out that I just blurted the first words my dumbass brain threw at me.

I picture the look on Micah's face after I said it. She looked shocked and annoyed. And that look in her eyes…

She was hurt at how dismissive I was.

I was going to apologize, but she was glaring at me, looking like she wanted to get the hell away from me as fast as she could.

I exhale sharply. God, I really fucked this up.

A banging sound behind my half-open office door gets my attention. I hear Dr. Wauncho's muffled voice. I wince and glance down at my lap. Nothing like the sudden sound of your boss's voice to kill your boner.

More muffled sounds and grunting. I hop up and walk over to my door and open it all the way, surprised when I see Dr. Wauncho on the floor, picking up a bunch of papers.

"Everything all right?" I ask.

"Oh, yes. All fine." He winces as he leans up, on his knees. "I was reading as I was walking and missed my footing. I really should know better by now." He chuckles.

I bend down to help him up anyway, then crouch on the floor and grab the papers he missed.

"Thank you," he says when I hand them to him. With his free hand he straightens his tie and smooths a hand over his gray hair. "So. I noticed you and Ms. Mila stayed in the conference room the other day after everyone left."

My stomach bottoms out. Shit. Did he hear us? I thought we were being quiet, but…things got pretty filthy. Both of us were struggling to stay quiet. Maybe someone overheard…

My eyes start to widen, but I blink and rein in my expression, hoping I look unbothered and not like I'm totally losing my shit.

"We did." I clear my throat and tell myself to stay calm as I try to decipher the look on his face.

He frowns slightly. I hold my breath.

"And did you two use that time alone to work out your differences?" he asks.

I almost choke at his wording. If only he knew.

"We didn't."

He sighs. "That's unfortunate."

"Uh, yeah. It is." I study Dr. Wauncho's expression. He looks bothered but not upset. I don't think he knows what Micah and I actually got up to in the conference room but I can't say for sure, and it's making me nervous as fuck.

He starts to walk off but turns around after a moment. "You know, it's a shame you two can't get along, Professor Scott. I know Micah's job conflicts with yours in a way, but she's very diligent, focused, and hardworking. Just like you. Under different circumstances, I feel like you two could get along."

I let out a surprised chuckle. He has no idea how right he is. "I don't know about that. She is the most stubborn, relentless, harsh person I've ever met. We'll never get along."

That's a lie. I know just how well Micah and I can get along when things get hot and dirty…

But I don't want him suspecting that anything went on between us.

Dr. Wauncho turns the corner and walks off. And that's when I see Micah standing several feet away, glaring at me... probably because she just heard me talking crap about her. Again.

Shit.

Twenty

Micah

I stand there and stare at Aidan, stunned at what I just heard him say about me.

She is the most stubborn, relentless, harsh person I've ever met. We'll never get along.

I can't be too surprised to hear those words come out of his mouth. Except for our rendezvous in the conference room, we've spent the entire time we've known each other in near-constant conflict.

I'm not under any illusion that Aidan suddenly is mad about me after one hookup. But I was hoping that he wouldn't still hate me after we were so physically intimate with each other.

I think back to him on his knees in front of me in the conference room, that look in his eyes. How it was soft and pleading and fiery all at once.

How he looked like he wanted me. How he looked like he actually liked me.

How in that moment, as he touched me and kissed me and drove me wild with his hands and mouth, it *felt* like he actually liked me too.

And if I'm being honest with myself, I was starting to like Aidan. A lot.

My throat aches when I try to swallow.

But that moment and that feeling were fleeting for him. If he ever even felt that way to begin with, it didn't last. It disappeared right after he came into my mouth and regained clarity.

He wanted to leave right away. He wanted to pretend like it never happened.

I let myself be intimate and vulnerable with him—I let myself start to like him—and then he trashed me.

God, I'm so stupid for thinking he'd act like anything other than a total jerk.

Aidan's eyebrows crash together as he aims a panicked expression at me. When he starts to move toward me, I walk off.

"Micah, wait." He touches my arm.

I yank away and turn around. "Don't touch me."

He holds up his palm, like he's surrendering. "Okay. I'm sorry. I just… I didn't know you were standing right there."

I let out an annoyed laugh. "Oh, well that makes it okay, then, for you to talk shit about me."

He shakes his head. "No, that's not what I mean. I'm sorry for what I said."

"Don't even bother with some half-assed apology."

His jaw bulges as he bites down. "I'm not trying to half-ass this. I'm trying to tell you how sorry I am, but it's coming out all wrong."

I stare at him. "You're an English professor. You deal with words all day, every day, and you can't figure out how to convey a sincere apology?" I let out a bitter, annoyed laugh.

Frustration flashes in Aidan's ice-blue eyes as he looks at me.

And that's when I know. Any affection he had for me in the conference room when he was touching me, kissing me, and driving me wild with his mouth is long gone now.

"I think we both know that what happened in the conference room was a mistake," I say.

He stares at me, his expression unreadable. "Yeah. It was. Let's just forget it ever happened."

I swallow through the tightness in my throat. "It's forgotten."

And then I turn away and walk off, knowing full well that I won't ever be able to forget hooking up with Aidan.

"Mom, that's way too much food for one person."

I stare at the pot full of leftover *pansit* sitting on my sister's stove.

Mom glances at the pot and waves her hand. "Oh, *anak*, it's not really that much. That's for the whole week. You can portion it out."

"She's right," Jordan says from my phone screen. "You've got the appetite of a horse, Micah. You'll demolish that in no time."

I roll my eyes and laugh as I tell my sister to shut up.

My mom frowns at me. "*Anak*, don't talk like that."

Jordan laughs. So does Dad. He sets some leftover in the fridge and walks over to Mom, pulling her into a hug. "Come on, Anita. You know our girls are just joking around. They've always been like that."

Mom smiles at Dad and tiptoes up to kiss him. She's five-one and he's six-one, so even in her heels she has to reach.

I quickly turn the phone away as Jordan mutters, "Gross!"

"Save it for when you get home," I holler.

"You girls need to grow up," Dad teases. "How do you think you two got here in the first place?"

I make a gagging noise. So does Jordan. In the background, Mom cackles.

We're just finishing up family dinner at Jordan's place. Mom and Dad came over to cook an early dinner while I was at work. While we ate, we FaceTimed Jordan. We try to do this once a week ever since Jordan moved to London. Even though it's not the same as when we all spend time together in person, it's the next best thing.

Dad and Mom kiss once more to annoy my sister and me. We both groan and laugh. It feels really good to joke around after such a crummy day at work.

I think about that argument with Aidan. How he talked crap about me behind my back. How quick he was to admit that he wanted to forget about our hookup completely.

That familiar ache lands at the center of my chest. I swallow it back and push the thought from my brain. I don't want to waste another second thinking about Aidan.

Jordan says she's tired and needs to head to bed, so I turn her back to our parents. They exchange *I love you*s and say good-bye to Jordan. I blow her a kiss and hang up the phone, then I help my parents gather their things.

I walk them to the front door and give my mom a hug.

"Next week, how about I make my grandpa's schnitzel recipe for dinner?" Dad says as he hugs me.

"Sounds yummy," I say.

"You haven't cooked that one in a while. You sure you can still make it?" Mom teases.

He frowns at her. "That recipe is in my genes. Just like my adobe recipe from my mom's family. No way I'll mess it up."

"Too bad I didn't get your cooking skills," I say to Dad.

He laughs, his eyes bright. "You got my height and my nose—that's good enough for me."

Mom reaches up and ruffles his gray-brown hair. "Come on now, you know our girls look more like me."

He smiles adoringly at her. "They're your clones, Anita. Thank goodness for that."

Mom smiles sweetly at him and drops a quick kiss to his mouth.

Despite how my sister and I give our parents a hard time whenever they display some PDA, my chest always goes gooey at how in love they still are with each other after decades of being married.

I smile at them. "Thanks so much again for everything."

They tell me of course and head out. I close the door behind them and lock it.

I finish cleaning up, plop onto the couch with the remote, and try to find something to watch. Now that my family is gone, my mind floats back to Aidan. I exhale sharply. I really, really need to stop thinking about him.

I turn off the TV and opt instead to jump on the exercise bike for a hardcore sweat session. But that backfires…because all the panting and sweating reminds me of every filthy thing we got up to in the conference room…

Between my legs, I feel that faint pulse. I groan out of sheer frustration.

I'm still so turned on.

I'm ashamed to admit that I've played with myself a handful of times while thinking about my hookup with Aidan. I can't help it. Despite what a jerk he is, despite what a mistake it was, it was still the hottest moment of my life. And the only way I can feel some sort of release is by grabbing my favorite vibrator, closing my eyes, and imagining Aidan's mouth and hands all over me.

I make annoyed sound as I finish my session on the bike and hop into the shower. I brush my teeth and get ready for bed. When I settle under the covers, I grab my phone from the nightstand and pull up the one thing that I'm certain will distract me.

I tap on the Scribble Share app and navigate to @ShakespeareInLove's posts. When I see they've posted a brand new story, I'm giddy. I immediately read it.

Trina gazed at Petra. She took in the feral look in his eyes, the way his chest rose and fell with each breath he took. He took one step forward. Her heart raced.

She hated this man. She hated him with every bone in her body, every beat of her heart.

But she also wanted him. She wanted his mouth on hers, she wanted his hands all over her body, she wanted his face buried between her legs, licking her pussy until her entire body trembled with pleasure.

"Tell me to stop, Petra, and I will."

He took another step forward and stopped.

She let out a shaky breath, her gazed fixed on him standing less than a foot away from her. She didn't speak. She just stood there and looked at him, daring him to take another step forward.

He did. And then another and another, until he had her backed against the wall. His massive hand gripped her waist. His mouth hovered over hers. He exhaled, his hot breath ghosting over her lips. Her mouth watered and her eyes fluttered.

Petra's eyes were ink-black pools ringed in ice blue.

"This is your last chance, Trina," he growled. "If you don't tell me to stop, I'm going to kiss you. And then I'm going to drop to my knees and kiss you between your legs until you're screaming my name."

Trina gasped. A hard swallow moved down her delicate throat. Her entire body was on fire, aching for Petra's mouth.

She looked Petra straight in the eye. "Do it."

A half second later, Petra's mouth was on hers. He kissed her like a mad man, like he was starving and the only thing keeping him alive was Trina's mouth. She could barely keep up, barely breathe. But she loved it. He was rabid and desperate, like he couldn't get enough of her mouth, enough of her taste.

She tugged her hands through his hair, pulling hard. He groaned, smiling at the pull and the pain.

"So rough. I like it," he growled against her mouth.

"I can't help it. You drive me wild."

It wasn't long before they had torn off each other's

clothing. Petra stepped back, his eyes fiery and intense as he ran his gaze down Trina's body

A smug smirk tugged at his lips as he zeroed in between her legs. Her clit jumped at the way Petra devoured her with his gaze.

A second later, he dropped to his knees. He pressed his hands gently on her thighs, spreading her apart. Trina gasped, her pussy pulsing. Judging from the way he kissed, she knew it wouldn't take long for her to come once Petra's mouth was on her.

He pressed a soft kiss to the inside of her thigh. Her knees buckled.

"I'm going to enjoy this—watching you unravel," he said against her skin.

Trina tried to scoff, but she was too turned on.

Petra slowly kissed her pussy lips apart. Trina gasped. Pleasured jolted through her entire body like a lightning bolt.

Once more she was pulling her hands through his hair as he licked and sucked her clit. Pleasure and pressure converged inside of her, winding tighter with each swirl of his tongue.

Suddenly he pulled away and looked up at her, smirking.

She whined at the loss of his mouth, breathing hard.

"You hate me, don't you, Trina?"

She nodded, and Petra's smirked morphed to a full-on grin.

"But you love my mouth."

Again she nodded.

Eye still on her, he kissed her thigh once more. "Say it, Trina. Say you love my mouth."

This arrogant bastard. She said it anyway though. Because it was true.

"I love your mouth."

With those magic words, Petra brought his mouth back to her pussy. His tongue moved in an achingly slow and teasing rhythm, the pleasuring building and building until Trina's whole body was trembling.

Her entire body was aching, begging for release. This sweet torture Petra was unleashing on her with his mouth was heaven.

"Petra…please…"

He flicked his tongue faster. Seconds later Trina came, screaming and thrashing as the most powerful orgasm she'd ever had claimed her body.

I kick off the bedsheets, suddenly hot. I immediately message ShakespeareInLust.

Just finished reading your latest post and first of all, excellent Taming of the Shrew fanfic. I love that play! And second, HOLY HOTNESS!!! My phone is on fire! That was incredible!

I toss my phone aside and fan myself with my hand. Reading this fanfic reminded me of the good parts of hooking up with Aidan in the conference room.

Just then I see a notification on the screen. ShakespeareInLust just replied to my message. I smile as I read it.

ShakespeareInLust: Aww thanks! I'm so happy you enjoyed it! Inspiration hit so I decided to go for it.

Hot4Hermia: Well, I'm thrilled that you did because that's the hottest thing I've read in a long time. Well done!

ShakespeareInLust: You're making me blush haha

Hot4Hermia: It was the perfect way to end a crummy day, so thank you

ShakespeareInLust: Shoot, another bad day at work?

Hot4Hermia: Yeah :/

ShakespeareInLust: Ah damn. Was your annoying coworker causing you problems again?

I smile at my phone, heartened that they remember.

Hot4Hermia: Yeah, they were.

ShakespeareInLust: Really sorry to hear that.

Hot4Hermia: It's okay. That's work, sometimes it sucks. How are things going for you at work?

ShakespeareInLust: Kind of the same sadly. She still hates me. Oh well.

ShakespeareInLust: Writing this was a nice distraction though. And reading your message turned the day around for me. So thanks for that :)

Hot4Hermia: Anytime! Always here to fangirl over your stuff :)

ShakespeareInLust: I'm just happy to meet another Shakespeare superfan who also loves filthy fanfic. There are so few of us LOL

ShakespeareInLust: Do you write at all?

Hot4Hermia: I used to, but I kind of stopped.

ShakespeareInLust: Why?

Hot4Hermia: It's a long story, not sure if I want to bore you to death lol

ShakespeareInLust: Aww come on, I love long stories. I write them, remember?

Hot4Hermia: Haha okay good point. So I've honestly always loved writing stories, ever since I was a kid. Romance especially. It's always been a dream of mine to publish my writing, but I was always better at more analytical stuff. So I focused on that in college and started my career. I kept writing in my spare time though. And then I dated this guy. He was a pretty successful author. When I shared some of my writing with him, he outright laughed at me. Told me that writing romance was lowbrow and that I should aspire to something better. Ever since then, I just stopped writing all together.

As I wait for them to reply, my nerves crackle in my tummy. Are they going to think I'm a loser because I gave up on my passion so quickly?

ShakespeareInLust: He seriously did that? What a piece of shit.

I smile, comforted at their response.

Hot4Hermia: Yeah, he definitely was.

ShakespeareInLust: I'm really sorry, Hermia. You didn't deserve to be treated like that. Your partner should support you and lift you up, not tear you down. And hey, I'd bet anything your writing is really good. Some people, especially writers of other genres unfortunately, love to bash romance. Probably because it's a women-dominated genre. And some people are sexist assholes and feel the need to minimize something just because women like it or excel at it.

Hot4Hermia: I never thought if that way, but you're totally right.

Hot4Hermia: He was pretty awful all around. I wish I had dumped him when he criticized my writing. He ended up cheating on me with his coworker.

ShakespeareInLust: Okay, fuck this guy. What's his address? I'm heading over there so I can leave a bag of flaming dog crap on his porch.

I cradle my tummy as I laugh.

Hot4Hermia: I almost peed my pants, I laughed so hard. Thanks for that :P

ShakespeareInLust: I'm not even kidding, I'll do it ;)

Hot4Hermia: You need to stop, I'm seriously going to piss myself!

ShakespeareInLust: Okay okay, I'll stop :P

ShakespeareInLust: I don't mean to tell you what to do…but I think you should start writing again.

That nervous feeling bubbles up in my chest.

Hot4Hermia: I want to. I'm nervous though. What if it's terrible?

ShakespeareInLust: I get that feeling, I really do. I struggle with it sometimes. But what if it's amazing and you're depriving readers of some incredible stories? ;)

Hot4Hermia: Fair point :) How do you deal with those doubts?

ShakespeareInLust: I have a mantra: Fuck the haters

I burst out laughing.

Hot4Hermia: Bahaha that is perfect and brilliant!

ShakespeareInLust: As fun and rewarding as writing is, it's also a roller coaster. Because what one person loves, another person hates. You could write the most perfect piece of prose and I guarantee some sad sack would find some ridiculous reason to dislike it.

Hot4Hermia: Okay yeah, I see your point. You're right. I think I'm still kind of disappointed with myself for letting my exboyfriend rattle me like that.

ShakespeareInLust: It's understandable. It can be really unsettling when someone you love and care about hurts your feelings.

Hot4Hermia: Yeah :/

Hot4Hermia: Men can be the fucking worst, am I right?

ShakespeareInLust: As a man, I definitely agree LOL

My eyes go wide as I stare at my phone screen, shocked at what I just read. ShakespeareInLust is a guy? I had no idea.

Hot4Hermia: Crap, I'm so sorry! I assumed you were a woman because you write such amazing romances!

Hot4Hermia: Ahhh I feel like such an idiot. And a jerk. So sorry!

ShakespeareInLust: It's okay. Really. Don't apologize, I swear you didn't offend me :) I assumed you were a woman too LOL

Hot4Hermia: Haha fair enough

ShakespeareInLust: But you're totally right, men can be massive jerks. I've met plenty of them myself.

I let out a breath, relieved. I guess he could be lying to spare my feelings. But we don't even know each other. We're anonymous users on this app. There's zero incentive to lie to each other.

Hot4Hermia: Thanks for being so great about this :)

ShakespeareInLust: Of course :) And thanks for being so amazing. Your comments and DMs always make my day.

ShakespeareInLust: Can I ask you to do me one favor though?

Hot4Hermia: Sure

ShakespeareInLust: Will you at least think about writing again? I hate to think that your ex is holding you back.

Warmth blooms in my chest. This guy is so kind and sweet to encourage me.

Hot4Hermia: I promise I'll think about it :)

ShakespeareInLust: *fist pump*

Hot4Hermia: You might be the last person in the world who's still fist pumping

ShakespeareInLust: Aww really? And I thought I was so cool. I mean, I write Shakespeare fanfic, that's the coolest thing a person could ever do

I burst out laughing again.

Hot4Hermia: I think still you're very cool

ShakespeareInLust: That's all that matters to me :)

My stomach does a little flutter as I read his reply. This feels a lot like flirting…

I instantly shove that thought out of my mind. I shouldn't be thinking of him in that way. I don't even know this guy. We're strangers on an app. And he's going out of his way to be kind to me and encourage me. I shouldn't read anymore into it.

He mentions that he has an early day at work tomorrow, so we say goodbye. I set my phone on the nightstand and turn off the lamp. As I snuggle into the covers, I'm smiling. ShakespeareInLust may be a stranger on an app, but one conversation with him turned my entire day around.

Those stomach flutters hit once more. I close my eyes and try to ignore them as I fall asleep.

Twenty-One

Aidan

I smile down at my phone as I reread my conversation with Hermia on Scribble Share.

I think back to how fun and easy it felt to talk to her, how we vented about our frustrations of the day, how she admitted that she's a writer too, how her asshole ex had made fun of her writing.

How I instantly felt angry for her and protective over her, and told her that her ex was a piece of shit for doing that and that she should keep writing.

Maybe it's weird that I had such a reaction. But it was instant. I've never even met Hermia, but from all of my chats with her on Scribble Share, she's such a kind and supportive person. Everything she says feels so genuine. She's never mean or cruel, like some people are when they're online or on an app. She didn't deserve to be treated like that, especially by someone who's supposed to care about her.

Even now as I read back that part of our conversation on my phone, I can feel that anger spark up inside of me. What a pretentious, self-important prick. I'd bet anything he writes literary fiction. Those guys are the fucking worst.

Jason elbows me. I glance up at him, but then I hear a crashing sound.

We look up just in time to see Liam smash a player from the opposing team into the boards and steal the puck. The home crowd around us cheers.

We holler as he takes off down the ice.

"Everything okay?" Jason asks, his eyes on the ice. "You keep looking at your phone."

"Yeah, sorry, just got a little distracted." I really shouldn't be glued to my phone right now. I should be focused on watching my brother play.

I type a quick message to Hermia.

Just wanted to slide into your DMs and see if you've written anything? Because I'm dying to read something from you :)

I put my phone away and spend the next few minutes watching the game. But the whole time, I'm thinking about Hermia.

Maybe it's silly, but that conversation we had the other night completely changed my mood. I was so upset and frustrated from arguing with Micah that day. Even writing a new post on Scribble Share wasn't enough to clear my head. But then Hermia messaged me to compliment my post and I was all smiles. The conversation from there flowed so naturally. It felt like talking to an old friend…and a little like flirting too.

That probably sounds so pathetic. It was just a pleasant and fun conversation with an internet stranger. I shouldn't read more into it.

But there was definitely a different vibe…it was more playful and more teasing. And she seemed into it too.

I shake my head, annoyed at myself with how much I'm thinking about this right now. Liam, who plays center for Nashville, speeds down the ice toward the opposing team's net with the puck. He takes a shot, but it's blocked by the goalie. The crowd lets out a collective disappointed "Ahhh."

"Kendall didn't want to come tonight?" Jason asks.

I shake my head. "You know she hates hockey. She'd rather drink a shot of vinegar."

He laughs. "Good point. She came to a lot of Liam's games

with us when he played in college though. She seemed to have a good time then. I wonder what changed."

Jason is right. Kendall attended hockey games with us when Liam played for Vanderbilt. But after that house party we all went to, she started acting pretty frosty to Liam. She went to a few games after that but then stopped altogether. When he started playing professionally for the Nashville Wolves, she went to one game, and that was because Jason and I practically begged her to come. But that game was it. She hasn't been to one since.

"Yeah, I wonder that too," I say to Jason.

The opposing team's defender steals the puck from Nashville and speeds down the ice. Liam takes off after him, checks him, then swipes the puck and takes off in the other direction. He weaves around a few opposing players, then shoots, sinking the puck into the net.

Jason and I jump up and holler in celebration, along with the rest of the crowd. The goal siren blares, and along with the cheers from the crowd, the sound in the arena is deafening.

Liam skates past his team box, high-fiving everyone. Then he flashes a smirk at the opposing team as he skates by their box. One of the players shoves him, but Liam just laughs.

Jason shakes his head and chuckles. "Your brother is a shit stirrer."

"He really is. It was annoying as fuck to grow up with."

After the game, we head to a pizza place in the 12 South neighborhood to meet Liam for drinks. We settle into a booth and order beer and pizza while we wait for him. I snap a photo of the menu and text it to him, asking what drink he wants so I can order it for him.

A notification from Scribble Share pops up on my screen. I tap it and see it's a new message from Hermia. I'm grinning.

You are relentless :P But okay…*deep breath* I wrote something. It's probably terrible, so you have to promise not to laugh when you read it. It's not even fanfic…it's just a random idea that popped in my brain earlier and I just kinda went with it. Here goes nothing!

Mischievous caramel eyes peer over a handful of playing cards. "What do you have?"

I cross my legs, then uncross them, then cross them again. My bare thighs stick against the hard wood of the chair. I wonder if this hand will cost me my tank top.

I spread the cards face up onto the table. "Three of a kind," I say.

Gavin raises an eyebrow. "Not bad."

I smile. It's about damn time. I've lost everything other than my panties and top in this game.

He tosses his cards down. "Beats my pair."

I squeal and pump my fist in the air.

"Don't get too excited," he tuts. "From what I can see, you've only got a couple of items left on you. It's still anyone's game."

He's right. This night of strip poker has tested many things for us. My ability to learn a new card game. Gavin's ability to tell if I'm lying or not by simply looking at my face. Our abilities to restrain ourselves while half-naked, just inches away from one another.

This past hour is the longest we've ever refrained from touching each other when this close, while wearing this little clothing.

I shrug. "True. But right now it's my game, my win, and I want your shirt."

His crooked smile—my favorite smile—makes an overdue appearance. He tilts his head to me and stands up.

"As you wish." His gray cotton T-shirt drops to the

floor. He stays standing for an extra few seconds. He knows this is my favorite state of undress. Him in nothing but boxers, his sculpted torso on display.

My eyes fall to his chest first, then his arms. An impressive amount of chiseled muscle rests under that honey skin. I lick my lips, suddenly unconcerned with who wins or loses. All I really want is his body on top of mine.

"Control yourself," he advises with a mock frown. "We've got a game to finish."

The next hand goes to him. "Your top," he says with a slight growl at the end.

My heart thuds at the thought of being topless in front of him. Not because I'm nervous or embarrassed, but because the anticipation is killing me. I wonder just how long we can keep up this charade of a card game before we attack each other with our mouths.

I stand and slide the thin white cotton over my head. It joins the puddle of gray on the floor. Gavin's tongue runs along his bottom lip. The faintest pink hue covers his cheeks; his eyes display a familiar haze. My missing tank top has him in a tizzy. I flash him my most seductive smile.

"I'll deal this round." My breasts skim the polished tabletop as I reach for the cards. I don't have to look at him to know he's gawking.

Before I can lean back into my chair, Gavin's hand covers mine, pinning it to the table. "Wait," he whispers.

When I gaze into his unblinking eyes, I know I have him.

"Screw this," he says. With a single slide of his forearm, the cards fly off the table and onto the floor.

In an instant he's at my side. With both hands encircling my waist, he sets me on top of the table. We're kissing before I can utter a word. Our tongues resume the filthy rhythm we employ whenever we kiss.

He leans forward, arms caging me, pressing me down flat.

"But who won?" I say with a desperate gasp.

His silky lips glide along the side of my neck and down my chest. He gives attention to both of my breasts, encircling my nipples with his tongue until I'm crying out. He trails wet kisses along my stomach all the way down to my panties. He hooks both his thumbs over the sides and pulls them off.

I already know the answer to my question. I just want to hear him say it.

He smirks. "You won. You got me to fold without even dealing the cards."

His mouth falls to the inside of my left thigh. He presses a single soft kiss to my skin, then repeats the move on my other thigh. Air pushes out of my lungs in a shaky exhale. I close my eyes, my head rolling to the side. I've never come on top of a table before.

I bite back the grin crawling across my face. The steam of his exhale on my skin sends a shiver through me.

"Now lie back and relax like a good girl while I eat your pussy."

I stare at my phone screen, eyes wide and unblinking.

Holy shit. That was hot as fuck.

I try to swallow, but all that comes out is a strangled noise. It's then that I realize just how tight my pants feel. Reading Hermia's flash fiction made me half hard.

"Aidan? Aidan?"

I jerk my head up and see Jason, who's frowning at me.

"You okay?" he asks. "Your face is red."

I clear my throat three times before I feel confident enough to speak. "Yeah, I'm fine. I was just reading an email."

Jason chuckles. "You looked like you were about to pass out."

I try to laugh, but I end up making an awkward barking sound. I'm turned on in public. Goddamn it.

With my free hand, I gesture to my glass. "I think it's the beer. Tastes really hoppy," I lie. "Not sure I like it."

Jason aims a thoughtful glance at his glass. "Hmm. Maybe you're right." He takes a long sip, and I quickly type a message to Hermia.

Hermia, are you kidding me? Your writing is amazing! So damn good. Seriously. This whole time you've been able to write like this and you've been hiding it?? Please post your fanfic on the site. Pretty please? The readers on Scribble Share will lose their minds over it, I promise :)

I exit out of the app and set my phone aside, right as Liam walks in. I wave at him and he walks over. He slides into the booth seat next to me.

Jason and I congratulate him on the goal he scored tonight.

He grins. "Thanks." He glances at the pitcher of beer. "We just drinking beer tonight?"

And that's when I remember I forgot to put in his drink order. I was too distracted reading Hermia's flash fiction.

"Oh, sorry," I say. Our server walks by, and I order the vodka Red Bull Liam texted me that he wanted.

Liam laughs as he looks at me. "You okay? You look a little out of it."

"Right?" Jason chuckles. "He's been glued to his phone the whole night. Even during your game."

My little brother raises his eyebrow, a gleam in his eyes. "Really? You sexting or something?"

I make a grossed-out face and shake my head, feeling defensive and embarrassed at the same time. "Hell no. Just had to catch up on some emails."

They both laugh. Liam pats my shoulder. "Oh, definitely. You can't let those emails pile up."

I roll my eyes at him and take another drink of my beer.

He smacks his palm against my cheek. "Aww, are you blushing? I didn't know emails made you blush, big brother. Unless they're…dirty emails."

Jason laughs. I shove Liam's hand away.

"So. How did post-game press go?" I ask, wanting to change the subject.

Liam laughs again, and we talk about the game. But the whole rest of the night I can't stop thinking about Hermia.

I'm so happy she's writing again. Just from reading that short scene, I can tell how good she is. Pride swells in my chest that she has the courage to write again after her douchebag ex insulted her dream.

I start to smile, then take a drink so Liam and Jason don't give me more shit. I don't even know Hermia and I'm proud of her. I get excited every time I see a new message from her. I grin like an idiot when we message each other. I like her. A lot. And when we joke and tease each other, it feels a lot like flirting.

I'm probably reading into this too much. She probably sees me as a fun internet friend, nothing more.

For the rest of the night, I try to remind myself of that. But I can't help the excitement that sparks in my chest every time I think about her.

Twenty-Two

Micah

When I see a Scribble Share notification on my phone, I'm instantly smiling. My stomach does a familiar flip as I pull up the app and see a new message from ShakespeareInLust.

Sitting on the couch, I let out a squeal when I read his compliments on my writing and his encouragement to post it. The nerves that were swirling through me ever since I sent him my writing ease and turn warm. It's not that I thought he'd be mean, even if he didn't like my writing. He's been so sweet and supportive so far, and I knew he'd react kindly, regardless if he liked or not.

But to see him get this excited and rave about it was a total surprise. The best surprise.

I quickly type a response.

Hot4Hermia: You really think so? You're not just being polite?

I head to the kitchen to pour myself a glass of wine. When I'm back on the couch, I pick up the remote, turn on the TV, and try to find something good to watch this Sunday night. My phone buzzes with an alert. I set the remote down and swipe it from the coffee table.

I grin when I see it's a message from ShakespeareInLust. I'm surprised he answered so quickly. I figured since it's Saturday night, he'd be busy.

ShakespeareInLust: Come on, Hermia. You think I'd do you

dirty like that? Of course I think you're that good. You're incredible.

Hot4Hermia: I'm officially blushing. Thank you. I'll think about posting some fanfic then.

ShakespeareInLust: Nope. Not good enough. You gotta post. ASAP.

Hot4Hermia: LOL I'm nervous though...

ShakespeareInLust: Okay, how about this? If your post isn't a hit with readers, I'll do something super embarrassing.

Hot4Hermia: Hmm, now that's a tempting offer...

ShakespeareInLust: You choose the embarrassing thing and I'll do it.

ShakespeareInLust: What'll it be? Drunk dialing my boss? Streaking through my neighborhood?

Hot4Hermia: Okay well, since you put it out there, I'll take the streaking

ShakespeareInLust: Deal! Now post that fanfic ;)

As I navigate through the app, I'm smiling so wide my cheeks are starting to ache. He's the sweetest.

Butterflies flutter in my stomach. I can't remember the last time I had such a fun and flirty conversation with someone.

Don't get too carried away and make up some romantic fantasy in

your head, Micah. He's just a charming stranger on an app. Don't let it mean anything more than that.

I pull up a new post and paste the text of my flash fiction piece into it. And then I take a deep breath and post it.

A wave of nerves and excitement crashes through me. I did it. I published my writing on a public platform. Even if no one reads it or likes it, I did it. I didn't let my fear and anxiety get the best of me.

I navigate back to my chat with ShakespeareInLust.

Hot4Hermia: Okay! I did it!

ShakespeareInLust: Hell yeah!! Way to go!

ShakespeareInLust: I just left a comment on it and tagged it as one of my top recommended posts :)

ShakespeareInLust: People are going to lose their minds over your writing, Hermia. Just wait and see ;)

Hot4Hermia: You really think so?

ShakespeareInLust: I know so :) I'm so proud of you for doing this.

Warmth pools in my chest. He doesn't even know me, and he believes in my writing that much.

Hot4Hermia: That means everything, truly. Thank you.

ShakespeareInLust: Always here to pump you up :)

ShakespeareInLust: I hope you make the time to write again soon. I want to read more of your work!

Just then an idea hits.

Hot4Hermia: I think I'm going to write some more tonight actually.

ShakespeareInLust: Really? That's awesome!

Hot4Hermia: Yeah. Inspiration is hitting hard :)

ShakespeareInLust: I'll stop messaging you then so you can get down to business :)

Hot4Hermia: Will you post again soon? I'm dying for more of your fanfic!

ShakespeareInLust: Absolutely!

Hot4Hermia: Yay! Happy writing, ShakespeareInLust!

ShakespeareInLust: Happy writing to you too, Hermia!

I turn off the TV and grab my laptop. My fingers fly across the keyboard as another fun and filthy fanfic idea swirls around in my brain…inspired by my hookup with Aidan.

A weird tension works its way through my body as I type. I can't stand him, but there's no denying he was the hottest sexual experience of my life. I may as well write about it.

I change some key identifying details to make sure that no one would be able to identify him or me.

Not like Aidan will ever read this. I'd bet anything his pretentious self wouldn't be caught dead reading steamy romance.

When I finish, I skim through what I've written. I smile. Wow. It's honestly pretty good. And hot.

"Don't move." I cup my hand over my skirt, right on the mound of my pussy.

I watch as he immediately stills. His crystal-blue gaze falls between my legs. A hard swallow moves down along his thick, stubbled throat.

I rest my other hand on my breast and squeeze.

His gaze flits to my chest, then back down to my pussy, like he can't decide where he wants to look.

I still can't believe we're doing this. We're in the storage closet down the hall from our offices. We're right across from a classroom full of people.

If one person walks by and hears us, if someone opens the storage room door, it's over. We'd be caught. And fired.

My clit jumps against my palm. I have to hold back a moan.

Something about that is so thrilling though. It turns me on even more.

I narrow my gaze at the handsome, infuriating man standing just inches from me, taking me in with a hungry gaze.

I've hated him since the first moment I met him. Our first conversation was an argument in the middle of a staff meeting, when he made a quip about my credentials. It's been a full-out war since then.

Every day we toss dirty looks back and forth. We trade snide comments like we're opponents in a match, trying to wear the other down.

Today things reached a head. He walked behind me,

caught a glimpse of my computer screen, and made fun of my lesson plan.

In that moment, I had had it.

I looked at him and said the most outrageous thing I could think of.

"You don't have to keep playing these childish games. You know you want to fuck me. Just say so."

He stopped dead in his tracks, his eyes wide as he gawked at me.

"You're right. I do want to fuck you. So bad."

I was floored. I couldn't believe it. I was shocked…and intrigued. And I thought maybe this is what we need to resolve the tension between us once and for all.

One hate fuck to get it out of our systems.

Sweat beads along the back of my neck in this stuffy storage room. I fix my gaze on him.

"I mean it," I say, my voice barely above a whisper. "If you so much as reach for me, I'll stop everything, get dressed, and leave."

He frowns but nods. He understands.

I see his hand twitch at his side, like he's trying to keep from touching me. I smile. He just can't help himself.

"Ready?" I ask.

"Yes." He speaks through gritted teeth.

"Tell me again what we agreed to." I slip my hand down my skirt and into my panties.

His Adam's apple moves with a single swallow. His pale skin glows red. Everything from his face to his toned chest flushes crimson.

"I get to watch first," he says, his voice guttural. "Then I can go down on you, when you tell me to."

"Good." I shut my eyes and focus on the waves of cool air coming from the vents above us. Each burst of air that hits my skin feels like heaven. I slide my fingers through my wet folds. I tap my middle finger against my clit and moan. So warm and wet.

I swirl my finger in tiny circles. A strangled gasp leaves his mouth.

I open my eyes and pin him with my gaze.

"You have to be quiet," I say in a breathy voice.

Heat flashes in his eyes. He looks pissed and turned on. He nods.

I smirk. It's heaven tormenting him like this, making him watch, knowing every muscle in his body is aching to ravage me.

As I work my pussy and my tits in my hands, the pleasure inside of me builds. My mouth falls open as I let out a ragged breath.

I watch him watch me. I spot the unmistakable bulge of his hard cock in his pants. His hands are balled into fists at his sides, and his knuckles are stark white with how hard he's gripping. Every muscle in his jaw bulges through his peaches-and-cream skin. If the AC weren't going right now, I bet I could hear him grinding his teeth in aroused frustration.

My gaze falls between his legs once more. His pants do little to mask the hard angle underneath. He's barely hanging on by a thread.

I tilt my head to the side with a soft whimper. I relish this feeling, knowing I'm making him this hot.

He can't stand me, but he's so turned on by me that he's about to lose his mind.

My fingers work at a frenzied pace. My breathing becomes more labored and desperate. It's only been a couple of minutes, but I won't last much longer.

I force myself to drop my hand from my body. My legs are shaking, I'm so tense from pleasure.

I look him square in the eye as I catch my breath.

His chest heaves as he slashes his tongue along the seam of his lips. His pupils are completely blown out, ringed in ice blue.

"Can I?" he rasps. "Please?"

I nod.

He steps up to me and drops to his knees. He pushes my skirt up, hooks his finger over the crotch of my panties, and yanks it to the side. The second his mouth is on my pussy, my jaw plummets to the floor. I have to clamp my hand over my mouth, I'm moaning so hard.

His tongue swirls around my clit, the heat and pressure winding tighter inside of me. My heart races and my skin burns hot.

Holy hell, his tongue…it's like a shower massager… How is he this good?

The heat builds, then crests. When my climax crashes over me, I'm cursing and moaning into my own hand. My legs tremble, but he holds me up, his mouth and tongue working me over. When I start to come down, I drop my hands from my mouth and gasp for air.

I glance down, annoyed and amused when I see that smug smile.

"Still hate me?" he asks.

"Of course I do. Now bend me over and fuck me against that wall."

He grins. "Gladly."

It's not till I finish reading it that I realize just how hard I'm breathing…and how wet I am between my legs.

I touch a hand to my face. Whoa. My skin is fiery hot. I shake my head and laugh, embarrassed. Is it normal to turn yourself on like this with your own writing?

I was going to send it to ShakespeareInLust first to get his opinion on it, but now I'm not sure if that's a good idea. I mean, he writes steamy stuff too…but I doubt his steamy stuff is based on the filthy things he got up to in real life, unlike me.

I hop up from the couch and get ready for bed. The whole time, I wonder if I should even send it to him.

When I crawl into bed, I set my phone on the nightstand. I'm about to turn out the light when I think *Screw it*. We both write steamy stuff. He doesn't know this is based on something I did in my real life. He'll just think I have a filthy imagination, just like him. I grab my phone and send what I wrote to him.

Hey! Here's my latest! I know we both write steamy stuff, but be warned, this is extra steamy haha. Happy reading :)

And then I set my phone to vibrate, turn off the light, and burrow into the covers, hoping I haven't weirded him out.

Twenty-Three

Aidan

I blink at my phone screen, stunned.

Holy shit. That post Hermia just sent me? Hands down, the hottest thing I've ever read.

And that's a problem. Because I currently have a raging boner because of it.

I toss my phone to the other side of the couch. Clearing my throat and shifting in my seat, I frown down at the hard angle of my lap.

I'm not naive. I know there are plenty of people on Scribble Share who get turned on by the sexy writing that I and other authors post on there. I'm sure that some readers have even pleasured themselves during or after reading one of my posts. And I'm completely fine with that.

They're strangers. We don't interact; we don't know each other.

But I know Hermia. Yeah, we've never met, and yeah, I don't even know her real name. But we've been messaging back and forth for the past couple of weeks. We've been getting to know each other. We vent about work and joke around and talk about writing. She feels like a friend at this point. After being too scared to write, she finally did, and she trusted me enough to share it with me.

And here I am, getting turned on by it.

I huff out a breath. My hard-on starts to lose steam. I shake my head at myself. Nothing like a little self-loathing to kill a boner.

The other reason why I was so turned on? Because Hermia's flash fiction reminded me of Micah.

I absentmindedly tug a hand through my hair, but then that reminds me of the way Micah pulled my hair while I went down on her and how fucking hot that was, and I start to get hard again.

I pull my hand away and roll my eyes. Jesus.

I reach over, grab my phone, and pull up Scribble Share. I navigate to Hermia's profile and smile when I see how popular her first post is with readers. She just posted it a few hours ago, and already she has more than two dozen comments from readers raving about her writing.

There's a burst of pride in my chest. I knew she'd be a hit. Her writing is amazing. I still can't believe her ex shamed her for writing romance. I know romance isn't for everyone, and that's fine. But why would anyone want to shame someone for liking something just because they don't? That's such a pompous and arrogant attitude to have.

I navigate to my messages and pull up my conversation with Hermia.

Two things: One, HOLY FUCKING HOTNESS. Hermia, that was incredible. My phone practically caught on fire. It was amazing, I loved it! Two, have you seen your first post? Readers are going nuts over your writing! Just like I told you they would ;) You HAVE to post the scene you sent me, okay? Readers are going to lose their minds over it, it's seriously so good.

I get up from the couch and head to my bathroom to get ready for bed. When I walk back out into the living room to grab my phone, I see a notification from Scribble Share. Hermia just replied to me.

I'm smiling as I read her message.

Hot4Hermia: You like it? Like, really liked it? You're not just being polite?

Hot4Hermia: I just saw all the likes and comments on my first post! Oh my gosh! I can't believe it!!

Hot4Hermia: Okay, I'll post the most recent scene I wrote tomorrow :) Thank you for encouraging me through all of this. I would have never had the guts to write again, let alone post my writing on a public forum like this, if it weren't for you. So thank you :)

I type her back while I head down the hall and climb into bed.

ShakespeareInLust: You're an amazing writer. It would be such a shame if you didn't share your writing with the world.

Hot4Hermia: I was scared you'd think the scene I sent you tonight was too much *sweating emoji*

Hot4Hermia: I was sure you'd think I was a deviant lol

ShakespeareInLust: What's wrong with being a deviant? ;)

ShakespeareInLust: You've read my writing. Clearly you know I'm a deviant too lol

Hot4Hermia: True haha. But the stuff you write is fiction

My eyes go wide as I read her message. Wait, does…that she mean that she's writing from personal experience?

As curious as I am, I don't want to outright ask her that. That would be creepy.

ShakespeareInLust: Yeah, I write fiction. You do too right?

Hot4Hermia: Yeah, of course. But my latest post was based on a personal experience I had.

There's a flicker of heat in my chest reading what Hermia has just admitted.

Hot4Hermia: Still think I'm not a deviant? :P

I stare at my phone. Tone in text can be so hard to decipher, but I'm getting an undeniable flirty vibe from Hermia's messages.

ShakespeareInLust: You're not a deviant. You're just adventurous :)

Hot4Hermia: Truth ;)

I let out a breath. My heart is thudding faster. I zero in on the winky face she just sent me. Okay yeah, that's a strong flirty vibe too. I start to smile. It's been a while since I've had such a fun and flirty chat with someone.

I rack my brain to think of something charming and witty to write back to her, but then I see that she's logged off. A ping of disappointment hits. I would have liked to keep chatting with her, but it's late. She's probably tired. And honestly, maybe it's better that we left the conversation on that cute-and-flirty note. That way I didn't ruin things by overthinking and sending an awkward message back to her.

I exit out of the app, put my phone on the side table next to my bed, turn out the light, and pull the covers over me. What a random and awesome night this turned out to be.

I think about how much work is going to suck tomorrow morning when I have to deal with Micah while she observes my class. Dread starts to seep into my good mood, but I try not to think about it for long. I'll deal that that tomorrow.

Twenty-Four

Aidan

Micah aims her death glare at me after the last student leaves my classroom. She stands up from where she was sitting at the far end of the lecture hall and makes her way over to me.

All the muscles in my torso tense in anticipation of whatever verbal ass-kicking she's about to unleash on me. I take a long sip of coffee from my *O happy dagger* thermos to buy myself another moment of peace before she lays into me.

Ever since we argued in the hallway after she overheard me bad-mouthing her to Dr. Wauncho, she's been her usual biting, no-nonsense self. If we pass each other in the hallway, she doesn't even say hi. She just glowers at me. We hardly ever talk to each other. When we do, it's strictly work, mostly her offering up criticism about whatever I did wrong after observing me in class or analyzing whatever statistics she's gathered about me and my work.

She stops just a few feet in front of me, notebook in hand. "I don't think we need to bother with a verbal wrap-up of your class today. I'll just type up my observations to you and email them to you later."

I try and fail to hold back a scoff. "That's fine."

Her glare on me sharpens. "It sounds like you have more you'd like to say."

I turn away and start to gather my things from my desk. "You wouldn't like what I have to say, Micah."

When I turn back to her, I see that her mouth is parted open and her brow is lifted, like she can't believe what I just said.

Satisfaction swells inside of me. It feels really, really good to piss her off a little.

I frown at her. "Don't act so surprised. You really think I'd have anything positive to say to you? Your job is to figure out how to get me fired."

She presses her eyes shut for a second, her shoulders rising and falling with the breath she takes. "That's not what I'm trying to do. Like I've said before, the purpose of my job is to make observations and recommendations. It's up to the university what they do with that information. It's not my job to get you fired. I resent how you keep saying that."

"Cut the crap, Micah. Of course that's your job. So fine, type up whatever you want in your little report and send it to me. But I'm not going to change how I teach or how I conduct myself as a professor."

She purses her lips like she's tasted something bitter. I'm sure she's about to go off on me. Before she can utter a word, I stomp out of the lecture hall and head up the stairs to my office and shut the door behind me. I drop all my crap onto my desk and plop down into my chair, then grab a stack of essays I need to grade along with a pen. I turn off the notifications on my phone and close my email.

That was my last class of the day, so I could just head home and work, but I don't want to run into Micah in the hall or at the building entrance. Better to just hide out in my office until she hopefully heads home and I don't have to see her again for the rest of the day.

For the next few hours, I block out the world as I read and grade. My neck starts to ache from hunching over my desk for so long. I groan as I lean back and stretch my neck out. Movement out of the corner of my eye catches my attention.

When I turn and look out the window, all I see is white.

"What the…"

I stand up and step over to the window to get a better look at the snow falling outside. All of the trees are covered in white. I can't even see the pavement. It's all snow.

I grab my phone and turn the notifications back on. I see a campus-wide alert from hours ago canceling all late-afternoon and evening classes due to snow in the forecast. I must have missed it because I was holed up in my office.

A second later, my phone is beeping with texts from both Jason and Kendall. I tap on our group chat.

Kendall: Snow day! Can you believe it? Woo-hoo!

Jason: I know! We were only supposed to get rain today.

Kendall: See you guys later!

Jason: Be careful when you're driving, it won't take long before the roads get bad. And you know how people in Nashville drive whenever we get even a dusting of snow.

Kendall: Okay, just got home, it's an ice rink out there. You guys make it home okay?

Jason: Yeah. I slid down the street in front of my house, but luckily I didn't hit anything

Kendall: Phew!

Kendall: Aidan, you alive? You haven't answered in hours.

I quickly text them back.

Aidan: Yeah, I'm okay. Still on campus though

Kendall: Shit, really?

Kendall: Yikes. Are you gonna be able to get home? It's getting dark. I'm watching the local news and there are accidents all over the city.

I huff out a heavy breath and gaze out the window at the snow dumping out of the sky. No way am I going to attempt driving in this.

Aidan: I think I'm stuck here. I'll just hunker down here overnight and wait it out.

Kendall: :(The snow is only supposed to fall for another couple of hours. Then in the morning it's supposed to be like forty degrees and sunny, so it'll start melting.

Aidan: Okay yeah, I guess I won't try going home until then

Kendall: Be safe. And if you get hungry, feel free to head to my office and break into my snack stash.

Aidan: I just might. Thanks.

Jason: Just now seeing your messages, damn Aidan, sorry you're stuck.

Jason: If you need liquor to help you power through, you know where I keep my stash. You're welcome to it.

I text him thanks, set my phone on my desk, and rest my hands on my hips with a sigh. I guess I'm stuck here for the night. I'm tempted to grab some snacks and liquor and settle in, but I should probably see if anyone else is in the building.

I open my office door and step out. "Hello?" I holler.

No answer. Well, at least I have the place to myself for the night.

I start to turn around, but then I hear the squeak of a door down the hall. When I step back out to see what that sound was, disappointment slashes through me.

There's Micah standing a few doors down from me.

She frowns. "What are you shouting for?"

"Did you know it's snowing?"

"No. I don't have any windows in my workspace. How could I have known?"

I sigh at how annoyed she sounds.

"It's snowing pretty bad right now," I say. "The university cancelled all classes a few hours ago, but I had my notifications on my phone and computer turned off while I was working, so I didn't find out until just a few minutes ago. Jason and Kendall texted me to say that the roads are pretty bad. I don't think I can get home tonight."

Micah walks over to me, then darts into my office and heads straight for the window.

I roll my eyes. "Sure, come on in."

Her eyes are wide as she gawks out the window. "Why did no one tell me? I would have left hours ago."

I cross my arms over my chest and shrug. "Maybe because you're working to put us out of a job, so there's really no incentive to help you out."

She glowers at me.

"They sent out a campus-wide alert via email," I say.

"I don't get the university emails, remember? Someone should have told me."

I shrug. "They probably forgot.

"Right. Kind of how you forgot to tell me when there was only decaf coffee in the break room."

I can't help but smile at her frustration. "Pretty much."

She glowers at me. "You think this is funny?"

"A little."

She scoffs and pulls out her phone, checking the weather. She turns back to the window.

"Staring at the snow isn't going to make it stop," I mutter as I check the weather report on my phone.

"Shut up," she bites.

I let out a breath. Tonight is gonna suck.

Twenty-Five

Micah

I gawk out the window of Aidan's office, stunned into silence at the sight of giant snowflakes falling from the sky, blanketing everything in sight. The ground, the roads, the buildings, the cars in the parking lot…everything is covered in snow.

"So were stuck here together? For the whole night?" I turn to Aidan.

That annoyingly sexy mouth of his hooks up in a smile. Not a happy smile though. More like exasperated. Like he's so irritated with me in this moment that he can barely take it.

He rolls his eyes. "Yeah, Micah. Looks like it," he mutters. He huffs out a breath and runs a hand through his chestnut hair.

With that single movement, I'm thrown back to that afternoon in the conference room. Even though I'm standing a handful of feet away from Aidan, I can feel the thick silk of his hair in my hands…

My heart starts to race as the memory of our hookup replays in my brain like an X-rated highlight reel.

I feel his soft lips kissing me breathless, his hot breath dusting my skin… I savor the taste of his tongue, the feel of his hands gripping my waist…his firm, muscled body pressed against mine…

I do a slow scan of his tall, lean form hidden behind the crisp white dress shirt and blazer he's wearing.

Even through all that fabric, I remember perfectly just how cute Aidan is. It's like I've got X-ray vision. I blink and see that mass of hard lines and bulging muscle, the golden glow of his skin, how hot he felt when I touched him...

How thick and massive his cock felt in my mouth, hitting the back of my throat...

Aidan clears his throat sharply, and my gaze flies up to his face.

He frowns at me. "You okay?"

I blink quickly, feeling the heat of embarrassment cook me from the inside out. Judging by his annoyed stare, he's over our rendezvous in the conference room.

I think about how after we hooked up, he could barely maintain eye contact with me for more than two seconds. I think about how when I tried to bring it up, he shut me down, told me to forget it ever happened.

Clearly he's not been obsessing over it, replaying it in his head again and again, using it as self-pleasure material almost every night, like I have...

Clearly our hookup meant a lot more to me than it did to him. I mean, I wrote fan fiction about it. So pathetic.

The longer Aidan stares at me, the harsher his frown looks. Yup. He's forgotten all about that day. I should try to forget it too.

I clear my throat. "Yeah. Fine. Just trying to figure out how the hell I'm going to get through the evening."

A humorless laugh falls from his mouth. "Why, because I'm here too?"

"Well, yeah." I don't know why he sounds so upset. It clear as crystal that he can't stand to be around me. I figured he wouldn't be thrilled to be stuck with me either.

"Tough life for you, having to occupy the same building as me," he mutters.

Anger flares through me. "It is actually. Especially when you're constantly acting like a jerk. Look, I know you don't like me, Aidan. I don't like you either. But our jobs are forcing us to be around each other. Can you at least try to act professional?"

Another bitter laugh falls from his lips. "Professional? Really? Like the way you lunged at me in the conference room?"

My jaw drops. This son of a bitch. Is he really gonna sink that low?

I step into his space and poke my index finger into his chest. He stumbles back, surprised at that move.

"I didn't lunge at you!" I practically shout.

Aidan aims a hard stare at me as he works his jaw, like he's silently, reluctantly accepting the fact that he played a role in instigating our hookup too.

I wait for him to admit it, to say the words. But he just stands there, quietly glaring at me like I've offended him by pointing out the truth.

I tug a hand through my hair and make a frustrated noise. "God, you're the worst. I can't believe I'm stuck here with you. Literally anyone else in the world right now would be better."

"Really, Micah? Are you gonna be *that* dramatic? You'd rather be stuck here with a murderer or an evil dictator than with me?"

"Yup." I say it without missing a beat while looking him straight in the eye.

He clenches his jaw. "You know what, Micah? You're free to drive home in this wintery mess, if you want. I'm sure as hell not gonna stop you. So if you wanna test your luck driving your car in the worst snowstorm Nashville has had in the last five years, go right ahead. It's pretty much guaranteed you'll get into a wreck given that this city has zero snow-removal equipment. But hey, better than staying in the same building with me, right?"

He grabs his phone from his pocket, falls into his office chair, and frowns at the screen.

I stand there, just now noticing my racing heartbeat and the way my breath has quickened. God, I can't take this anymore.

I stomp out of his office, then head back to my workspace. Best if we stay far apart from each other for however long we're stranded on campus.

I pull my phone out of my bag and pull up Scribble Share. I instantly brighten at the number of notifications on my profile. It looks like my latest post was a hit with readers. Just like ShakespeareInLust promised it would be.

I smile as I read through them.

Holy hotness gimme MORE

Hooking up in a storage closet on campus?! Why couldn't my uni days be this wild and sexy?! *crying face*

Okay, a hot, well-endowed professor with a tongue like a shower massager? I'd gladly go back to college for that LOL

I smile to myself, giddy at how much readers are enjoying my writing. I think back to when ShakespeareInLust convinced me to take the plunge and post some fanfic on the site. I remember how nervous I was when I sent him some of my writing, when I assumed he'd insult my lack of skill…and then I remember how shocked and elated I was when he ended up actually liking it.

I skim our message exchange from that day, chuckling when I reread him promising to go streaking if readers didn't love my latest post.

I also read the message he wrote encouraging me, the one that gave me butterflies in my stomach and made me grin so wide, my cheeks hurt.

Hermia, are you kidding me? Your writing is amazing! So damn good. Seriously. This whole time you've been able to write like this and you've been hiding it?? Please post your fanfic on the site. Pretty please? The readers on Scribble Share will lose their minds over it, I promise :)

I still can't get over how kind and encouraging he is.

I skim a few more comments.

I'm gonna need Hot4Hermia to write a whole book, I need more!

I stare at the comment, stunned and flattered. Just thinking about writing a steamy romance book makes me so excited and happy. But then reality sets in. No way could I do that. Making a living out in a creative, unstable field like writing is impossible for most people. Better for this to stay a hobby and keep working as an auditor…even though I'm a million times happier writing than I am working my job…

That's not the point. So what if I'm not happy all the time as an auditor? That's normal. A lot of people aren't happy all the time at work. I'm good at what I do, and it's stable and pays well. That's what matters.

An alert pops up in my messages. When I see it's from Shake-speareInLust, my stomach does a flip. I roll my eyes at myself, but I can't help the smile tugging at my lips. Yeah, it's border-line pathetic that I, a thirty-two-year-old woman, have a crush on a random internet account, but I do.

ShakespeareInLust: Phew! Looks like I don't have to go streaking in my neighborhood after all. You killed it, Hermia! Just like I knew you would. So damn proud of you!

My chest swells with joy. Yeah, I don't even know this guy. He could be a creep living in his grandma's basement for all I know. But honestly? I don't care. Because it doesn't matter who he is in real life; all that matters is the way he makes me feel. And he's been sweet and supportive in a way that no one else in my life has when it comes to my writing. He makes me feel like I'm special, like I'm good enough.

And deep down, I honestly don't think he's a loser or a creep in real life. I'd bet anything he's kind, sweet, and cute, just like he is on this site.

Hot4Hermia: Aww, thanks! I honestly can't believe it...my little story getting so much love

ShakespeareInLust: "Little"? Come on now, Hermia.

Hot4Hermia: My story is little, but she's fierce. As hell ;)

ShakespeareInLust: That's the spirit!

ShakespeareInLust: You're a vixen schooling us all on love with that mindblowing story you wrote

Hot4Hermia: LOL I see what you did there

ShakespeareInLust: Had to. You put your own spin on a line from A Midsummer Night's Dream. I had to do one too

Hot4Hermia: I would have never had the nerve to post my story without you. Seriously. You gave me the confidence boost I needed. Thank you :)

ShakespeareInLust: Anytime you need a boost, I'm here for you. Anytime you need anything, Hermia, I'm yours.

It feels like butterflies are swarming in my stomach as I read that sentence.

Anytime you need anything, Hermia, I'm yours.

There's been a flirty vibe to our conversations pretty much from the get-go. And our last exchange was pretty flirty, which was all due to me. He's just so funny, sweet, charming, and easy to talk to.

But that sentence…something about it seems like more than flirting. It feels bolder, like he's trying to convey that this thing between us, whatever it is, means something to him too. And I really, really like it.

It makes me want to amp things up between us even more, to see just how far we're both willing to take things…

I quickly type back a response before my nerves get the best of me.

Hot4Hermia: Gotta say, I'm disappointed you didn't end up going streaking. I was going to ask for a photo as proof

ShakespeareInLust: Is that so?

Hot4Hermia: Yup. I would have needed to see it with my own eyes.

ShakespeareInLust: Well, you'd definitely get an eye full…of pasty skin. I'm pale AF

I burst out laughing.

Hot4Hermia: Aww come on, I bet you look great in your birthday suit!

ShakespeareInLust: Haha you're too kind. But I would have needed a shot of the hard stuff to work up my nerve to get naked and run in public.

Hot4Hermia: Oh gosh haha really?

ShakespeareInLust: Yup. A long swig of vodka straight out of my O happy dagger thermos would have done the trick LOL

My fingers freeze, hovering over my phone screen. *O happy dagger* thermos...like the one Aidan has?

My heart rockets to my throat. No way. That's gotta be a coincidence, right? I mean, there are a lot of Shakespeare fans in this world. I bet some of them have a similar thermos.

But no matter how many times I tell myself that, doubt digs into me. I need to know for sure.

I stand up on shaky legs and walk toward Aidan's office. Nerves blast through me like firecrackers. But I have to find out. I have to know if Aidan is ShakespeareInLust, if he's the fanfic writer who I've been flirting with these past few weeks.

When I make it to the open doorway of his office, I stop. He clearly hasn't heard me walk up. He's sitting facing the window in his office so he can't see me. But I can see the side of his face. I can see his gorgeous grin and how he looks completely engrossed with whatever is on his phone.

I slowly, quietly walk up to his desk, my eyes on his phone screen the whole time. And then it comes into view. The familiar Scribble Share logo...

I spot his username at the top: ShakespeareInLust.

My stomach bottoms out completely.

"You're ShakespeareInLust?" I say, breathless.

Aidan's head whips up. A lethal frown appears on his face as he looks at me.

"What the…how did you…"

When I hold up my phone to him, he falls quiet. His blue eyes go wide as he registers the sight of my Scribble Share profile. And my username.

A hard swallow works along the length of his throat.

His gaze cuts back to my face. He goes pale. "Hermia?"

I nod despite the embarrassment and disbelief burning through me.

No way. This can't be happening.

Twenty-Six

Micah

All I can do is stand there and stare at Aidan. My brain can't process the reality. It's too shocking, too humiliating...

The guy I've been chatting with and flirting with for the past few weeks is Aidan.

The guy I've been confiding in, the guy who set me at ease with his sweetness and humor, the guy who I have a crush on is Aidan.

It feels like my entire body is on fire with how exposed I feel. I may as well be standing naked in front of him.

I told him so many personal things. The guy who loathes me, who can't stand the sight of me now knows my biggest insecurities. He knows about my biggest heartbreak. He knows about my failed dreams.

I wrote fanfic about our hookup. I never thought he'd see it. Ever.

But he read it.

Oh god...

It feels like a billion invisible needles are pricking into my skin.

Aidan stares back at me, his eyebrows wrinkled together, like he's as shocked and horrified as I am.

He shakes his head, as if he's trying to pull himself out of a daze. When he opens his mouth to speak, nothing comes out. He closes his eyes and falls forward, his elbows on his knees. He buries his face in his arms.

"No fucking way," he mutters in a muffled voice. "It can't be you."

My breathing picks up. I tug at the collar of my blouse. It's not even buttoned all the way, but I feel like I'm burning up and choking all at once.

"Of all the people in the world…" I let out a laugh that's crazed and sad all at once.

When Aidan finally looks up at me, his cheeks are red and his eyes are shy. For a long moment, we just stay like that, him sitting and me standing while staring at each other. The air between us thick with the mutual awkwardness and shock we feel.

"I gotta be honest with you, Micah. I have no idea what to say or do right now."

I nod. "Same."

Aidan gestures to the chair on the other side of his desk. I plop down. He takes off his blazer, stands up, and steps over to Jason's desk, yanks open one of the drawers, and pulls out a bottle of bourbon and two small shot glasses.

He holds up the bottle in his hand. "Drink?"

I nod. He sets the shot glasses at the end of his desk, sits back down in his chair, and pours a generous shot in both glasses.

We grab our shots and down them in silence. I wince at the hot burn in my throat. When I glance over at Aidan, I see that he does the same.

He wipes his mouth with the back of his hand. His crystal-blue gaze cuts to me. "Another?"

I nod. He splashes more of the amber liquid into our glasses, and we knock them back.

When I set my glass back on his desk, he catches eyes with me. "Another?"

"You really think that's a good idea? The two of us shitfaced in your office during a snowstorm after finding out we've been secret pen pals the past couple of weeks?"

He pauses. "You're probably right." He sets the bottle back on Jason's desk.

Another quiet moment passes. I clear my throat. "We should probably talk about…this."

He hunches over slightly and rubs the back of his neck. His gaze cuts to me. "This is really fucking weird."

I let out an awkward laugh. "Yeah. It is. But we can't just ignore it."

Aidan's broad shoulders rise and fall as he exhales. "You're right. But god's honest truth? I'm terrified of you, Micah."

I lean back, stunned at his admission. "Why?"

He chuckles like he can't believe I'm asking him this question. "Because you have the power to put me out of a job. And you're also the woman I've been flirting with via chat for the past two weeks. And I'm honestly having a hard time reconciling those two parts of you."

I'm quiet while I process what he's said. I completely understand where he's coming from.

"How about this? Can we, just for tonight, ignore our work relationship? Can we just talk to each other as Hermia and ShakespeareInLust?"

His brow lifts, like he's intrigued at what I've proposed.

"For the rest of tonight, we're not Aidan and Micah. We can talk about whatever we need to in order to clear the air between us. Nothing is off-limits. And neither of us will hold anything we say against the other later on."

He nods and looks me in the eye. "Okay. I'm good with that."

Nerves crackle in my stomach. I fiddle with the hem of my skirt, but I stop myself and fold my hands in my lap.

As nervous and anxious as I feel, I should be the first to start this conversation, since it was my idea.

I work up the nerve to hold Aidan's gaze. "I like you. You're really sweet. And funny. And really easy to talk to. I always look forward to our chats to help me get through a stressful day. And I'm a huge fan of your writing on Scribble Share. You're really talented."

For a long second, Aidan just looks at me, like he's stunned at what I've said.

"Really?" he asks.

"Yeah."

"Thank you," he says softly.

His throat works as he swallows. The hint of a smile dances across his lips. "I like you a lot too. And I feel the exact same way about you. Flirting and chatting with you is a blast. You make me feel really comfortable. I feel like I could talk to you about anything. I don't feel that way with a lot of people."

"You don't?"

He shakes his head and taps his finger on the side of his empty shot glass. His eyes cut to me, the corner of his mouth lifted in an easy half smile. "You seem surprised by that."

"You have a lot of friends in the English department. You're always hanging out with Jason and Kendall. I guess I just assumed you'd feel comfortable talking to them about anything."

"I do. But talking to you on the app was different. They don't know that I write steamy fanfic in my spare time. No one does. You're the only one."

Intensity flashes in his crystal-blue eyes as he holds my gaze. My stomach flips.

"Why haven't you told anyone else about your writing?" I ask.

"Jason and Kendall would be cool about it if I told them, but it's kind of nice to have something that I do just for me. I can just focus on writing what makes me happy without worrying about what people in my life would say about it."

"Yeah, I understand that."

"I also keep it to myself because people in my field can be really fucking pretentious and judgmental assholes when it comes to writing romance and erotica. And I don't want to deal with their bullshit if I don't have to."

I think about my ex. "I definitely can't blame you for that."

When I look back at Aidan, he's frowning. "I know I said this on the app, but your ex was a piece of shit for insulting your writing. And for cheating on you."

He furrows his brow like he's pissed on my behalf for being cheated on. I feel myself start to soften.

"Thanks for that," I say to him. "It was his assistant. It had been going on for a while, I think."

His expression turns to disgust. "This fucking guy. What a creep, to cheat with his own employee."

"Yeah." I let out a breath. "She really admired his work and would rave about him constantly. He was really into that. Obviously."

Aidan's looks to the side, shaking his head. He mutters a curse word before looking back at me. "You're a talented writer, Micah. He was probably jealous that you were so good."

"I don't know about that. He was pretty full of himself and his writing."

"What's his name?"

"Ashton Rutherford."

Aidan's brow hits his hairline. "Seriously?"

I nod, my stomach sinking. He's probably a huge fan of his.

A beat later, the shock on his face turns to a grimace. "I hate that guy. His writing sucks."

I burst out laughing so hard, I almost fall out of my chair. A few seconds later, I hear Aidan laughing along with me.

"I'm not kidding," he says. "His writing is so dense. Does the guy get off on purple prose?"

I clutch my stomach, laughing even harder.

"I'd rather read a thousand-page instruction manual than another one of his books," Aidan says. "I couldn't even finish reading the one and only book of his that I tried. I made it fifty pages, then I gave up."

I'm laughing so hard I'm crying. It's a minute before I'm able to talk again. I wipe my face and look at him.

"Which book was it?" I ask.

"*Primal Resurrection.*"

I grimace. "Oh god, yeah. That one was rough. I only read it because we were dating at the time."

"Even the title was terrible." Aidan grimaces.

"I didn't have the heart to tell him it was all bad. Not like it mattered. His publisher loved it. So did his superfans."

I catch Aidan looking at me.

"You're a way, way better writer than your ex."

"You don't have to butter me up."

"I'm not. Micah, you're an incredible writer. I love everything you've written. I'm not the only one either. Your posts are a hit with readers. They love them too."

I take in the sincerity in his eyes, the seriousness of his tone. He's being honest.

"Thank you," I say softly.

"Your ex is a typical literary douchebag," Aidan says. He shakes his head. "I should know. I'm kind of one too." A heavy sigh falls from his lips. He aims a pained gaze at me. "I'm really sorry, Micah, for what I said to you when we met."

I wave a hand. "You already apologized for making fun of my name when we were in the elevator—it's fine."

"No, that's not the only thing I have to apologize for." A hard swallow moves along the length of his throat. "I'm sorry for speaking to you so dismissively during that first staff meeting. That was really rude of me. It was just that..." He pauses to take a breath. "Some of the things you said brought up a really upsetting memory. I know you didn't mean to do that, but my reaction was almost like a reflex. I automatically went into defensive mode when I spoke to you. And that was pretty messed up. You were just doing your job. I'm sorry for that."

I blink at him, stunned at what he's said.

"That means a lot. Thank you." I pause. "I owe you an apology too. I came into this situation with a pretty harsh attitude. I was curt and short with you when we first spoke at that meeting. I'm sorry for that. I've done this job for so long that I've gotten used to disconnecting from it. Like, I know that at the end of the day, people's jobs are at stake because of what I do. And that's really shitty. I shouldn't blame you or anyone else for being upset with me. If the roles were reversed, I wouldn't be happy about it either."

He nods like he understands and appreciates what I've said.

"And I'm sorry that the way I spoke to you triggered you," I say.

"It's really okay."

I pause for a second before I work up to what I want to say.

"Do you want to talk about it? What upset you that day?" I ask.

He hesitates for a second.

"I spilled my guts to you about my ex. Just now *and* on Scribble Share. You can vent to me too."

A small smile tugs at his lips. For a long moment, we're quiet. The air between is us different now. The thickness is gone. Things feel lighter, more natural.

His gaze falls to the floor as he rubs the back of his neck. "It's just…when you said that thing about how you'll be able to figure out the exact value of me during your audit…" He clears his throat. "My dad said something similar to me years ago, right before we had a falling out."

I still. "That's awful. I'm so sorry."

He shakes his head. "It's not like it's your fault that my brain made that association."

"But still. I'm sorry you fell out with your dad. That must have been really painful."

There's a flash of rawness in his eyes. "It was." He blinks and it's gone. He's gaze is focused again. "I was a pretty serious hockey player when I was a kid, all the way through college."

"Oh." My voice hitches up.

He smiles. "You sound surprised."

"I just wasn't expecting you to say that. But I guess it makes sense."

My gaze trails down his torso. Even through that crisp white dress shirt and tie he's wearing, I can picture his ripped torso perfectly. All those hard lines and cut muscles. It makes sense now why he's in such good shape—he's an athlete. In addition to being a sexy, nerdy professor who loves Shakespeare and secretly writes erotic fanfic.

God, he is unfairly hot.

I blink, snapping myself out of that daze and focus back on his face.

"Both my younger brother and I played hockey growing up, to our dad's delight. He was a hockey superfan. I'm assuming he still is."

There's an ache in my chest at the way Aidan says that last sentence. He sounds so sad.

"For a lot of my life, he felt like more of a coach than a dad. Always talking about how well we played and what we could do to improve our skills. Every conversation was about hockey and training. I enjoyed playing, but I was never good enough to make it into a career. Unlike my brother."

"How long did he play for?" I ask.

"He still plays. Professionally now, for the Nashville Wolves."

"Oh, wow. That's impressive."

Aidan smiles, like he's proud of his brother. "Yeah, he's really good." His smile fades. "I hit the end of my rope in college. I was tired of making hockey my whole life. I was sick of all the injuries, of feeling sore and beat up all the time. And I was starting to get really into my English and literature classes at that point. I quit the team and started researching grad schools so I could study literature and eventually become a professor. When I told my dad, he was pissed."

Aidan winces like he's in pain before he continues. "He said, 'You think that because you got A's in all your English classes, you're a genius? You suddenly think your value is in your brain instead of your body now? Pathetic.'"

My jaw falls open. What kind of parent would say that to their own child?

My chest aches as I imagine college-aged Aidan listening to those words from his own dad.

His head droops and his shoulders slump, like just reliving that memory is throttling him.

Before I can stop myself, I reach over and touch my hand to his forearm. He closes his eyes, like he's savoring my touch, like it gives him comfort.

My palm tingles against his warm skin.

"He shouldn't have said that to you," I say in a soft voice.

Aidan nods. A second later he lifts his head and glances off to the side. "We haven't spoken much since then. Things have been pretty strained between us. I don't really want to see him."

"I understand." I'm quiet for a moment. "You're a great teacher, Aidan. That first class of yours that I observed was really enjoyable. You're passionate about literature, and you care about your students. And I thought the way you had your students compare Romeo and Juliet's love to their own feelings about their first relationships was honestly brilliant."

His brow lifts in surprise. "Really?"

"Yeah."

"That means a lot coming from you. Thank you." He flashes a smile. His eyes are soft and warm.

Then he quirks an eyebrow, his expression amused. "We broke the rules."

"What do you mean?"

"We were supposed to just be ShakespeareInLust and Hermia. We weren't supposed to talk about anything else."

I chuckle, but then I start to second-guess myself. "But it was okay though, right? I just mean, I hope you don't regret telling me anything…"

He shakes his head. "It was more than okay. Thank you for listening to me. And for understanding."

Warmth pools in my chest at the sincerity in Aidan's eyes, at the softness in his voice.

"Of course. Thank you for trashing my ex with me. That was fun."

His head falls back as he laughs. And then he glances down at my hand on his arm. And then he smiles.

That smile.

It's different from all the ones I've seen from him so far. This one is gorgeous. It reaches his eyes. They're practically sparkling. It's easy and relaxed, and it makes my heart do funny things.

I just now realize that I've been touching him for a while. I pull my hand away but accidentally smack my elbow against his thermos. It topples over, splashing all over Aidan's lap and stomach.

"Crap!" I jump up from my chair. "I'm so sorry!"

He lets out an embarrassed laugh. "It's okay. Really."

I shake my head, feeling like an awkward idiot. "I can't believe I did that. God, I'm so clumsy."

I swipe the tissue box from the other desk, grab a few tissues, and step over to where Aidan's sitting, but then I trip over a loose piece of carpet.

I yelp, and my ass falls into his lap. He lets out an "Oof!" I grip his shoulders to steady myself. He rests his hands on my waist.

And that's when I realize that we're nose to nose, our mouths barely a few inches apart.

I gaze at those crystal-blue eyes wide with surprise. His lips are parted. The hot breath he lets out dusts my lips. My mouth tingles, aching to kiss him.

I flex my hands, savoring the hard feel of his muscled shoulders. Between my legs, my clit is throbbing.

Suddenly the air in the room is thick and buzzing. I let out a shaky breath.

The urge to kiss Aidan pulses through me like an electrical current. But I don't want to do it unless I get a clear sign from him that he wants to too.

Just then I have an idea.

I bite my bottom lip.

I watch as his pupils dilate and the corner of his mouth kicks up. I start to smile too.

A half second later, his mouth is on mine.

Twenty-Seven

Aidan

A growl rips from my throat as I capture Micah's mouth with mine.

I'm desperate as I swoop my tongue through her mouth, teasing and lapping at hers.

I'm instantly hard, just like the last time I kissed her.

To be honest, I was hard the second she fell onto my lap. Because this woman...god, this woman. She drives me wild in the best way.

This isn't how I thought the night would go, with Micah on my lap, tugging her hands through my hair as we kiss each other senseless, but here we are.

It's unexpected and hot and fuck, I'm loving it.

We started the night as enemies, but we're not anymore. She opened up to me about her ex. I opened up to her about my dad. It felt raw and vulnerable and scary...but good.

I've talked about my dad before with a couple of my exes, and they always tried to get me to reconcile with him. They'd tell me that family is the most important thing in the world and that I should leave it all in the past. It always upset me, how they tried to push me to get me to do something I wasn't comfortable with. It felt like they didn't listen to my feelings. It felt like they didn't care.

But Micah didn't react that way at all. She understood my feelings. She empathized with me. And she didn't push me to do anything. She just listened and supported me.

That's all I've ever wanted.

I realize now that we had each other pegged wrong. Micah was tough with me because she felt like she had to be. And I was curt with her because something she said reminded me of my dad.

But we talked it out. We let our guards down. She let me see her softer side. I laughed with her. I saw her shy and insecure when she talked about her ex. And I saw the way she lit up when I raved about her writing.

She's incredible. Bold and smart and sweet and kind and funny.

My chest squeezes in a weird way when I think about how she's letting me see all these sides of her.

Micah moans against my mouth, and my whole body shivers.

Fuck, that sound. So whiny and pleading and hot.

I grip my hands around her waist as she runs her hands up and down my chest.

She leans back, breaking our kiss and catching her breath. Her deep brown eyes are cloudy and dazed. The corner of her mouth quirks up.

"You have no idea how bad I wanted to kiss you again," I rasp, cupping her cheek in my hand and bringing her back to my mouth.

We kiss until we're panting.

"How bad?" she murmurs against my mouth.

"So fucking bad, Micah."

She tugs at my shirt before undoing the buttons. I pull my tie over my head, then I help her out and work on the bottom buttons while she gets the top ones. She pushes the fabric off my shoulders, and I take a second to tug the sleeves off.

I slide my mouth along the side of her neck, and she whimpers. My cock pulses. That sound. I could listen to it over and over.

She leans to the side and lets out a shaky breath. Under my mouth, she shivers.

"I wanted this too," she mumurs. Her eyelids flutter. "I can't stop thinking about you, Aidan."

"Good. Because you're all I can fucking think about."

I run my mouth along her collarbone, savoring her sweet skin. I unbutton her blouse and glide the soft fabric off her even softer skin.

I lean back and stare at her gorgeous tits, which are spilling out of the blue lace bra she's wearing.

"Fuck, they're so pretty." I skim my thumb along the soft fabric and circle her nipple. She gasps.

"I can't get that day in the conference room out of my head," she rasps, chest heaving as I circle my thumb faster. "I keep thinking about it."

The corner of my mouth hooks up. "Yeah?"

She nods. A gorgeous red flush paints her full cheeks. It glides all the way down her pretty, delicate neck.

I give her nipple a gentle tug. She whimpers again.

"I touch myself thinking about that day with you," she says in a whiny, breathy voice.

Pleasure rockets through my dick. "You do?" I growl.

Micah looks at me, those beautiful brown eyes big. She bites her lip and nods.

I reach up and thumb her lush bottom lip. "You thought about me when you played with yourself?"

"Yes."

I have to take a moment, close my eyes, and breathe. Because the thought of Micah thinking about me while she touches her pussy, making herself come over and over has me on the verge of losing it.

I open my eyes and lean my face close to her. "Show me."

Her mouth parts open. There's a wild flash in her eyes. She looks excited and giddy all at once.

I grab her by the waist, lift her up, and set her on the edge of my desk. She hikes her skirt up and spreads her legs wide open. I fall back into my chair, groaning when I see how wet her baby-blue panties are.

I lean my face down, resting my cheek against her inner thigh so I can get a closer look.

"Fuck, baby. So pretty," I murmur.

Micah cups her hand over my cheek, and I glance up at her. She smiles. "I like that you call me baby."

I grin. "Take off those panties and touch yourself, baby."

She bites back a wide grin before lifting her hips up and sliding off her panties. They fall to her ankles, and I reach down to help her take them off.

When I sit back up, I almost choke. Her pussy is so wet and pink and swollen, and I can't fucking take it…

She pulls her blouse all the way off, leaving her in just her bra.

I reach up and pull the delicate lace fabric down, her perfect tits spilling over. And then I just sit there and stare.

I shake my head, in utter disbelief. "I can't handle how stunning you are, Micah. Just looking at you makes me lose my mind."

A shy smile pulls at her plush mouth. I pinch her nipple between my fingers. Her head falls back as she moans.

"The first time I saw you, I was speechless," I say. "You're the most beautiful woman I've ever seen."

She gasps and grips the edge of my desk. "I had no idea," she admits in a breathy, desperate voice. "You looked so pissed when you saw me."

"Oh, I was. But I also thought you were fucking hot."

She chuckles. A second later it turns into a moan. And then she moves her hand between her legs and starts swirling her fingertips around her clit. Her jaw falls open as she gasps. Her whole body shivers, and she moans.

I sit there, my brain overloaded as I watch the hottest image

I've ever seen. The crotch of my pants is on the verge of ripping, I'm so fucking hard.

"Is this how you touched yourself when you thought about me?" I rasp.

She nods, her stare turning glassy. "Yeah. Sometimes I'd use a toy."

A strangled noise rips from my throat.

"A vibrator?" Please god say yes, that would be so fucking hot...

She nods. "I use my vibrator a lot when I fantasize about you."

My brain melts. I scoot closer and pull my hands away from her breasts, then grip the tops of her legs. I lean down and press another kiss to her inner thigh. My dick is throbbing so hard it hurts.

"I want to see you do that, Micah. I want to see you use a vibrator on yourself. But for now, I need to see you come. What would send you over the edge?" I murmur against her impossibly soft skin.

She glances down at me with pleasure-drunk eyes. "Your fingers inside of me."

I sit up and gently slide my middle two fingers inside her pussy, growling at how tight and hot she feels. I lean closer to her and drop a kiss onto her shoulder.

"Fuck baby, you're soaked," I say against the base of her neck.

Her pulse hammers against my mouth. A rough breath falls from her lips.

"Oh my god," she murmurs, like she's in a trance. "Your fingers feel so good inside of me."

I pump my fingers in and out of her. It's not long before her breathing picks up and I feel her tighten around me.

And then she says, "Will you suck on my tits?"

Twenty-Eight

Micah

Aidan looks like he's about to pass out.

He swallows. "I've been aching to have your tits in my mouth."

I bite back a smile, but soon it disappears because I'm too busy gasping and moaning as he pumps his fingers in and out of my pussy.

He leans forward and dips his head to my breasts, capturing my nipple in his mouth. Pleasure pulses through my tits and my pussy.

Oh my god.

I've always gotten turned on when past partners have played with my boobs. But the way Aidan works me over with his mouth and tongue is a whole other level of hot. The movements he's capable of doing with his tongue are mind-blowing.

He was like this in the conference room when we hooked up. His tongue and mouth played my pussy like a fiddle. I had never come that hard or that fast from oral except with him.

And now he's on the verge of making me explode with just a few second of his mouth on my nipple.

My head falls back as the pleasure and pressure ramp up inside of me. "Oh god… Aidan…"

I swirl my fingers faster and faster around my clit. I'm soaked between my legs. I don't think I've ever been wetter playing with myself than right now.

"Are you close, baby?"

"Yes," I whine. "So close."

"Good." He flicks his tongue faster against my nipple. Sparks fly across my skin.

Aidan picks up the pace, pumping his fingers harder and faster. His long, thick fingers hit my G-spot, and something inside of me starts to unravel.

That pressure intensifies. Heat simmers inside of me. My legs are shaking so hard.

"Right there?" he asks.

"Yeah."

He hits that spot over and over.

"That's my good girl," he growls. "You're gonna come so fucking hard for me, aren't you?"

"Yes!" I yelp.

Aidan gently grazes his teeth against my nipple, and I snap, plummeting over the edge.

My entire body is thrashing as I scream and moan. Pleasure thrashes through me, like waves crashing against a shore. With my free hand, I grip around Aidan's bicep to steady myself as he pumps his fingers faster through me. It feels like my entire body is tingling and on fire all at once.

It feels too good and too intense but just right at the same time.

I'm powerless. Every part of me is overtaken with pleasure, and god, I love it.

I start to fall back, but Aidan leans up and wraps his free arm around me, holding me close. I slink my arm around his neck and bury my face in his shoulder. As I start to come down, I hug him tighter.

My head feels like it's about to fly off my shoulders. I've never come that hard from someone's fingers before.

Aidan's warm body flexes against me.

"Watching you play with yourself is the hottest thing I've seen in my life, Micah." His voice is low and rough.

There's a flutter in my chest. This guy.

He's shattered my expectations when it comes to finger fucking in the most glorious way, *and* he made me feel like a goddess.

He pulls his fingers out of me. When I lean back, he locks his gaze with mine and slides his fingers into his mouth. My stomach flips as I watch him lick my wetness off his fingers.

Insanely hot.

He flashes a wicked smile as he hums.

This is so filthy and flirty and sexy. And I want more.

I grip his shoulders and gently push him back into his chair.

"You watched me get off. Now I want to watch you."

Aidan grins. "Okay."

I cross my legs as I sit back on the desk and watch him loosen his belt and undo his pants. He lifts his hips up and pulls down his trousers, revealing a pair of black boxer briefs and a massive boner.

My mouth waters. "Wow…" I murmur.

His stubbled cheeks redden, like he's flattered and embarrassed. It's so cute and sexy.

He slides off his boxers, and for a moment I just stare at his impressive dick. I've seen it before, but I still can't get over how hot it is.

His muscled quads twitch as he grips the base of his cock.

I run my tongue along my bottom lip and glance up at him. His gaze is hot and focused as he looks at me.

"You thought of me too? When you touched yourself?" I ask.

"Yeah," Aidan rasps.

I can't help but smile at the thought that this insanely sexy man pictured me to get himself off.

He gives himself a slow, rough stroke. I gasp softly as I watch.

"What did you think about?" I ask, watching him slowly work himself in his fist.

He doesn't answer at first as he pumps his hard cock.

"I thought about your mouth. The way you bite your lip. It's so fucking sexy…" He makes a growling noise.

His throat works as he swallows. He takes a breath.

"I thought about how wet you get when you're turned on. I thought about how sweet you taste."

I start to moan. Hearing him admit that is such a turn-on.

His gaze falls to my chest, where my breasts are still spilling out of my bra.

"I thought about your tits. Your gorgeous tits. The most perfect tits I've ever seen in my entire life."

He works himself faster in his hand, grunting. He closes his eyes and leans his head back against his chair, slowing his hand. Like he's pacing himself. "Fuck… If I'm not careful, I'm gonna come too fast and embarrass myself."

That giddy feeling blooms in my chest. "It is hard not to come too fast when you think about me?"

Yeah, it's a shameless question, but I'm curious.

He opens his eyes and looks at me. "Yeah. It is"

My chest flutters at his admission.

I move my hands to my nipples and start to play with them. Aidan's eyes go wide.

"Holy shit…" He pumps his hand along his shaft harder and faster.

Intensity flashes in his eyes. The muscles in his chest and arms flex. I can tell he's close.

Just then the filthiest idea pops into my head.

I bite back a grin and look Aidan in the eye.

"Do you wanna fuck my tits?"

Twenty-Nine

Aidan

My brain has gone offline.

All I can do is sit there and stare at Micah as I attempt to process what she's just said.

Because that's the single hottest question anyone has ever asked me.

My cock throbs in my hand. A second later, the gears in my brain finally start to work.

"Hell yeah, I wanna fuck your tits."

Beaming, Micah hops down from my desk and falls to her knees between my legs.

She reaches behind herself, unhooks her bra, and tosses it to the side.

My eyes feel like they're about to pop out of my head as I stare at her. This is the first time I've seen her gorgeous tits totally naked, completely free of any clothing, and fuck if it's not the most stunning image I've ever laid eyes on.

She cups her breasts in her hands and leans forward, then presses my dick between them.

My eyes roll back. The satin feel of her skin against my dick is almost too much…

"Jesus, baby. You're gonna give me a stroke."

She giggles, then works her tits up and down the shaft of my dick. I open my eyes and look down, instantly mesmerized by the image of her breasts swallowing up my hard cock. I take in the hungry look in her eyes, that teasing grin, how she looks like she's genuinely turned on by this.

I'm a boob guy—that's no secret. And I've always wanted to do this before, but I've never had the nerve to ask. I always thought it was too weird…

But then Micah comes along and offers it right up, and good god, this woman. If I'm not careful, I could fall hard for her.

I reach over with my free hand and brush her hair out of her eyes. Her gaze connects with mine, and she flashes a sweet smile.

My chest aches. She's the perfect combination of feisty and bold and sweet and filthy…

"Does this feel okay?" she asks.

I run my thumb along the seam of her mouth. "More than okay. Your tits feel like heaven around my cock."

It's not long before my dick is aching for release, but I need a harder grip than her breasts can offer.

"Can you finish me with your hand? Please?" I rasp.

That sweet grin turns wicked as she nods. She leans back, grips me with her hand, and works me so hard and so fast that my brain starts to splinter.

That tightness in my lower abdomen intensifies. Liquid heat pools at my spine. All the muscles in my quads and calves start to tremble.

"Can I come on your tits? Please?"

She grins. "Yeah."

With her other hand, Micah gently grips my balls. And that's the moment I break.

Pleasure rockets through my body like a lightning bolt. I'm grunting and cursing as I shoot reams of hot come all over. Micah leans closer, and I paint her gorgeous tits with my release.

White stars cloud my line of vision. My cock is aching by the time I finish.

I blink a few times and look at Micah. She's still on her knees, between my legs, covered in my come.

I reach over and grab her, pulling her to me, and crash my mouth against hers.

I kiss her until she's moaning and breathless. When we finally break the kiss, we're both panting. I pull her to sit on my lap and wrap my arms around her. She slides her arms around my neck. We stay like that for a minute, quietly cuddling and catching our breath.

Micah glances down at her chest and then at me. "We're a mess."

I laugh. "I guess we are."

I grab the box of tissues from my desk, pull out a bunch, and do my best to clean up Micah. When I finish, she stands up and steps away while I wipe up my lap and legs and stomach.

We could probably use a shower, but since we're stranded on campus in the middle of a snowstorm, that's not happening anytime soon.

I glance up at Micah, who's standing in front of me, glancing down at herself. It's a second before she notices me looking at her.

"What?" she says with a sweet smile.

I shake my head. "You look really beautiful right now."

She beams and cups my face with her hand. She leans down and presses a kiss to my lips. Then she glances to the side and her eyes go wide. "It stopped snowing."

"Oh yeah?"

Together we stand up and walk over to the window. It's nighttime now. The sky is dark blue, but there's a soft glow from all the snow.

In the distance, I hear the sound of trucks removing snow. I spot a couple of campus maintenance crew members guiding a snowplow through the pavement below us.

We both step back from the window, then laugh.

Micah looks up at me. "Could you imagine they're just doing

their jobs and then they happen to look up and see two naked people in a random window?"

I laugh. Then I scoop Micah's hand in mine. She glances at our joined hands, the look on her face warm.

"We should get some rest. It's late," I say.

"You're right." She glances around my office. "Sleep on the floor, then?"

"I have a better idea."

I head to my desk and pull out an old hoodie I keep as a backup. I hand it to Micah. "So you don't have to sleep in your dress clothes."

"Thank you," she says sweetly.

I throw on my boxer briefs and pull my shirt on, then walk out of my office. A minute later, I'm back with an armload of couch cushions and a couple of pillows.

Micah laughs. "Where'd you get those?"

"Dr. Wauncho's office and Kendall's office. They're the only ones with couches. They're too small to sleep on, but I figured the cushions would be better than sleeping on the floor."

I drop them to the floor, then arrange them into a makeshift bed. And then I step over to Jason's desk and pull out a plush fleece blanket from one of the bottom drawers.

"Wow. Jason's desk is stocked," Micah says.

I drop the blanket on top of the pillows. "There's your bed."

Micah frowns. "You don't want to sleep with me?"

"Oh… I mean, yeah, of course I do. I just didn't want to assume or make you feel uncomfortable."

She smiles. "I'm not. I want you to sleep next to me."

We crawl into the makeshift bed. It's a tight squeeze, but then Micah cuddles into my chest. I instantly relax. The warmth and softness of her body feel like heaven.

She lets out a satisfied hum as she snuggles into my chest. I kiss her forehead. She peers up at me.

"This is wild, right? A couple hours ago we were at each other's throats. And now look at us."

I chuckle. "*Wild* is a good word for it."

Her eyes are shy as she looks at me. "Earlier, when you said you wanted to watch me with my vibrator…" She pauses to swallow. "Did you mean that? Or was that something you said in the heat of the moment? Because that's okay if it was."

I gently grip her chin in my hand. "Of course I meant it." I press a soft kiss to her lips. I feel her smile against my mouth.

"Mmm. Okay, good." She leans back slightly after kissing me. "Because I don't want this to be the last time we're together."

"Same. I want to keep seeing you, Micah."

"I want that too. But you also should know something…"

She blinks quickly and pulls her lips into her mouth, clearly nervous.

"What is it?" I ask.

"I'd like to keep hooking up with you, but I'm not ready for anything serious. Or full-on sex. I'm trying to take things slow after my breakup, and for me that means no sex outside of a relationship. But anything else goes. If that's okay with you?"

I kiss her. "Of course that's okay." I'll give her whatever she wants. I just want to keep seeing her.

And not just because it's fun as hell to fool around with her. I like spending time with her, talking with her and laughing and joking. I like the way she makes me feel.

Warmth gathers in my chest when I think about how she listened when I talked about my dad, how she understood me and didn't judge me. I want more of that feeling. I want more of her.

Micah smiles at me like she's relieved. A beat later, her expression turns serious. "We still have to work together. We need to be professional."

A gentle frown rests between her eyebrows. I press a soft kiss to her brow, and it instantly fades.

"Yeah, we do. But we can do what we want in our free time."

She flashes an embarrassed smile. "I just don't want to get in trouble with my job. I don't want you to either. Especially after all the…unprofessional things we've been getting up to lately."

I smile and brush her hair out of her face. "I don't know what you're talking about," I tease.

She chuckles. "I mean it. We brought quite a bit of attention to ourselves with the hot-sauce incident and the coffee incident. If we decide to keep seeing each other, we need to be discreet about it at work so no one notices anything."

"I agree. It's no one's business what we do in our private time. We keep work at work. And outside of that, we can do whatever we want."

Micah smiles. "That sounds perfect."

She cuddles back into my chest. I blink, my eyelids heavy. All the muscles in my body relax as I hold her. I can't remember the last time I felt this comfortable, this content sleeping next to someone. Soon I hear Micah's breathing turn steady and gentle as she falls asleep. It's not long before I'm asleep too.

Thirty

Micah

Jordan gawks at me through my phone screen, her eyes bulging out of her head. "You hooked up with Professor Douche Canoe in his office? During a snowstorm?"

"Stop calling him Professor Douche Canoe. I like him now."

My sister closes her eyes and shakes her head. "Right, sorry. My brain is playing catch-up." She looks at me. "And that wasn't even the first time you hooked up?"

My face feels like it's on fire. "Nope. It wasn't."

It's a couple days after I hooked up with Aidan while snowed in on campus. My sister called for our usual FaceTime session and asked how things were going with Aidan...so I filled her in. On everything.

"Wow," she says through a breath, eyes bright. She holds up a hand. "Just so I have everything straight—you had a hate hookup up with him after arguing with him one afternoon. And then you were trapped on campus with him during a snowstorm, you hashed things out, realized you actually like each other, and then hooked up again."

"Pretty much, yeah."

She lets out a crazed laugh. "Micah, you legend."

I burst out laughing.

"That's an impressive one-eighty you managed."

"Very funny."

"In all seriousness, I'm happy for you. You went through a lot with Fuckface. You opened up to him about your ex, and he opened up to you about his dad. That's honestly really sweet, how you two were able to be there for each other. If things are good now between you and Professor Douche—I mean, Aidan. Sorry. Then that's all that matters. Have fun."

"Thanks."

My mind flashes back to that night on campus, how, other than our first time together, it was the hottest hookup of my life...and we didn't even have sex.

But it was way, way hotter than any sex I've ever had.

I shiver when I think about the way he looked at me with that hungry gaze, like he was aching to devour me.

I think about how he showered me in compliments, how he raved about my body.

I think about how turned on he was watching me. I think about how hard he made me come with his mouth on my breasts and his fingers inside of me. I think about how hard he came for me...

And then I think about how sweet he was afterward, how he made a bed out of couch cushions for me, how he made sure I was comfortable. How tight he held me in his arms as I melted into his body and fell asleep.

Warmth pools in my chest. If I'm not careful, I could fall hard for Aidan...

But you won't. Because you're not interested in a relationship, remember? This thing with Aidan is just a casual good time. You both agreed to it.

That heat inside of me dissipates with that little reality check I've given myself.

This is exactly what happened with my ex, Ashton. I was smitten from the get-go, and I let myself get carried away. I fell hard for him, and then he shattered my heart.

I can't let myself fall for another literary d-bag.

I halt that thought the instant it forms in my brain. Aidan's not like Ashton—not even close. Yeah, we didn't like each other at first, but we hashed things out and we apologized to each other. And now that I've gotten to know him—who he really is—I see how sweet and kind he is. He supports my writing and encourages me to keep at it. He's a million times better than Ashton ever was.

That warmth puddles inside of me once more.

"So! Guess who almost got hit by a double-decker bus this morning because I forgot cars drive on the other side of the road here?"

I snap out of my thoughts and refocus back on the conversation with my sister.

"Crap, really? Are you okay?"

Jordan reassures me she's fine. We chat for a couple more minutes before we end the call so she can go to bed.

When I set my phone aside, I grab my laptop, eager to write some fanfic inspired by the other night with Aidan.

When I finish, I read over it to make sure it sounds okay and there aren't any typos. And then I post it.

Unlike the first two times I posted to Scribble Share, I don't feel nervous. Just giddy and excited for people to read it. I've got a few hundred followers on the app already, just from my two posts. Pride swells in my chest knowing that there are people out there who actually enjoying my writing.

I navigate to my messages and type a quick message to Aidan aka ShakespeareInLust.

Hey. You were the inspiration for my latest post. Happy reading ;)

He mentioned that he's hanging out with his brother tonight, so I'm sure it'll be a while before he even sees my message or my post. Not even an hour later, my phone is blowing up with notifications from the app. I tap on the comment sections of my latest post to see what readers are saying.

Okay, I had no clue that mutual masturbation could be SO HOT

Y'all, I am on fire after reading this glorious smut

You just wrote the man of my dreams! Hot professor who's amazing with his hands AND his mouth? Sign me up!

Hermia, you and ShakespeareInLust need to do a collab. Who else wants to read some dual POV sexy stuff from these two?

OMG yes pleaseeeee

Pretty please!

A million billion times yes!

I'm grinning so wide my cheeks are aching. Not only because of the amazing response from readers, but also at the idea of writing something with Aidan. I'd love that.

I tap on the comment and Reply.

I'm up for it :) What do you think, @ShakespeareInLust? Should we write something together?

Thirty-One

Aidan

When I finish reading Micah's latest post on Scribble Share in my office, I have to undo the top button on my shirt and loosen my tie.

Damn. That was crazy hot.

I message her back on the app.

Holy FUCK. My phone caught on fire. So hot and so good. Well done :)

Then I spot the comment she tagged me in at the end of her post.

What do you think, @ShakespeareInLust? Should we write something together?

I grin and type my response.

Hell yeah. Let's do it.

I check the clock and see that I have some time before my next class starts, so I reread my favorite lines from her story. She based it on our night together when we were stuck in my office a few days ago during that freak snowstorm. It's not an exact retelling, since she used fake character names and changed a lot of the details. But the passion is spot on.

His fingers pump in and out of me. The pleasure and pressure builds so intensely, I can barely take it.

My eyes roll back. God, he feels so big and so thick. I wonder if his dick would feel this good.

Who am I kidding? I know it would.

His gaze locks with mine. A storm brews in those crystal-blue eyes. "You're soaked."

"I can't help it," I whine. "You turn me on so much."

He pumps harder and faster, until it's almost too much. And then he lowers his mouth to my nipple, capturing it in between his lips. He drags his tongue over the sensitive bud, sending electricity through my body.

"That's my good girl," he growls. "You're gonna come so fucking hard for me, aren't you?"

With those growled words, I explode.

Jason walks into our office, and I smack my phone onto the desk. I shuffle through a random stack of papers, trying to look busy. I clear my throat, hoping he doesn't notice how red my face is.

"Want some coffee?" he asks as he stands at my desk.

"Uh, sure. Thanks."

He sets the cup on my desk before sitting down at his chair.

We work in silence for a few minutes. Then Jason gathers his things and stands up to head to his class.

"Wanna check out that new distillery in Franklin this weekend?" he asks.

"Yeah. Sounds good."

"Hey, have you noticed that Micah's been a lot more pleasant these past couple days?"

I look up at him shoving pens into his laptop bag. "Oh. Really?"

"Yeah." He loops the strap over his shoulder and smiles. "She was observing my class this morning, and I caught her smiling while she was reading something in her notebook. I think that's the first time I've ever seen her smile."

I hold back a grin. I wonder if she read that funny poem I scribbled in her notebook earlier this morning when I walked by her workspace. She was in the break room getting coffee, so I wrote a dirty poem to hopefully make her laugh.

"I'm just thrilled she's not staring daggers at me anymore," Jason says before chuckling, and I laugh along with him.

My gaze falls to my desk, and my brain instantly brings up the image of Micah naked on it, writhing and shouting as I finger fucked her and sucked on her tits. My dick stirs in my pants.

I glance at the floor and remember how we fell asleep on that makeshift bed, her cuddled in my arms, sleeping soundly. How when she woke up, she flashed the sweetest sleepy smile. How she snuggled closer to me and let out the softest moan, like she's never been so cozy and content.

I think about how happy and comfortable I felt just lying with her as we slowly woke up. I don't really like to fall asleep cuddling. But with Micah, it felt so good, so natural.

Warmth flashes through me. It's never been like this with anyone before. I've never felt so much passion and comfort at the same time.

As I think about Micah, I feel a pull in my chest. This thing with her is supposed to be casual. We haven't even had full-on sex yet, but my heart does funny things when I think about her...

I refocus on the moment and look at Jason. "You're right. It's definitely a nice change," I say.

Jason heads out, and I start to load up my bag to head to my class. There's a soft knock at my half-open door. I look up and see Micah standing there, a playful smile teasing at her lips.

I grin and motion for her to come in. She shuts the door as I stand up and walk over to her. I grab her by the waist, pull her to me, then crash my lips against hers.

She moans softly into my mouth. Fuck, I love it when she does that.

She drags her fingers through my hair. I tilt her head back, deepening our kiss.

After what feels like a solid minute, we finally break apart. Both of us are gasping and chucking softly.

That playful smile is back. "Hi."

"Hi."

Micah straightens my tie and gazes up at me. "We already broke the rules."

"We did?"

She nods. "We said we'd keep things professional while we're at work. That kiss wasn't very professional."

I grin and shrug. "Can't help it. I was dying to kiss you."

She sinks her teeth into her lush bottom lip as she grins.

I swallow back a groan. "You can't do that. Not when I'm on my way to teach class. Now all I'll be able to think about is that hot little mouth of yours."

She giggles. "Thanks for the poem, by the way."

"You liked it?"

"Oh yeah. Very romantic. I was swooning hard. 'Roses are red, violets are blue, your tits are amazing, I want to wine and dine you.'"

She chuckles and shakes her head. I laugh and shrug. "What can I say? I'm an incredible poet."

She playfully smacks my shoulder. "Oh, yeah. Your poem was right up there with Orlando's love letter to Rosalind in *As You Like It*."

I grin. "That's exactly what I was going for."

She laughs even harder.

"I was serious about the wining and dining part though. Let's go grab dinner tonight after work."

One corner of her mouth lifts higher than the other when she smiles this time. I notice she does that when she gets ex-

cited about something. That means she's excited to get dinner with me.

I feel that pull in my chest again, wondering what that
means…if maybe she's feeling the same about me.

I tell myself not to get carried away. This thing between us
is supposed to be casual and fun.

"Then afterward maybe we can head back to your place or
mine and brainstorm an idea that we can write for Scribble
Share," I say.

She kisses me. "That sounds perfect."

Thirty-Two

Micah

I unlock the door to my sister's townhome and walk in, Aidan following behind me.

"I'm just going to charge my phone really quick, and then, I'll be ready for dinner."

"Sounds good—whoa…" Aidan glances around the open-concept kitchen and living room with wide eyes. "This is place is amazing. And huge. Damn."

"It's my sister's. I'm just house-sitting while she's out of the country for work for the next few months."

I spot my phone charger on the kitchen island and plug in my phone. "Wanna have a glass of wine or something before dinner…" I trail off when I see Aidan gawking at the floor-to-ceiling windows on the far side of the town house.

"Damn, that's a nice view." He gazes out at the nighttime sky glittering with all the city lights in the distance. "Holy shit, there's a balcony?"

I laugh as he rushes over to the sliding glass door and opens it. When he steps out, a gust of cold air whooshes in.

I cross my arms. "Get back inside—it's freezing!" I say through a laugh as I watch him peer over the edge of the balcony.

"This is sweet!" he hollers. He turns back around to look at me, grinning. "Think of how many ways you could reenact the balcony scene from *Romeo and Juliet*."

My head falls back as I laugh. I walk over to the open door but stay inside.

He clutches his hand over his chest and leans back on the balcony. "Romeo! Oh, Romeo!" he yells.

I burst out laughing.

A second passes and someone outside in the distance hollers, "Juliet! I love you, girl!"

Aidan and I laugh. He walks back inside and closes the door. He grabs my waist and pulls me against him. I cup my face round his cheeks, which are red from the cold. He lets out a soft, satisfied hum, then he kisses me.

"You're ridiculous," I murmur against his mouth.

"I think you mean charming. And entertaining." He kisses down the side of my neck. I shiver and gasp.

Just then my phone buzzes. Aidan groans against my neck.

I giggle. "One sec."

I step out of his embrace and walk over to my phone and see a text from my sister.

Jordan: Hey! Wanna FaceTime later?

Me: Sorry, I made dinner plans with Aidan, we're leaving in a sec. Can we do tomorrow?

Jordan: Oooohhh sounds hot! Yeah, no problem :) Have fun!

Jordan: Oh hey, can you water that succulent over the fireplace? I don't think that's been watered since I left, oops lol

Me: Yeah, sure thing!

I leave my phone on the kitchen island to continue charging. I grab a glass, fill it with water at the sink, and then walk over to the fireplace, where a potted echeveria plant sits on the mantle above it.

"House-sitter duties," I say to Aidan.

He flashes a sexy, lopsided smile. "Pretty nice gig."

I chuckle. "It is. I just have to make sure the place doesn't catch on fire or flood, and I get to stay for free."

"Will you go back to living at your place when she comes back?"

I still as I set the glass in the sink. "Um, I don't really have a place of my own."

"Oh." He flashes a concerned frown. He walks over to me. "Is everything okay?"

"Yeah, it's just…" Embarrassment bubbles up inside of me. He's going to think I'm so stupid when I admit this.

"So I lived with my ex for most of our relationship. I gave up my place at the time to move into his house. And, um, well, he was doing a lot of renovations and I spent a lot of my savings to help him with that. I thought we'd be together long-term and get married someday, so I didn't think twice about helping him with his house. But then we broke up. And I didn't really have money for a place of my own because I had spent so much of my savings on him. So I got into some debt trying to live on my own. Once my parents found out, they paid it off for me. And then my sister insisted I live at her place while she was gone. When she moves back, I'll hopefully have enough money saved that I can get my own apartment again."

My shoulders hunch as I cross my arms over my chest. Aidan's gaze sharpens. He looks pissed.

"Your ex didn't offer to pay you back?" Aidan asks.

I shake my head. "He wasn't really obligated to. He owned the house. I was just his girlfriend at the time—it's not like I was his spouse and entitled to any compensation when we split."

He tugs a hand through his chestnut waves. "What an asshole."

I shrug. "I should have known better."

"Micah, no." He steps forward, grabbing my hand in his.

"He's a piece of shit for doing that to you. You were kind and generous, and he took advantage of you and your money. He deserves to rot for that."

I'm quiet as I take in the fierce look in his eyes, the firmness of his tone. Warmth gathers in my chest at how Aidan defends me.

He leans closer, wraps his arms around me, and presses a kiss to my forehead. "I'm sorry that happened to you. It's not right."

All the muscles in my body relax. I sink deeper into his embrace. "Thank you."

"If I ever see that guy, I'm going to kick his ass."

I chuckle. "You will not," I say, even though I can tell he's joking.

"You're right. I'll get my brother to kick his ass. He's a hockey player, so he loves to fight."

I burst out laughing. When I step back, Aidan's flashing that teasing grin. Inside, I'm melting. He's so sweet and funny and supportive, and he defends me…

He's all the things I'd want in a boyfriend…

Except you don't want a boyfriend, remember?

This thing with Aidan is just supposed to be fun, nothing serious. And even if things got serious, how could we ever last as a couple? My job could put him out of work. Which means things with us will probably end when I'm done with my audit…

Emotions surge through me. I still at how intense and raw it feels…how rattled I feel at the thought of ending things with Aidan.

"You ready to grab some food?" he asks.

I nod at Aidan and shove those feelings aside. I can't get caught up in all that now. I just need to focus on enjoying the moment.

I grab my phone. "Let's go."

★ ★ ★

Aidan stares at me, mouth half open in surprise as I devour the last fry on my plate.

"Wow. If the whole financial-auditor thing doesn't work out, you'd kill it as a competitive eater."

I cover my mouth as I laugh and chew. I reach over the table in the booth we're sitting at and shove his shoulder.

I swallow. "You're making fun of the way I eat? Not cool," I joke.

His mouth curves up in a teasing smile, and he holds up a hand. "I'm not making fun of you. I'm impressed. I've never seen anyone demolish a burger and fries so quickly. It was pretty hot."

I chuckle. "I skipped lunch today, so I was starving."

"You eat faster than my brother, and he's a monster when he's hungry."

"Yeah?"

Aidan nods. "I want to set up an eating contest between you two. That would be epic."

I laugh into my Cherry Coke. He finishes his patty melt but leaves half of his fries. "The rest is for you."

I grin as I finish off his food. He grabs my glass and takes a long sip of my drink.

"So did you always want to be a financial auditor?" Aidan asks.

I raise my eyebrow at him. "I thought work talk was off-limits."

He chuckles. "I'm just curious how you got into it. It's not a job I hear a lot about. And hey, I told you about how I got into teaching. It's only fair that you tell me how you got into your career. I want to learn more about you."

I can't help but smile at how sincere Aidan sounds, at just how much he cares to know about me.

"One of my mentors in college suggested I look into it as a

job after getting my MBA," I say. "She thought it would suit my skill set, and it does."

As I wipe my mouth with a napkin, I catch him staring at me.

"What?" I ask.

He flashes a hesitant smile. "I thought you'd say you were passionate about it."

I shrug. "I mean, I like it just fine. It's the kind of job where if you work hard at it, it pays off. I've been able to move up over the years and earn a great salary. And I'm good at it."

He looks at me for a long moment. "But you're not passionate about it. You don't love it."

I pause for a long moment. "You're right. I don't love being a financial auditor. It's not my passion. It never has been. But not everyone has to be passionate about their job."

"Yeah, of course. But you're passionate about writing. I can tell how much you love it. When you talked about it on Scribble Share, you lit up. Even though we were exchanging DMs, I could tell just how much writing and reading brings you joy," he says.

I'm quiet for a moment as I process what he's said. He's right. I love writing and reading. I'm a million times more passionate about that than I am about my actual job.

"You could make that into a career with how good you are at it, Micah," he says.

I start to smile at his glowing praise, despite the uneasy feeling that builds inside me.

"Writing is such a competitive field. It's hard to make a living at it, even if you're good. Even if you work hard," I say.

He looks like he wants to say more, but after a second he nods. "Yeah, you're right. It's definitely not easy. But if your asshole ex can make a career out of it, so can you."

I chuckle. "Okay. God's honest truth? If I could magically have the stability of my current career with writing, then I'd quit my job and be a writer in a heartbeat. But that sort of stability doesn't exist in creative fields. And I'm not the type of person who can live in that kind of uncertainty."

I'm surprised at how empty the words feel when I speak. Like I'm reciting a mantra I no longer believe.

Maybe I shouldn't ignore that feeling...

A second later, the logical part of my brain catches up. I'm just caught up in all the happy feelings that writing on Scribble Share has brought me recently. It's fun to write as a hobby, but I'll never be able to make it doing it for a living.

A weird unsettled feeling burrows in my tummy. I ignore it and take a long sip of my drink.

I glance up at Aidan, who's nodding at what I've said. For a second, I think he's going to say something, but he stays quiet.

I offer him more of my drink, but he holds up a hand.

"No, thanks. Gotta stick to water for the rest of tonight if I'm gonna hit it hard at the gym with Jason tomorrow."

"Wow. You're so hardcore," I tease. He laughs.

When the server walks by, Aidan hands him his credit card. I try to give him mine too so we can split it, but Aidan won't let me.

"Don't you dare. Tonight is my treat."

My stomach does a somersault at the firmness in his tone. "Thank you."

He smiles. "My pleasure."

When he finishes signing the receipt, we stand up and step out of the booth. He looks at me, his gaze catching on my lip. He reaches over and gently drags his thumb along my bottom lip.

"You had a little something," he says in a low, soft voice, his eyes fiery.

A tingling feeling spreads through my chest. Even when he's wiping food from my mouth, it's sexy.

"Aidan?"

We both look up. There's an older man standing a few feet away from our table, staring at Aidan.

I glance over at Aidan, who's looking at the guy with a weird expression on his face. Like he recognizes him, but he's not happy to see him.

And then he says, "Dad."

Thirty-Three

Aidan

I sit there, too shocked to move or speak.

It's been years since I've seen my dad. And somehow we run into each other at this random pub just outside of the Gulch?

A familiar uneasiness settles in the pit of my stomach. The muscles in my shoulders tense. Even though it's been a long time since we last spoke, my body remembers how to react to him.

He walks over to me. Now that he's closer, I see just how much he's aged since the last time I saw him. The wrinkles on his face are deeper. His hair is more gray than light brown now. When he blinks, the fatigue in his eyes is clear.

My dad doesn't stand as tall as I remember him. We've always been the same height. Six foot two. But I see now that his shoulders are hunched and his back is slumped.

He flashes a tired smile. "It's really good to see you."

I'm taken aback by the genuine joy in his voice. I haven't heard him speak like that to me in… I can't even remember.

He never used to sound that way when we talked. When I was a kid playing hockey, he'd always lecture me on how I could train and play better. His tone was always so hard and cold.

But he sounds warm when he speaks now, and it's throwing me off.

I nod at him. "Yeah. It's been a while." I almost flinch at how detached I sound.

My dad's smile falters at what I've said. He glances over at

Micah, who's glancing between the two of us. The look in her eyes seems pained and pitying.

After a second, she smiles and sticks out her hand for him to shake. "I'm Micah. I work with Aidan."

He shakes her hand and gives her a warm smile. "Lovely to meet you."

He turns back to me. "I, uh, saw you at your brother's game the other day."

"You did?"

He nods. "I see you a lot. Almost every time I go to a game, I see you there too. But, uh, I don't wanna bother you, so I don't say anything. I know you'd hate that." He flashes a sad smile. "How's work going? Liam says you're a professor at East Nashville University."

I tense when he mentions my job. Inside I feel so jumbled, like my body can't decide how to feel in this moment.

"Yeah, it's good. I teach literature there."

He grins wide. There's a brightness in his eyes. He almost looks…proud of me.

"That's really great, Aidan." He pats my shoulder, but then he quickly pulls his hand away, almost like he didn't mean to do that.

Another quiet moment passes. His smile turns sad as he looks between Micah and me.

"Sorry for interrupting."

"It's okay," Micah says quickly, but my dad shakes his head.

"I don't want to intrude more than I already have." He looks at me. "It was good to see you, son."

Sadness flashes in his blue eyes. My chest aches.

I nod without saying anything more. He walks off.

Micah touches her hand to my arm. I turn to her.

"Are you okay?" Concern and sadness flash in her deep brown eyes.

I let out a shaky breath. "I don't know."

★ ★ ★

I unlock the door to my place and let Micah in.

"Thanks for driving me home," I say as I close the door behind her.

She grabs my hand in hers and squeezes tight. "Of course."

After that run-in with my dad, I was so out of it that she insisted on driving me back to my place. I was quiet the whole ride here, but it didn't seem to bother Micah. She didn't pepper me with questions. She just seemed to understand that I needed a quiet moment to process what happened with my dad.

I glance up and see the sink full of dishes.

"Sorry it's a little messy," I say.

"Don't apologize. Do you want to sit for a sec?"

I nod. She leads me over to the couch, and together we sit down.

I squeeze her hadn't in mine. "I'm sorry things were so awkward at the pub with my dad."

She shakes her head, a small smile pulling at her mouth. "Stop apologizing, okay? You don't need to be sorry for anything."

I scrub a hand along my scruffy jaw. "I just…it was weird running into my dad. I wasn't expecting him to be so happy to see me."

Micah looks surprised. "Really?"

"The last time we spoke to each other was years ago. He was so angry with me. But tonight…" He huffs out a breath. "My brain is kind of all over the place right now. Sor—"

She smiles when I stop myself. "It's okay," she says softly.

"Whenever I talk about my dad with anyone else, I always feel on edge. I always feel like they're judging me. But with you, it's different," I say. "I feel comfortable with you. Like I can tell you anything."

Her expression turns warm as she looks at me. "You can.

Tell me anything you want. Or nothing. Whatever you need, I'm here for you."

A warm feeling settles in my chest. I feel so much comfort being with Micah right now. She's giving me the support I need after that jarring interaction with my dad—the support I've never gotten from anyone else whenever I talked to them about my strained relationship with him.

A pained look appears on Micah's beautiful face. With her free hand, she cups my cheek. "I'm so sorry you're having these feelings right now about your dad."

I close my eyes, humming softly at her touch, how comforting it is.

"My brother still has a relationship with him, and every so often he tries to talk me into reconnecting with our dad, but I always shut him down. I just can't get past the things he said to me. I'm too hurt, even now, even after all these years. But maybe he really has changed…"

Micah's quiet as I trail off and work out the mess of thoughts in my brain.

"But even if he has, I don't know if I can move past what happened. I don't know if I want to have a relationship with him, even if he's changed for the better now. That doesn't erase the hurtful things he said and did before."

She nods like she understands. "Of course." She hesitates for a second. "Look, I don't know your brother, obviously, but I'm sure he means well. It probably hurts him to see a rift between his brother and his dad. But even so, your feelings are valid, Aidan. It's okay that you're still hurt over what he did to you. And it's okay that you need time to process your feelings. It's okay that you need time to figure out what you want to do when it comes to your dad. Take all the time you need."

I gaze at Micah, taking in the softness and sincerity in her eyes. Emotion surges through me like a tidal wave. In the past, when I've been in a relationship and my estrangement with my dad came up, my exes have always listened to me and said they understood, but I could tell they didn't really get it. They didn't really empathize with what I was going through. I couldn't blame them. It's complicated, this thing with my dad.

But this is the first time I've ever felt truly heard, truly understood. With Micah.

My heart thuds in my chest. There's a strange ache that I don't think I've felt before.

The longer I look at her, the more that ache intensifies, burrowing deeper in my chest.

Right now I don't need anything or anyone except her.

I grab her face in my hands and pull her to my mouth, kissing her hard. When we break apart, we're both panting. I rest my forehead against hers as I catch my breath.

"I need you in my bed. Now."

Thirty-Four

Micah

I take the wild gaze in Aidan's eyes, the rawness and intensity as clear as the crystal-blue color.

"Are you sure?" I ask.

He nods without even blinking.

My heart is thudding and my skin is hot.

I listened to Aidan while he poured his heart out to me. I could tell how difficult it was for him to see his dad. I could tell he was struggling to process it all.

I wasn't expecting him to spill his feelings to me. I was happy to give him the space he needed while he worked it all out in his head. But then he opened up to me. And that felt so special.

He admitted that he hasn't talked about his dad a lot. That it's too overwhelming, too painful. So the fact that he chose me to share that with means the world.

That ache in my chest intensifies. I let the feeling settle and wash over me.

This thing with Aidan doesn't feel like some casual thing anymore. It feels deeper, more meaningful.

I cup his face in my hands and kiss him. Up to this point, our kisses have been rabid and filthy. But this kiss is slower. Achingly slower. I can feel everything in this kiss. His heart, his emotions, his pain…

He hums against my mouth, and my stomach flips. We break the kiss, and I grab his hand and stand up.

"Take me to your bedroom."

Aidan leads me through the living room of his Craftsman-style home and down the hall to a bedroom at the far end. He flips on the light and walks over to the king-size bed in the middle.

I stop to kiss him in the same slow and teasing rhythm as before. I run my hands all over his chest, savoring all the hard muscle under his crisp dress shirt. I unbutton it and push the fabric off his shoulders. He untucks my blouse and pulls it over my head. A second later, his pants and my skirt are on the floor.

I skim my fingertips along the waistband of his boxer briefs. "What do you want from me right now, Aidan?"

He cups my cheek in his hand, then a second later gently runs his thumb along my lips. "Your mouth."

My pussy aches at the roughness in his voice. I bite my lip. "You want my mouth on your cock?"

The side of his jaw bulges as he exhales. "Yes."

"Do you want to fuck my mouth? And my throat?"

His eyes widen, and the corner of his mouth lifts. "Fuck, yes."

I'm giddy and turned on all at once. I start to move to the bed, but Aidan stops me with a hand on my waist. "You have no idea how badly I want to fuck that sweet little mouth. But I need to make you come first."

As if on cue, my pussy aches and my inner thigh muscles twitch. Just hearing the need in Aidan's voice, how badly he wants to make me come has me soaking my panties.

With his hands on my hips, he turns me and backs me up to the edge of his bed. He reaches behind me and unhooks my bra, then tosses it aside before dropping to his knees and sliding down my panties.

I sit down on the edge of the bed. Aidan moves closer to me, rests his palms on my legs, and gently coaxes them open. He leans his face down and presses a trail of soft kisses up my inner thigh. Goose bumps break out across my entire body. My clit pulses, and my eyes roll back. God, he's so sweet and sexy with the way he kisses me. When his mouth makes it all the way up, instead of kissing my pussy, he moves his mouth to my other thigh and dusts a trail of light kisses there too.

My head falls back as I let out a shaky breath as he takes his time with me.

I glance down right as he runs his thumb gently along my soaking-wet slit. Pleasure throbs in my clit and pussy, and I gasp. And then he plants his massive hand on my stomach and gently pushes me to lie back onto the bed.

The second my body hits the mattress, he runs his tongue up my pussy. Pleasure pulses through me, pooling between my legs and up my abdomen and chest.

"Aidan...god, how are you always this good with your mouth?"

He groans as he works his tongue in slow circles. My eyes roll back, and I fist the sheets on his bed, whimpering.

He eases back and kisses the inside of my thigh.

"Fuck, Micah. I can't take it when you make that sound."

Aidan moves his mouth back to my pussy. He flicks his tongue against my clit. The pleasure amps up with each passing second.

When he pulls his mouth away again, I whine. I glance up and see that smug, sexy-as-hell smile on his face.

"Do you know how long I've wanted to do this to you in my bed?" He slides his index and middle fingers into his mouth, wetting them. Then he slides them into my pussy. I gasp and my eyelids flutter at the sensation of being filled up with his thick, strong fingers. Just like before, he pumps them in and out, slowly at first.

"Oh god..." I whimper. My entire body is trembling, pulsing, aching...

When he lowers his face back down between my legs and starts tonguing my clit again, I scream. His tongue and his fingers working in tandem is too much. I'm overloaded with pleasure. My brain can't form a single coherent thought and my entire body is on the verge of exploding.

Aidan pumps his fingers faster and harder. I'm shouting so loud, my throat is sore.

"Are you close, baby?" he asks. He swipes his tongue along my clit.

"Yes."

"Good. Say my name when you come."

His growled words shove me to the edge. And then he swirls his tongue on my clit. Orgasm thunders through me. I thrash against the bed as Aidan works me over with his mouth and fingers. I've lost all control of my body. My limbs are spasming, my back arches off the mattress, and my eyes roll back.

I scream his name so loud, my ears ring. I don't know how long I come, but it feels like minutes. When I finally start to come down, I look at him. He locks eyes with me as he slips his fingers in his mouth, licking my wetness.

"Mmm," he groans as the corner of his mouth quirks up. "You taste so fucking good, baby."

I shiver at the raw want in his voice, at just how much I turn him on, at the way he calls me baby.

I've never really liked that pet name when guys have tried to use it on me before. But I like it when Aidan says it. I like that he only says it when we're fooling around, when he sheds his hot-nerd-professor image and unleashes his filthy side.

He climbs onto the bed and pulls me against him. He kisses my forehead, and I hum as I cuddle into his chest. We stay like that for a minute, and then I reach down, gently gripping his hard cock in my hand. A strangled noise rips from his throat.

My mouth waters. I'm aching to take my turn with him now. I'm aching to see him come undone.

I glance up at him, eyeing his dick. "You have a gorgeous cock."

His cheeks flush pink. My chest tingles at how bashful he looks at being complimented.

"Thank you. And you have a gorgeous everything." He leans down and captures my nipple in his mouth. He swipes and swirls his tongue around the hard nub. I run my fingers through his hair, moaning at how good it feels. He moves to my other nipple and works it in his mouth until I'm trembling and gasping. And then he straightens back up, the look on his face hungry. Like he's just getting started.

"Are you ready to throat fuck me?" I ask in a sweet voice.

A wicked smile tugs at his lips. He kisses me, then slides off the bed. I maneuver myself so my head is hanging off the edge.

I look up. He's upside down in my view. He smiles down at me and grips his rock-hard cock in his hand. "Open that pretty mouth for me, baby."

He moves closer, the head of his dick hovering over my lips. "Will you touch yourself with my cock in your mouth?"

I grin and nod. "Would that turn you o—"

He pushes his cock into my mouth, cutting me off. I close my eyes and moan around his dick. So thick and so hard and so, so good.

Aidan stills for a few seconds. I can feel him shudder. Above me, he lets out a rough groan. God. He sounds downright feral. That tingling feeling intensifies. I love knowing that just a few seconds of using my mouth on him is enough to drive him wild.

He slides deeper into my mouth. I relax my throat and jaw, letting him go even farther.

His breathing picks up. I watch as his eyelids flutter. He runs his tongue along his bottom lip.

"Is this okay?" he asks, his voice rough and raw, on the verge of pleading.

I nod slightly and hum, "Mmm-hmm."

His throat works as he swallows. The side of his jaw bulges as he bites down.

"Jesus Christ, Micah…"

His gaze slides to between my legs. "Now, be a good girl and play with your pussy for me."

Thirty-Five

Aidan

Holy fucking FUCK.

I close my eyes, my entire body trembling with want.

It's been ten seconds of having my cock in Micah's mouth, and already I'm on the verge of exploding.

I slide the rest of my length into her perfect, soft, wet mouth and still. I close my eyes and take a second to breathe. My heart is hammering in my chest, my breathing is ragged, and my brain is mush. Her mouth, her tongue, her throat—it all feels incredible.

When I open my eyes, I glance down and see her circling her fingers slowly against her clit. My knees buckle and my balls tense. Good fucking god, that's insanely hot.

She moans, the vibrations in her throat and mouth pulsing through my cock. I grunt.

I could come right here, right now. She just feels so good; she just looks so fucking sexy.

But I can't. Not yet. I want to pace myself. I want to make this last a little bit longer.

Gripping the base of my cock, I ease out of her mouth slowly, then slide back in. I'm slow and gentle with my thrusts, and not just for my sake. I want to make sure this is good for her too.

"What a good girl you are, taking my dick in your mouth while you play with your perfect pussy."

Her eyes roll back, and she moans around my cock, which is hard as steel.

"Fuck, I wish I could see you with your vibrator right now."

She stills and taps my arm. I ease out of her mouth. She takes a breath. "I, um, have a vibrator. In my purse. If you want to see me play with it…"

I march out of the room instantly. Micah's laugh floats behind me. I grab her purse from my living room, bring it back to my bedroom, and hand it to her.

She chuckles. "That was quick." She pulls out what looks like a small silver lipstick.

"You keep a vibrator in your purse?" I ask, my mouth curling up in a smile.

She flashes a shy grin. "It was a gag gift from a friend years ago. But it comes in handy."

Micah holds the small vibrator to her clit and turns it on. A low buzzing sound fills the room as her mouth falls open and she moans.

For a second, I just stand there and watch her, savoring the gorgeous image of her pressing that vibrator to her pussy.

I step up to her and gently grip her chin in my hand. "Are you ready to take my cock again?"

She nods and opens her mouth. When I push the head of my cock past her lips and slide into her mouth, she moans even louder than she did the first time. Just like before, I start off with slow thrusts. But it doesn't take long for me to pick up speed. I'm getting so turned on, watching her pleasure herself with that vibrator while she takes my hard dick in her throat.

Her legs start to tremble and her moans grown louder.

"Are you gonna come, Micah? Are you gonna come with my cock in your throat?"

She whimpers around me and nods.

"Good girl."

Slowly, I slide out, then in. Her pussy is soaked with her wetness and my saliva. God, that's sexy.

The feral part of me doesn't want to just stand there and

watch, so I reach my free hand between her legs. "Do you want me to fill you up with my fingers again?"

Another whimpered moan as she nods her head. I slide in two fingers, then three. She kicks up the speed on her toy and groans. I grit my teeth as the vibrations from her throat and mouth amp up the pleasure pulsing through me. I can't come. Not yet.

I focus on her and pump my fingers in and out of her tight, wet pussy. Not even a minute later, she comes screaming around my dick.

The vibrations are full-on pulses now. My cock is throbbing. I'm on the razor edge of coming. Just another few thrusts into her mouth and I'm there.

"Can I come in your mouth? Is that okay?" I rasp.

She hums, "Mmm-hmm." And then she reaches her free hand behind her, grips my ass, and pulls me closer, deeper into her throat.

Fucking god YES.

It only takes two thrusts before I unload into Micah's sweet throat. My brain shatters as I come. Pleasure thrums through my entire body. It's so hard and so intense that I can barely stand up straight. I pull my hand away from Micah's pussy and plant it on the bed, bracing myself. The sound that falls from my mouth isn't human. It's rough and wild and deafening.

When I finish, I ease out of her mouth.

She lets out a shaky breath. I stare at her lying on my bed, face red and lips swollen. For a second, I'm scared it was too much, but then she aims that beautiful smile at me.

"That was okay?" she says softly.

I grin, lean down, and slide up her the bed so that she's against the pillows now. I climb up next to her, then pull the comforter over us. I slink my arms around her and hug her against me.

"Not 'okay.' That was incredible. Beyond incredible. Holy shit, Micah."

Smiling, she kisses me. The rest of the night we stay like that, cuddled together.

As she falls asleep in my arms, I think about earlier. I think about how vulnerable I was in front of her, how she didn't shy away when I divulged all that emotional baggage with my dad. I think about how much closer I felt when I shared all that with her, how feeling her care and support made me want her even more.

Is that weird? To feel so turned on after such an emotion-ally vulnerable moment?

But then I realize that I don't care. All that matters is the way Micah makes me feel, the way I make her feel, the way we feel about each other.

That ache in my chest from earlier resurfaces, only this time it's deeper, more intense.

And that's when I know: I'm falling hard for Micah.

Thirty-Six

Micah

When I wake up, I'm cuddled in Aidan's arms.

As I open my eyes, I look up at him, still sleeping. I take in his messy bed hair and how the stubble on his cheeks is even thicker in the morning.

Damn. Even when he's not conscious he's hot.

I snuggle back into his chest, savoring how tightly he holds me even when he's sleeping. I've never been much of a cuddler when I sleep. I always like to have my own space. But with Aidan it's different. He holds me like he wants me, like he can't fall asleep without me right there with him.

Warmth bursts in my chest. I love that about him. I love a lot of things about him.

That feeling in my chest intensifies. This thing with Aidan isn't casual anymore. Maybe it never was and I was kidding myself. I'm starting to feel something deep for him.

I think about last night, how it was one of the hottest nights of my life, and we didn't even have sex.

Between my legs, I feel that telltale ache.

I want to have sex with him. So, so bad.

I think of my no-sex rule, how I told Aidan that when I hook up with a guy, full-on sex is off the table. It's too intimate.

But things between us feel really intimate right now. And I like that.

He starts to stir. I press a kiss to his chest.

He opens his eyes and peers down at me. He flashes a sleepy smile.

"Good morning," he murmurs.

"Good morning."

I lean up and kiss him. As our tongues get filthier and filthier, I feel his dick harden against my thigh. I reach down and grip him gently, then stroke him.

Aidan groans into my mouth, then pulls away. "You keep doing that and I'm going to have to fuck your mouth again."

"I'd rather ride you."

He smiles. "Really?"

I bite my lip and nod.

His grin turns wicked before he gently grips my face and pulls me in for a hot kiss. His tongue swoops into my mouth, hard and teasing all at once. I whimper. I lose track of the seconds and minutes when Aidan kisses me like this.

When we finally break, he tosses off the covers and reaches to open the drawer of the side table by his bed. He pulls out a condom, rips it open with his teeth, and rolls it over his cock, which is hard as steel.

He holds my chin and looks at me, his eyes a crystal-blue bonfire. "Ride my dick, baby."

I move to straddle him, then position myself over the head of his cock. When I lower myself onto him, I gasp. For a few seconds, I just sit there, relishing the feel of him stretching me out. He feels so big and so good.

He mutters a curse. His eyes roll back and he digs his fingers into my hips.

"God, Aidan…" I moan.

A low growl rips from his throat as he focuses is gaze on me. He reaches up and teases my nipples between his fingers. I whimper at how good it all feels.

Slowly, I glide up and down his cock. The pressure and heat between my legs spreads up my abdomen to my chest.

"So good…" I murmur.

"That's it, baby," he growls, pinching my nipples. "Ride me harder."

I bounce harder and faster. The pressure builds and builds. It feels like my entire body is one fire with pleasure.

"Will you play with my clit? Please?" I whimper.

Aidan makes a feral sound. He drops his hands to my hips, stilling me.

"Hang on." He lets out a shy laugh. "I just need a sec. Hearing you beg like that when you're riding my cock almost sent me over the edge."

After a few moments, Aidan lets out a breath. He drops one hand to my hip and the other between my legs.

I cup my breasts in my hands, working my nipples between my fingers.

"Jesus fuck, look at you," he mutters. "You're the hottest thing I've ever seen in my life, Micah."

I'm floating at Aidan's praise. I start to move up and down his hard dick. Gently, he flicks his thumb over my clit. I gasp.

The muscles in my legs tense as heat pools between my legs. I lean forward slightly, stilling when I feel the head of his cock bump against my G-spot.

"Oh god…"

There's a wicked flash in Aidan's eyes. "Right there?"

I nod frantically as I glide up and down. With his dick filling me up and his thumb on my clit, I'm not going to last much longer.

I bounce faster, and my breathing turns ragged. I can feel my orgasm just on the horizon, barreling toward me.

"That's it," Aidan says in a sweet, rough voice. "Get so fucking loud when you come on my cock."

Seconds later, I do exactly that. Pleasure rams through me. I scream *Please* and *Yes* and *Oh my fucking god, Aidan.* My throat is aching, but I can't help it. I can't help but shout through this mind-blowing orgasm. I've lost all control of my body, and it feels incredible. I close my eyes as I come apart on Aidan's lap, thrashing and howling his name as climax absolutely wrecks me. Blood pumps hot though my body, and there's a ringing sound in my ears.

He moves his thumb quickly over my clit. I'm so wet between my legs that I can hear the slick sounds his fingers make.

After a minute, I start to come down. I fall forward, landing on his chest. He wraps his arms around me.

"Wow…just wow," I babble into his pec.

A low chuckle sounds above me. "Yeah?"

I smile into his chest. "Yeah."

"You came so fucking hard. That was insanely hot."

I smile, feeling the blush work up my chest to my face. I take a few seconds to catch my breath, and then I lean back and look up at him. "Now it's your turn to come. How do you want me?"

Smiling, he runs his tongue along his bottom lip. "On your hands and knees."

I grin and lean up, getting into position. He moves behind me, gripping my hips, and lining his dick up with my pussy.

He teases the head of his still-hard cock at my entrance.

I moan. "Will you fuck me hard? Please?"

Aidan responds to my request with a rough growl. "I'm going to pass out if you keep saying things like that."

I chuckle.

"Sure, baby. I'll go hard. But I'm not gonna last long. That okay with you?"

He massages my ass cheek in his hand. I lower my chest and face onto the mattress and groan. "Yes. That's exactly what I want."

A second later, Aidan slides into me and I yelp. Then he pulls out and slams back in.

"Like that?" he rasps.

"Yes!"

Again he pulls out and slams in. My eyes roll back at how deep he's hitting me. It's so intense and so fucking good.

Over and over he thrusts, gripping my hips. It's not long before he starts to unravel. His rhythm and his breathing turn desperate. He thrusts hard into me with a curse, his muscles tensing. He leans over me, pressing a kiss to my shoulder before slowly pulling out of me.

I fall into the mattress, feeling so full and so satisfied as he steps away.

A minute later, he crawls back into bed. He hugs me into his chest and pulls the covers over us.

I lean up to look at him, taking in pleasure-drunk look in his eyes. He smiles and kisses me.

"You're amazing," he says softly.

My heart hammers in my chest. A wave of emotion crashes through me.

I'm falling so, so hard for this guy. I shouldn't be.

We weren't supposed to be attracted to each other.

We weren't supposed to have this incredible connection.

We weren't supposed to have this secret romance.

He wasn't supposed to be this sweet, this caring, this doting.

I wasn't supposed to like him this much. I wasn't supposed to feel this connected, this close to him…

But I do. And I have no idea how things are going to work out between us.

An ugly feeling claws at the pit of my stomach. I will it away.

Don't ruin this moment. Just focus on the time you have with him now.

I snuggle into Aidan's chest and fall asleep.

Thirty-Seven

Aidan

I look up from my laptop at Micah, who's sitting on the other end of my couch with her own laptop.

"How's it going?" I ask.

She grins but doesn't take her eyes off the screen. "Good. I'm almost done. How about you?"

"Just a few more minutes, then I'll be ready to go."

When I finish typing, I glance at her. She looks up at me and grins. "Done!"

I smile. "Should we read each other's before we post to Scribble Share?"

"Good idea."

We swap computers. I'm instantly engrossed the moment I start reading Micah's story. When we woke up this morning, we decided it would be fun to write a dual-POV post for Scribble Share. So we came up with an idea for a sexy scene, and Micah wrote her POV and I wrote mine.

I make a few proofreading corrections, but other than that, it's good to go.

When we finish reading, we look at each other. I'm smiling like an idiot. Micah's cheeks are flushed bright red.

"Hot."

"Crazy hot."

We both laugh after speaking at the same time.

"This morning in bed gave us quite the filthy inspiration," she says.

I laugh. "It really did."

Together we make a joint post on Scribble Share. When we finish setting everything up, we look at each other.

"Are you ready?" I ask.

Micah nods, smiling. "Our first coauthored story. Let's do it."

I hit Post, and then I close my computer. Micah closes hers too.

"I can't look and see what people's reactions will be—I'm too nervous," she says.

I reach over to her and pull her onto my lap. She hikes up her skirt and straddles her legs over me.

"Don't be. I have a feeling readers on the app will love it." I cup my hand over her cheek and kiss her.

I think back to earlier this morning with Micah. That was the hottest sex I've ever had in my life.

But more than that, it was the fact that she broke her no-sex rule. For me.

There's a pull in my chest. She broke the rules for me. That must mean she feels something deep for me…something deeper than just this casual setup we initially agreed to have.

And if her feelings for me have changed, what does that mean for our work relationship? Her job is to essentially put me out of a job…has she changed her mind about that?

I halt the flurry of thoughts circling in my brain. We agreed not to talk about work when we're together outside of work. I need to stop thinking about it.

She leans down and kisses me. It's not long before we've shed our clothes and our hands are all over each other. I grip my arms under her ass and stand up, carrying her. I walk out of the living room and down the hall.

Micah holds my face. "Bedroom again?" she murmurs as she kisses me.

I break our kiss and grin at her as I stop in the doorway of my bathroom. "Nope. Shower."

A giddy smile tugs at her lips. I set her down, and we walk into the bathroom. I push back the sliding glass door, flip on the water, and stick my hand into the stream to make sure it's warm enough. Taking Micah's hand, I lead her into the shower. Together we stand under the spray. I slink my arms around her and pull her close as I kiss her.

I slide my hand between her legs and gently glide my fingers between her folds.

She whimpers into my mouth. I pump my fingers in and out, just how she likes it, making sure to keep my palm pressed against her clit.

Micah runs her fingernails down my back and bites my shoulder. My eyes roll back at the burn. It feels amazing to know that I make her feel so good that she's getting this rough.

"Aidan…" The way she moans my name makes me crazy.

I pump my fingers faster.

"So good…" she whines.

She starts to shudder around me, and that's when I know she's close. I lean my head down and take her nipple into my mouth. I drag my tongue against the hard nub. When her moans turn to screams and she starts to shake, I gently press my teeth to her sweet, soft skin.

"Oh my god!"

She unravels completely, shouting and thrashing against me. When her movements start to ease, I release her tit and gently pull my fingers out of her. I press a kiss to her mouth.

"Good?" I ask.

She flashes a giddy smile at me and nods. "So good."

"Turn around and put your hands against the wall so I can fuck you."

Fire burns in those beautiful burnt-umber eyes. She bites back a grin as she does what I tell her. I slide the shower door open and step out to grab a condom from the cupboard under the sink. I wince as I roll it on. My cock is so hard, it's throbbing. I step back in, admiring the sight of Micah's gorgeous ass. I step up to her and palm her ass cheek in my hand. She moans.

"You ready for my cock, baby?"

"So ready."

I grab her hips and pull her ass closer to me. I fist the base of my dick and tease the head at the entrance of her pussy.

"Don't tease me, Aidan. Please."

Raw want pulses through me at hearing her beg.

"You want this dick so bad, don't you, baby?"

"Yes," she says in a whiny voice. "I want it all. Please give me your dick. Please."

I slide the head inside of her and groan. "Your pussy feels like heaven."

She lets out a whimper as I slide all the way in. I pump slow and steady at first. The pleasure is instant. I can feel it radiating through my entire body.

I pick up speed, thrusting harder. I reach up and thread my fingers through Micah's soaking wet hair.

"Yes…" she moans.

I curl my fingers, careful not to pull too hard. I keep thrusting until I feel that telltale pressure inside of me intensify. Liquid heat pools at the base of my spine.

The last of my self-control hangs by a thread. I can't hold off much longer.

Just then Micah reaches back and grips my ass with her hand, pulling me closer. I take that as my cue.

I thrust hard until I come. My brain shatters as the pleasure overtakes me. Bursts of light cloud my vision and my ears start to ring. God. This is so fucking intense and so fucking good.

A growled curse rips from my throat as my head falls against her shoulder. I kiss her satin skin.

"Baby…you should come with a warning label."

Micah giggles. I lean my head up and gently grab her face

and kiss her before I slide out of her and pull off the condom. I lean out of the shower and toss it into the nearby trash can.

We wash up, rinse off, and step out. I wrap a fresh towel around her and pull her close for another kiss. She dries off, and I grab another towel from the rack to dry myself.

When she finishes, she asks if she can wear some of my clothes. "I want something a little more comfortable than my work clothes."

A happy feeling bubbles up inside of me. I smile at her. "Yeah, of course."

I wrap the towel around my waist, grab her hand, and lead her into my bedroom. I pull a T-shirt and a pair of boxers and hand them to her. She smiles and says thank you, then gets dressed.

When I see her wearing my clothes, my heart skids.

God. She looks so fucking adorable and so fucking perfect wearing my clothes.

A strange protective feeling pulls in my chest. I don't want to see Micah wear another guy's clothes. I don't want her hooking up with anyone else. I don't want her in another man's bed.

I want her to be mine.

That feeling inside of me sharpens and intensifies.

She smiles at me as she smooths a hand down the front of the T-shirt she's wearing. "I look okay?"

I pull her against me and kiss her. "You look amazing."

A shy smile pulls at her beautiful mouth. I kiss her one more time before walking back to the bathroom to finish getting ready, my heart pounding at my chest at just how intense my feelings for Micah have become.

Thirty-Eight

Micah

As I brew a pot of coffee in Aidan's kitchen, I'm smiling so wide my cheeks hurt. I can't help it though.

This morning with Aidan has been perfect.

He is perfect.

My stomach does a somersault when I think about what we just did in the shower. *God.*

Not only is he incredible in bed—and in the shower—but he's sweet and funny and kind and we can nerd out while writing fanfic erotica together—

Just then there's a knock at his front door. I contemplate knocking on the bathroom door to let Aidan know, but I don't want to bother him since he's busy getting ready.

I walk over to the front door. When I open it, there's a guy standing there who looks like a younger, blonder version of Aidan.

His brow hits his hairline. Clearly he's surprised to see me. "Sorry—um, is Aidan around?"

"Yeah, he's getting ready in the bathroom."

"Oh…" He tugs a hand through his hair, which is thick and wavy like Aidan's. "I'll come back later, then."

"I can let him know you stopped by."

"That would be great. Thanks." He frowns and shakes his head. "Sorry—I should say I'm his brother, Liam."

"Oh!" I chuckle. "I see the resemblance."

The corner of his mouth hooks up in a teasing half smile that looks identical to Aidan's half smile.

"I like to think I'm the handsome one."

I laugh. "I'll tell him you stopped by."

"Thanks…"

"Micah."

His eyes widen. "Wait, *you're* Micah?"

"Yeah…"

He looks down at the shirt I'm wearing—Aidan's shirt. Liam flashes a knowing smile.

Just then I hear footsteps behind me. Liam looks past my shoulder. "She's the hot auditor who hates you, right?"

My face instantly flushes hot. I step back and turn to see Aidan standing behind me, still clad in just a towel, looking annoyed.

"What are you doing here, Liam?"

His brother shrugs, a smug look on his face. "I was just dropping off the tools you let me borrow. Sorry—didn't mean to interrupt." He gestures to the toolbox on the porch next to him.

I chuckle at the smug look still on Liam's face. He doesn't look the least bit sorry.

Aidan moves to stand next to me. "Thanks for coming. Bye."

He starts to close the door, but Liam stops him.

"Whoa, wait—aren't you going to invite me in for some coffee? I'd love to get to know your lady friend."

"No," Aidan barks.

I step back and cover my mouth to keep from laughing so hard. This is such typical brother behavior.

"Aww, come on! Promise I'll behave," Liam says through a smile that's somehow smug and charming at once.

"No, you won't." Aidan sighs. He tugs a hand through his still-wet curls. He turns to me. "I'm sorry my little brother is such an annoying dipshit."

Liam clutches a hand to his chest. "Ouch," he says through a laugh. He steps back. "I was kidding. You really think I was gonna try and third wheel my way into this?" He flashes that handsome smile. "You two have a nice day. Micah, it was nice meeting you."

"You too."

"If you're not busy tomorrow night, you should come with Aidan to my hockey game."

I turn to Aidan. "That sounds fun."

"Really?" he deadpans.

"Hey, come on. Hockey is fun."

Aidan rolls his eyes. I laugh and give his arm a squeeze. "I'd like to go, if that's okay with you."

He smiles. "Of course it's okay." He turns to look at his brother. "You sure you want to watch this guy play? He's pretty awful."

Liam frowns like he's genuinely offended. I burst out laughing.

Liam shakes his head. "Come to the game tomorrow night and see for yourself, Micah."

"I will."

He waves bye and walks off. Aidan shuts the door and shakes his head.

"Sorry about him. He's obnoxious."

I chuckle. "I have a sister, remember? I know all about how annoying siblings can be."

He smiles. "Right."

I slink my arms around his neck. "I get to go to a hockey game tomorrow night with you. I'm excited."

There's warmth in his eyes as he smiles at me. "Me too."

Thirty-Nine

Aidan

I take a sip of my beer and glance over at Micah sitting next to me in the stands of the arena.

She stares ahead at the ice, watching the players fight for control of the puck. "Wow. Your brother is really good."

I watch him take possession of the puck from a defender on the opposing team, then speed down the ice. "Yeah, I guess he's okay."

She elbows me and chuckles, then grabs the beer from my hand and takes a long sip.

We both watch as Liam closes in on the goalie and sinks the puck at the back of the net. We jump up and cheer along with the rest of the home crowd.

Micah hollers "Woo-hoo!" and pumps her fist.

When I chuckle, she turns to me. "What?" she asks.

"I think it's really cute that you get so into it."

Smiling, she shrugs. "Sports are fun."

"You a big hockey fan?" I ask as we sit back down.

"Not really. But I can go to most sporting events and have a good time." She raises the plastic cup of beer, and I laugh. "Except for golf. So boring."

She hands me back the beer, and I take a sip. "You're right about that."

I run my gaze over the outfits she's wearing. She's in dark yoga pants, boots, and one of my hoodies with Liam's team logo on it.

"Thanks again for letting me borrow your hoodie." She smiles at me.

My heart beats faster in my chest. This the first time I've seen Micah in casual clothes, and I really, really like it.

She always looks beautiful no matter what she wears, but it feels different seeing her like this—drinking a beer, relaxed, letting loose, having fun.

I love that she's letting me see this different side of her. I love that she's comfortable being herself around me.

And I love that she's wearing *my* hoodie. That she feels comfortable wearing something of mine in public, in front of everyone.

That familiar pull in my chest hits yet again.

My brain pictures Micah sitting with me at all of my brother's home games, wearing my hoodie. I picture waking up with her in my bed every morning. I picture cuddling her on my couch after a joint writing session. My chest aches.

I want that. All of that. So bad.

I take another long sip of beer and quietly scold myself for get carried away and picturing a future with Micah. This is temporary. We're just messing around, having fun.

But even as I tell myself that, it feels wrong. Because that's not how I feel at all.

When the first period ends, I ask Micah if she's hungry and she says yes. I offer to run to the concession stand and grab her whatever she's craving.

She shakes her head. "I'm hungry, and I don't know what I want. I have to see what my options are."

I laugh as we stand up and head up the stairs to the nearest concession stand. She settles on popcorn and nachos. As we stand off to the side and wait for our food, I freeze.

There's my dad walking by.

He spots me when he's a dozen feet away. He stops suddenly,

and the person behind him runs into him. My dad apologizes and walks over to us.

Micah loops her hand in mine. I look over at her.

"You okay?" she asks.

I nod and turn back to him. "Hi, Dad."

He flashes a sad smile. "Funny running into you here." He laughs.

I try to smile, but it feels so weird, joking with him. "Yeah, I guess."

He stands there, shuffling his feet, clearly waiting for me to say something.

"Liam's playing well tonight," I finally say.

He blinks like he's surprised. "Yeah. He is."

I stand there, taking in the look on my dad's face. I can tell he's eager to talk to me, but he's scared too. Like he's worried he'll say the wrong thing.

He hesitates before aiming a pained gaze at me. "I just wanna say, Aidan, I'm really sorry for what I said to you all those years ago. I was a jerk."

I'm quiet as I process the shock of his apology. I wasn't expecting that.

"I was wrong to make you feel bad about giving up hockey. I should have supported you." His eyes turn glassy with unshed tears. He quickly blinks. "I'm embarrassed at how long it took me to realize that I was the one in the wrong. You're doing what you love, you're happy, and you're a good person. That's all that matters to me. Your brother tells me all about your work as a professor. I'm so proud of you."

That pain in my chest morphs into an ache. "You mean that?"

He nods. "Absolutely. Look, I know one apology doesn't make up for what I did. I missed a lot of years of your life because I was a stubborn jackass. But I'm different now. And I'd love it if you'd like to have me in your life again. Though I'd understand if you decide that you'd rather not."

He lets out a shaky breath. He looks at Micah and offers a sad smile before looking at me. "Bye, son."

I watch as he walks off, getting swallowed up by the surrounding crowd.

And that's when I realize I don't want things between us to stay this way. Yeah, he hurt me. But he apologized to me. I can tell he regrets what he did. And that's enough for me to at least try and repair our relationship.

I turn to Micah. "I have to go to him."

She flashes a sad smile. "Of course."

I make my way through the crowd, apologizing as I bump into people. After a minute, I finally spot him as he's about to head down the stairs to a different section.

"Dad, wait!"

He stops and turns around, eyes wide with shock when he sees me. "Aidan?"

I walk up to him. "Do you want to go to the next home game together?"

He blinks, like he's not sure if he heard me right. After a second, he starts to smile. His eyes light up. "I'd love that."

Before I can talk myself out of it, I hug him. He wraps his arms around me so tight. Emotion rushes through me as my dad hugs me tighter than he ever has.

When we finally break apart, his eyes are misty again. He claps my shoulder. "Thank you."

I nod and walk back to Micah, that ache in my chest gone.

Forty

Micah

As we walk through the parking lot after the game, I hold Aidan's hand tightly in mine.

I look over at him. "I'm so glad you're going to your brother's next game with your dad."

A gentle smile appears on his face. "I am too. Thank you for being so supportive. I'm sure that was really awkward, watching the two of us have an emotional moment in the middle of a hockey game."

"Hey." I gently tug on his hand. "It wasn't awkward at all. I'm so glad that you're trying to work things out."

"Me too."

I stop and squint out at the rows of cars in the lot. "Please tell me you remember where I parked because I totally forgot."

"Row ten, section C," Aidan rattles off without missing a beat.

I reach up, cup my hand along his stubbled cheek. "I knew I kept you around for a good reason."

He quirks an eyebrow. "Not just for sex?"

I laugh. "Well, obviously that too."

He drops a kiss to my mouth.

"What do you think about writing some hockey-inspired erotica for our next joint story on Scribble Share?"

Aidan makes a face. "No way."

I laugh at how grossed out he looks. "Why not?"

"Because I can't think about hockey without thinking of my brother, and that's just gross."

I grimace. "Okay, yeah, good point. Never mind."

"Micah? Is that you?"

When I turn around and see my boss, I freeze. I pull my hands away from Aidan and step away from him.

"Carl. Hello."

I walk over to him standing by his Mercedes.

He chuckles as he points to the hoodie I'm wearing. "I didn't know you were a hockey fan."

"I'm not." I say quickly. "I just…"

I trail off, my brain in full-on panic mode. There's actually no company rule that say I can't hang out with someone who works for the business I'm auditing…but it's messy. I know it wouldn't look good to my boss, who's as by the book as they come.

"I borrowed it from a friend for the game," I say. I turn around and gesture to Aidan, who offers a polite smile and wave but thankfully stays back. I don't want to introduce him to my boss and have to explain why we're together. It would make me look so unprofessional.

He nods. "How are things going with the audit for the university?"

"I'm on track to wrap things up next week."

"Good to hear. How is your report looking so far?"

I tense, knowing full well that Aidan is standing behind me and can hear this entire conversation.

"Exactly what I expected. They have the typical problems with retention and class size. My recommendation is going to be cutting low-enrollment courses and consolidating a portion of their classes."

"And what about staff cuts?"

A rock lodges in my throat. I nod. "I'll be recommending those too, of course."

Carl nods once, satisfied. "Well done, Micah. I can always count on you for an efficient, no-nonsense audit."

I open my mouth to say *Thanks*, but I don't. Because it feels so wrong to thank my boss for applauding me when what I just said could result in Aidan losing his job.

He says good-night, climbs into his car, and drives off.

When I turn around to look at Aidan, my stomach is in knots. It's dark now, but I can see his hard expression clearly in the parking lot lights.

"You're really gonna do it? You're going to recommend cutting classes and staff?"

Pain flashes in his eyes. I hesitate for a second before making myself speak. "Yes."

He shakes his head and looks off to the side.

"I'm sorry, Aidan, but I have to…"

He frowns at me. "You don't have to do anything, Micah. It's not like anyone is forcing you to hand in a report recommending that you annihilate the English department. You're doing this all on your own. So please don't act like that's the case," he says.

"That's not what I'm saying. I'm just trying to do my job."

He lets out a sad laugh. "Your job. Right. I forgot that your job is to put people out of work. Your job that you don't even like."

There's a sting in my chest. "Aidan, that's not fair."

"Yeah, it is. And you know what, if you honestly enjoyed doing that for a living, I could live with it. But you don't. I know you don't. There's no passion in what you do. You don't love it. You said it yourself."

I lean back, surprised at the way he's speaking to me right now. "Aidan, I understand that you're upset. And you have every right to be, but…"

He shakes his head, cutting me off. "You love writing, Micah. Why not focus on that? Why not try and make that your career? Why continue with this job that you don't even like? Why not pursue something you actually love that doesn't hurt people and cost them their livelihoods?"

I stare at him, frustration simmering inside of me at what he wants me to do. "Do you seriously expect me to throw away my stable, well-paying job to be a writer? Something I have no experience with? Something that I'll probably never make any money doing?"

He glances off to the side and lets out a sad laugh. He turns to me. "Why do you have to talk yourself down like that, Micah? You're such a talented writer. You see how many people on Scribble Share love reading your writing. Those readers would buy your books. They'd read anything you write. You're that amazing. You could turn this into a career. I know you could."

I shake my head, a confusing mix of emotions whirling inside of me. Heartened at the way he compliments my skills as a writer. Annoyed and pissed that he is pushing me to give up my career and pursue something uncertain, like it's so simple and easy.

I hold up a hand. "I'm not going to quit my job to be a writer, okay? Stop suggesting it." I drop my hand at my side and pause for a moment. "Look, I understand why you're upset. But honestly, Aidan, what did you think was going to happen? I'm an auditor, and my job is to find the fat to cut in any situation. I've been observing your department for weeks, and the problems are crystal clear. Do you really expect me to just ignore them because we're hooking up?"

Aidan's brow lifts, like he's shocked at what I've said. Pain flashes in his eyes. "That's what this is to you? Just hooking up?"

I let out a heavy breath, my chest aching at the pain in his expression.

"Yes." I say, despite how wrong it feels…despite how much it breaks me to say it.

But I have to say it. I can't let myself fall for him any more than I have. I'm already in deeper than I thought I'd ever be. I'm already feeling things for Aidan that I know I shouldn't…

Pain flashes through his beautiful blue eyes as he holds my gaze. "This thing between us started as just hooking up. I'll admit that. But it didn't stay that way. And you know it."

I hold my breath, gazing at him. He's right. But I can't admit it. I can't tell him how I really feel. Things are already so complicated between us right now. Bringing our feelings into this would just makes this a million times messier, a million times more painful.

Emotion flashes in his crystal-blue eyes. "I'm in love with you, Micah."

My mouth parts opens as I gasp. My heart hammers in my chest.

Aidan's broad chest heaves as he lets out a breath.

"What?" My voice is practically a squeal.

"I love you," he says without hesitation.

"Aidan…" I can barely get his name out. I'm too stunned. "We've known each other six weeks."

He shrugs. "So?"

"So? We don't know each other well enough for you to say that."

He doesn't even blink. He steps toward me, closing the space between us. He rests his hands on my hips, pulling me close. "I know you, Micah. I know you put on a tough front at work because you don't want people to see you as weak. But you're not weak. Not even close. You are so strong. But you're also soft. And sweet. And funny. You're the most talented writer I know. No one makes me as angry as you, but I love it. I love that you're fiery. I like that you're not afraid to fight me. You're passionate. You drive me wild in the best way. I've never met anyone like you. And I've never felt this way about anyone before."

I'm breathless, my heart thudding in my chest as Aidan stands there, holding me in his arms, telling me all the things he loves about me.

"You're the only person who I've really confided in about my dad. You're the only person who's ever made me feel safe enough to talk this much about my relationship with him." He pauses, the look in his eyes pained and pleading. My heart pounds in my chest as emotion wells up inside of me, hearing him tell me how much I mean to him.

"I know you're not ready to say you love me back. And that's okay. But can you at least admit that you have feelings for me too? Can you admit that this was more than just hooking up for you? I can handle everything else—I can even handle you getting me fired if I know that what you feel for me is real."

Intensity flashes in his crystal-blue eyes as I look up at him. The words rest at the tip of my tongue. Everything in me aches to say it. But I stay quiet.

Even if I say what I'm feeling, it wouldn't do any good. It would just make things between Aidan and me even more complicated, more painful.

I can't give him what he wants. And I'm about to cost him his job.

There's no way for us to work out long-term. This is all we can ever have. And it has to end now.

"I'm sorry," I say, my voice breaking. I close my eyes, feeling the sting of unshed tears.

When I open them and look at Aidan, his eyes are glassy.

His throat works as he swallows and nods. "Okay," he whispers.

His hands fall away from my body and he steps back. I'm instantly cold at the loss of his touch.

Aidan shoves his hands into his jacket pockets and aims his pained gaze at me. "Goodbye, Micah."

He walks off. I stand there and watch him until he disappears from my view before stumbling to my car. And then I finally let myself cry.

Forty-One

Micah

I stare at the computer screen in my office in downtown Nashville.

I've been finished with my final audit report of the English department at East Nashville University for days. I could have handed it in already.

But I haven't.

Because every time I get ready to submit it to my boss, I get this sinking feeling in my stomach. I feel like I'm going to be sick.

This is my job. I know I need to turn in this report. But I can't. Because deep down, I know it's the wrong thing to do.

I think about the night Aidan and I ended things in the parking lot of the hockey arena, how he called me out on what my job is really about…

He's right. I put people out of work for a living. And he was right when he said I don't even enjoy my job.

For the longest time, I was okay with all of that. I'm not anymore though.

An ugly feeling burrows in my gut, gnawing deeper and deeper the longer I sit here.

I don't want to do this anymore. I don't want to turn in this report because it means that people could lose their jobs—including Aidan.

And I can't do that to the man I'm in love with.

That gnawing feeling deepens at the same time as my chest aches.

I'm in love with Aidan. I tried to ignore this feeling, but I can't. I feel it with every breath I take, every time my heart beats in my chest.

I push away from my desk and let out a shaky breath. My skull throbs with the headache I've been nursing for the past week…ever since things with Aidan ended.

My chest feels like it's cracked open.

I miss him. I miss him so fucking much.

I love him so much.

Ever since we stopped seeing each other, I've been a wreck. I can't sleep. I don't feel like eating. It's a struggle to focus. I'm always thinking about him.

I think about the moment he told me he loved me…

I think about the emotion in his eyes, how sure he sounded when he said it.

I think about the broken look on his face when I didn't say it back.

My stomach churns. I hurt him so bad.

I pull my phone out of my purse. He hasn't called or texted me. Not that I have any right to expect him to reach out to me, not after the way I rejected him.

Not after the way I broke his heart.

I let out a shaky breath. When I blink, my eyes burn with the urge to cry.

I pull up the Scribble Share app on my phone. No messages from Aidan on there either.

I navigate to the post we wrote together. It was a huge hit with readers. I do a skim of the comments.

This collab was EVERYTHING!!

You two need to write more dual POV stories

We need more steamy stories from you two ASAP!

Okay, who else thinks that ShakespeareInLust and Hot4Hermia are dating? Because these two write like they're having crazy hot sex all the time

If these two aren't together, they need to be!

Yes!! We ship you, ShakespeareInLust and Hot4Hermia!

A sad smile tugs at my lips. Just then, my phone rings. When I see it's my sister, I'm confused. It's early morning here, which means it's the middle of her work day in London. She should be too busy working to call me.

I answer. "Hey. Is everything okay?"

Jordan lets out a heavy sigh. "I was calling to ask you that same question."

"Why?"

"Because every time this past week I tried to FaceTime with you or text you, you shut me down. Something's up with you, Micah."

I hesitate. This whole week I've been avoiding talking to her because I knew I would break down, and I'm sick of breaking down in front of my sister. I did that when I went through my breakup with Ashton. I don't want her to think that all I do is cry over guys.

Before I can say anything, she speaks.

"Micah. I'm your sister. You can tell me anything."

"I know." Emotion clogs my throat, but I push on.

I stand up, close my office door, then tell her everything that happened with Aidan. I tell her how my feelings for him deepened the more time we spent together. I tell her about how we both opened up to each other. I tell her about running into my boss at his brother's hockey game. I tell her about how Aidan told me he was in love with me but I was too scared to say it back, so we ended things.

By the time I'm finished, I've gone through a pile of tissues. I'm a snotty mess.

"Oh, Micah. I'm so sorry."

I let out a heavy sigh and sniffle. I wipe my nose. "Yeah, but I'll get through it."

There's a pause on her end of the line.

"What is it?" I ask.

She doesn't say anything at first. "Are you sure you're doing the right thing?"

"What do you mean?"

"Are you okay with the way things ended between you two?" she asks.

"Of course I'm not okay with it," I say. "But I have a job to do. There's no way Aidan and I can work out when my job is to potentially put him out of a job."

"Then why are you still working there?"

I pause, shocked. "What?"

"Micah, you said yourself this doesn't feel right. You're sick to your stomach. You've been sitting on this report for days, but you still haven't been able to hand it in to your boss. Doesn't that tell you something? That maybe you're not in the right job if it's making you physically ill? If it's forcing you to go against the man you're in love with?"

I'm quiet as I work out everything she's said.

"I know how hard you work, Micah. I know it means a lot to you to be successful in your career. But you should also be happy. And it sounds like your job is making you miserable."

"It didn't used to. I used to be fine with it," I say.

"It's okay to change your mind, Micah. It's okay to work at a job for a while and then lose interest. It's okay to want to try something else."

I think about what my sister just said. It's so simple. And true.

"What makes you happy?" she asks after I'm quiet for a while.

"Writing." I say it without even thinking.

"Really?" She sounds surprised, but not in a condescending way. More like she's intrigued.

"Yeah. I've wanted to be a writer for a long time. I just never told anyone because I was afraid of what people would think. I've never been a creative person. No one sees me that way. Everyone sees me as the no-nonsense, business-minded person."

"So? You can be whatever you want, Micah." I can hear the smile in my sister's voice.

"I write fanfic sometimes, for this one app." My nerves crackle as I admit this to her.

"Really? That's awesome." She's smiling even wider now. I can tell. "Can I read it?"

I let out a flustered laugh. "It's pretty steamy—not sure if you'd like it."

"That sounds fun, honestly. I'd love to read it, if that's okay with you."

I start to smile. It feels really, really good to hear my sister say that she wants to read my writing.

"Okay, sure." I tell her all about the app Scribble Share and promise to send her a link to my stories.

"My sister is romance writer. This is really freaking cool."

I laugh. There's another stretch of silence between us.

"You deserve to be happy, Micah. In your job, in your relationship, in everything that you do. I really hope you know that."

Emotion wells up inside of me. "Thanks, Jordan. You're the best."

"I know," she teases.

I promise to FaceTime her later this week. We hang up, and I look back at my computer screen. As I skim my report for the millionth time, that unsettled feeling burrows deep inside of me.

I can't do this anymore.

I stand up from my desk, walk out of my office, and go into my boss's corner office. He's on the phone, but he waves me in. I sit down in front of his desk as he wraps up his conversation.

When he hangs up the phone, he folds his hands on his desk and nods at me. "What can I do for you, Micah?"

I take a breath. "I won't be submitting my audit for the English department at East Nashville University. I quit."

Forty-Two

Aidan

"Hey, man. You okay?"

"Yeah, fine." I don't even bother to look up from my computer at Jason.

Out of the corner of my eye, I see him looking at me from his desk.

"You sure? You've been pretty closed off lately."

I finally glance up. "I've just been caught up in work. Sorry."

Lie. I'm heartbroken over losing Micah. But I'm not going to tell Jason that. He doesn't know that we were together. When we started seeing each other outside of work, we agreed to keep things a secret. Her sister and my dad and brother ended up finding out about us, but no one else needs to know.

Jason frowns at me, like he's studying me. "You know, when Micah wrapped things up and finally left, I thought you'd be happy. But you weren't. You actually seemed kind of upset."

I glance away, too uncomfortable at how my best friend is staring at me. I can't keep looking him in the eye and lying to him.

"Yeah, well. That audit kind of screwed with my head."

"Did it?"

I glance up at Jason, surprised at the hitch in his voice. "Was something going on between you and Micah?"

I blink at him, surprised at how quickly he put that together. I clear my throat. "Yeah."

Jason nods, a solemn look on his face. I glance up at our office door to make sure it's closed.

"I kind of suspected you two had a thing," Jason says after a moment. "Kendall did too."

"You did?"

He nods. "You and Micah were at each other's throats until that night you got stranded here during the blizzard together. After that we noticed you two didn't fight anymore. We figured you worked out your differences."

He tilts his head at me. I huff out a breath. "Yeah, you could say that."

I think about that night with Micah. It was hot as hell, just like every other time we were together. But that's not why I miss her.

I swallow through the tightness in my throat and that ache in my chest that's plagued me ever since we ended things.

I miss her smile. The most beautiful smile I've ever seen. I miss that gleam in her mahogany eyes whenever she got excited about something. I miss the way she let me cuddle her when we fell asleep together. I miss her smell. I still don't even know the name of her perfume—I never bothered to ask—but god, it was intoxicating. I miss the way she moans when she takes her first sip of coffee. I miss seeing her wearing my clothes. I miss sending her messages on Scribble Share.

I give Jason a brief rundown of what happened between us. "We ran into her boss at Liam's hockey game the other night. She made it clear that she was planning to recommend staff cuts to our department. I got upset. She did too. I told her my feelings for her, but she didn't feel the same way, so we ended it."

Jason frowns, his expression pained. "I'm really sorry to hear that."

When I take a breath, there's a sharpness in the center of my chest. It feels like someone rammed their fist into my heart.

"It wasn't going to work out anyway. How could I have stayed with someone who was trying to put me and all my friends out of work?"

Jason nods, the look on his face still sad.

Just then our work email alert sounds off. We both turn to our computers and click on the message that Dr. Wauncho just sent us.

Mandatory staff meeting at 11 a.m.

I frown. That's weird.

"Did you know we were having a last-minute meeting today?" I ask Jason. He says no.

We gather our things and head to the conference room. Once we're all settled, Dr. Wauncho shuts the door and stands at the front.

He claps his hands together. "Everyone. I've got some strange but exciting news. I'm sure you all remember when Ms. Mila was here conducing her audit."

I jolt at hearing Micah's name.

"I was just informed that she refused to submit her audit."

"She did what?" I blurt.

He chuckles. "Believe me, I was quite surprised to find that out as well."

"What happened?" Jason asks.

Dr. Wauncho shrugs and shakes his head. "I'm not quite sure. All I was told is that she refused to submit an audit, then promptly resigned from her position at the firm."

I sit there, stunned. Micah quit her job? Over auditing our department? But she told me she was going to submit her report...

"The university determined that the audit failed and was a waste of school money, so they've decided to stop with the audit of school for the time being. Now, we're not totally in the clear. The university might decide to do another audit next year or the year after. But as of now, we're no longer on the chopping block!"

Everyone cheers. Except for me. I'm still too shocked to speak.

Chatter fills the room. Kendall asks a question I don't hear.

Dr. Wauncho chuckles. "I'm not quite sure what happened, but I like to think Micah was charmed and impressed by our department, so much so that it led to her having a change of heart."

Jason turns to me and gives me a look. "Looks like your lady changed her mind." He hops up from his chair and walks over to Kendall. The whole room is buzzing. Everyone is relieved and thrilled.

I am too. Micah saved us. She went against her job and saved our department.

I shake my head in disbelief.

Just then my phone buzzes with an alert. I look and see it's from Scribble Share. I pull up the app on my phone and skim the notifications. I've been tagged in a new post written by Hot4Hermia.

My heart skids in my chest.

I stand up from where I'm sitting and head out of the noisy conference room back to my office. I sit at my desk, pull up the post, and start reading. It's a continuation of that enemies-to-lovers erotica between two professors that Micah has been writing.

I look him in the eye, every single one of my nerves firing off inside of me.

"I made the worst mistake of my life when I let you leave instead of telling you how I feel about you. So here I am, right now, telling you how I feel.

"I love you. So, so much. I love the way you hold me tight when you hug me. I love the gentle way you cradle my face when you kiss me. I love how you have to be hugging me to fall asleep. I love how you believe in me.

No one else has ever made me feel as safe or as loved as you. I even love fighting with you. You fight with me because you care. Because you want to fight for us and what we have."

My eyes burn. Tears threaten to fall down my cheeks. I blink quickly in an attempt to hold them back. But then I tell myself I shouldn't do that. This pain and regret coursing through me is how I really feel. And I'm tired of hiding my feelings from him. I want to show him everything.

When I blink, tears stream down my face.

"I was wrong to doubt us. You were right. It doesn't matter that we haven't been together very long. All that matters is how we feel. And when I'm with you, I'm the happiest. You feel like home."

I take a second to swallow and take a breath. "I know I'm probably too late telling you this. I know you're probably still hurt and angry. And that's okay. You have every right to be. I just needed to tell you how I feel. Even if you don't want me anymore, that's okay. I'll always love you. And I'll always regret that I let you walk away without fighting for you."

I stand there, holding my breath, and wait for him to say something.

I reach the end of Micah's post, my chest aching and my heart hammering in my chest. She wrote this for me. I focus on the three words that I still can't believe she wrote for me.

I love you.

She's sorry and she loves me. My heart hammers so hard, my chest starts to ache.

Micah loves me.

My body is buzzing and my head is spinning as I soak in her words.

I do a quick skim of the comments.

I'm ugly crying. That was heart-wrenching and amazing!

I need more tissues!

BRB gonna go cry in my car so my coworkers don't see

OMG SO DAMN GOOD

Not a cliffhanger! Noooo! I need to know what he says to her!

Why can't people apologize like this in real life? If they did, it would be sooo much easier to forgive lol

Oh damn, do you think Hot4Hermia and ShakespeareInLust are having a fight in in real life? Do you think Hermia is trying to apologize??

My pulse kicks up as I zero in on that comment. I want to leave a comment on Micah's story...but that would mean everyone on the app would know that we're a couple. Am I okay with readers knowing that about us? We've kept that to ourselves up to this point...

But then I realize, I don't care. I want everyone to know how I feel about Micah.

I type a comment on the post.

Hey. You're not too late. I love you too.

Forty-Three

Micah

I pump my legs faster on the stationary bike in my sister's workout room. My lungs are on fire, and it feels like my heart is about to burst through my chest.

This is exactly what I need though. I needed to distract myself after writing that post on Scribble Share and hoping that Aidan would read it.

I pump faster and faster until I hit the last hill sprint on my workout. I gasp and ease up on my pace. Beads of sweat stream down my forehead, so I wipe my face with my forearm as I catch my breath. I feel like I'm about to collapse, but it's better than that restless, broken feeling of missing Aidan.

I stop pedaling and brace my arms against the handles and close my eyes.

I hope he sees the post I wrote this morning after I quit my job. I hope he forgives me. I hope he still loves me.

My stomach sinks. I shouldn't get my hopes up. I grab my phone from the side pocket of my yoga pants and turn off Do Not Disturb. Seconds later, my phone is blowing up with notifications. When I see all the Scribble Share notifications on my screen, I pull up the app. I scroll through a load of glowing compliments. I start to smile. The readers on this app are so sweet.

But then I see it...

Aidan's comment on my post. When I read it, my mouth falls open. He loves me too.

Emotion bursts through my chest. I let out a giddy, breathy

laugh. And then I squeal, clutching my phone to my chest. And then I think, Why am I standing here freaking out? I should go to him now.

So I do.

Forty-five minutes later, I'm running into the English department building at East Nashville University. I head to the elevator but see that it's full.

Everyone frowns at me. Awareness hits when I realize they probably recognize me as the auditor who was trying to put them out of work.

I start to back up, but then Jason says my name.

I stop and scan the crowded elevator, finally spotting his face in the corner. "Micah, what are you doing here?" he asks.

"I, uh, came to see Aidan."

To my surprise, he smiles. "He's in his office. Here, come on in. We'll make room."

When people start to grumble about not letting me in, I hesitate to step forward, but Jason stops them.

"Micah quit her job, saving all of ours. The least we could give her is a ride," he says.

Everyone nods and murmurs their agreement. I smile at Jason and tell him thank you, then squeeze into the elevator, apologizing as I bump into people.

The elevator floats to the top floor and skids to a halt. The doors skid open, and I step out.

"Thanks, Jason!" I holler again as I jog out.

"Go get him!" he hollers back.

I run down the hall and turn the corner into Aidan's office. I step inside his doorway. He looks up from his computer, his eyes wide.

"Micah." He stands up and runs his gaze up and down my body.

And that's when I realize how ridiculous I must look. It's

the middle of winter, and I'm wearing yoga pants, a sports bra, and I'm soaked in sweat.

"I look ridiculous, I know," I say quickly.

He walks toward me, stopping just a couple of feet away from me. Intensity flashes in his gaze as he looks at me. "You look beautiful. You always look beautiful."

My chest squeezes. "I love you, Aidan. And I'm sorry. I'm so, so sorry. I know I've said that already in my post on Scribble Share, but I want to say it right now, in front of you, so that you know—"

Aidan grabs me, pulls me against him, and kisses me. I sink into his embrace and moan into his mouth. God, this feels good. *He* feels so, so good.

When we finally break apart, I'm dizzy. I run my tongue along my bottom lip as I catch my breath.

He cups my cheek in his hand. "Say it again," he rasps.

I smile. "Which part?"

The corner of his mouth tugs up. "The 'I love you' part."

"I love you. So much."

Aidan flashes the most beautiful smile. He closes his eyes, like he's savoring my words. When he opens his eyes, his gaze is bright and raw. "I love you too."

He kisses me again.

"I can't believe you quit your job," he says.

"I didn't love it. And I was tired of working a job I didn't love. It didn't make me happy. You do. And so does writing. I'm going to start looking for a different job. Something that makes me happy. Something that lets me be creative. And I want to try and write a book too."

He beams. "That's amazing, Micah. I'm so proud of you for following your dreams."

I'm giddy at the adoration in his voice, how he builds me up.

We kiss again. It's not long before our mouths get filthy. I'm clawing at his shirt, trying not to rip it from his body since we're standing in his office and any of his colleagues could walk in on us.

He breaks our kiss with a soft growl. He steps over to the door, shuts it, and locks it before stepping back over to me and pulling me against him.

I chuckle. "Really? Right now? You're at work."

The corner of his mouth quirks up. "You can use it as inspiration for your next Scribble Share post. Or maybe even your book."

Smiling, I kiss him. "Brilliant idea."

Epilogue

Micah

9 months later

I'm standing at the kitchen island typing on my laptop when Aidan comes up behind me, slinking his arms around my waist. He hugs me against him and nuzzles the side of my neck.

I close my eyes and shiver.

He kisses my cheek. "How's writing going?"

I smile. "Really well. I've almost hit my word count for the day."

"Good girl." He pats my ass, and I giggle.

He presses a kiss to the back of my neck that makes my eyelids flutter. He runs his tongue along the side of my neck before kissing me again. Heat puddles between my legs, and I moan.

"You're distracting me," I murmur.

"Can't help it," he says, his mouth on my skin. "You look really fucking hot wearing nothing but my T-shirt."

He palms my ass, and I squeal. I spin around, and for the next few minutes we make out in Aidan's kitchen.

Our kitchen, actually. Three months ago Aidan asked me to move in with him, and I, of course, said yes.

We haven't even been together for a year, but moving in felt right. Everything with Aidan has felt so right. Even when we worked together and couldn't stand each other, our chemistry felt right.

When we finally break apart, we're both breathing hard. He rests his forehead against mine.

"How's your writing coming along?" I ask.

He leans back and flashes that sexy-as-sin half smile. "Good. I'll hit my word-count goal later tonight."

"I still can't believe we're writing a book together."

Aidan and I have been writing and posting regularly on Scribble Share. We've been a hit with readers. All of our posts are consistently the most popular on the site. A few months ago, a literary agent reached out to us and pitched the idea of the two of us writing a full-length book. We, of course, said yes, and right now we're in the middle of writing it—a super steamy dual-POV mafia romance.

I've also been writing novellas on my own, which Aidan encouraged me to self-publish. A few months ago, I finally released my first one, then a couple more after that. To my shock, they took off. I'm not breaking any records, but I've been able to start earning enough money as an author to support myself.

Aidan leans over and taps my laptop keyboard. A second later he grins.

"What is it?"

"Have you seen your ranking on Amazon recently?" he asks.

"No. I haven't had the guts to look since I posted my last novella a few weeks ago. I'm nervous."

He smiles at me. "You should."

I twist around and focus on the screen. A second later, my eyes go wide. I let out a giddy laugh. "No way…"

Aidan kisses my cheek. "You broke top fifty in the entire Kindle ebook store. And your book is outranking Ashton's."

I can't stop staring at the screen. I'm grinning so wide, my cheeks hurt.

I take a screenshot. "I need to commemorate this."

Aidan winks at me. "Absolutely. You've got more reviews than him too. And a better overall book rating."

I laugh as he high-fives me.

"Is it petty for me to feel this good about beating him?"

Aidan beams at me. "Not at all."

I kiss him and turn back to my computer.

He clears his throat. "Hey, have you read my latest post on Scribble Share?"

"Not yet," I say as I type.

"Do you mind taking a look at it? There's a part in there I'm not sure about, and I'd like to get your thoughts on it."

"Sure. Just a sec." I finish typing, save the document, then grab my phone from the counter and pull up the app. I tap on Aidan's latest post and start reading.

I'm smiling the whole time. It's the latest installment from his Rome-and-Jia story aka *Romeo and Juliet* retelling with a happily-ever-after. It's still my favorite series that he writes on Scribble Share.

Rome grabbed Jia's hand, stopping her as they walked.

"Jia. I need to ask you something."

Before she could say anything, Rome dropped to one knee. Jia covered her mouth with her hand as she gasped while watching Rome pull out the most gorgeous diamond ring.

Tears glistened in his eyes as he gazed up at her. "I know our families are enemies. But I love you. I love you, Jia, with all my heart. I know a life together won't be easy. People will be after us constantly. But I promise to keep you safe. I promise to fight for you. I promise to guard your heart with my life. I can't imagine sharing my life with anyone else. Will you marry me?"

Tears streamed down Jia's face as she nodded and cried yes.

Rome let out a happy, crazed laugh. He slipped the ring onto her finger and hopped to his feet. She hugged him so tight, it made his heart ache. He could feel just how much she loved him.

She leaned up to kiss him. After they broke apart, she looked up and flashed him the most beautiful smile.

"You and me forever," she whispered.

He smiled at her. "I can't wait."

I'm beaming as I finish reading it. I start to turn around to look at Aidan. "That was amazing…"

I trail off when I see him on one knee in front of me, holding a black velvet box with a stunning diamond ring in it.

I gasp. "Aidan…"

He lets out a shaky breath as he smiles at me. "I'm so in love with you, Micah. I know we haven't been together long, but being with you feels right. You make happier than I've ever been. I'm the luckiest guy in the world to be with you. And if you'll let me, I'll spend the rest of my life trying to make you as happy as you make me."

His voice trembles as he speaks. Emotion blooms in my chest. Tears fall down my cheeks.

Aidan's crystal-blue eyes shine with tears. "Will you marry me?"

I'm nodding before he even finishes asking. "Yes!"

He hops up and hugs me, and we kiss.

He steps back and slides the ring onto my finger. I gaze down at it, mesmerized by how the princess-cut diamond sparkles in the light.

I slide my arms around his neck and kiss him. "You already make me the happiest, you know."

Emotion flashes in his eyes as he smiles at me.

"I can't believe you set up my proposal with fanfic." I smile.

Aidan chuckles. "Nerdy as hell, right?"

I cup my hands around his face and kiss him again. "So nerdy and so sweet and so perfect. I wouldn't want it any other way."

★ ★ ★ ★ ★

*Want to read a special bonus epilogue featuring
Micah and Aidan? Sign up to our Afterglow newsletter
and you'll get an email with the extra content!
bit.ly/AfterglowNewsletter*

*And, look out for Sarah Echavarre Smith's
next novel from Afterglow Books,
available winter 2026!*

afterglow BOOKS

Afterglow Books is a trend-led, trope-filled list of books with diverse, authentic and relatable characters, a wide array of voices and representations, plus real world trials and tribulations. Featuring all the tropes you could possibly want (think small-town settings, fake relationships, grumpy vs sunshine, enemies to lovers) and all with a generous dose of spice in every story.

♪ @millsandboonuk
⊙ @millsandboonuk
afterglowbooks.co.uk

#AfterglowBooks

For all the latest book news, exclusive content and giveaways scan the QR code below to sign up to the Afterglow newsletter:

SCAN ME

LET'S TALK

Romance

For exclusive extracts, competitions and special offers, find us online:

- **f** MillsandBoon
- **X** @MillsandBoon
- **O** @MillsandBoonUK
- **J** @MillsandBoonUK

Get in touch on 01413 063 232